RedBone 2:

Takeover at Platinum Lofts

RedBone 2:
Takeover at Platinum Lofts

T. Styles

www.urbanbooks.net

Urban Books, LLC
78 East Industry Court
Deer Park, NY 11729

ISBN 13: 978-1-60162-540-3
ISBN 10: 1-60162-540-5

First Paperback Printing April 2013
Printed in the United States of America

10 9 8 7 6 5 4 3 2 1

Distributed by Kensington Publishing Corp.
Submit Wholesale Orders to:
Kensington Publishing Corp.
C/O Penguin Group (USA) Inc.
Attention: Order Processing
405 Murray Hill Parkway
East Rutherford, NJ 07073-2316
Phone: 1-800-526-0275
Fax: 1-800-227-9604

I dedicate this to Charisse Washington.
Thanks for holding me down.
Always.

Ackowledgments

To every T. Styles fan who loves a little something different. If you guys weren't in my life, I am afraid to think where my sick mind would have sent me. I hope you enjoy my twist on street fiction. I love you all, and welcome to my crazy-ass world!

T. Styles
www.facebook.com/authortstyles
www.twitter.com/authortstyles
www.thecartelpublications.com

Prologue

Present Day

Mooney's House

The frosty November day came through with a vengeance. Icicles formed on Mooney's windowsill, yet she had it wide open. How else would she be able to ear hustle? The yellow chiffon curtains danced in the wind and the cigarette between her fingers threatened to light her apartment on fire. Spread hip to hip in her favorite chair, she was doing a horrible job of being the neighborhood watcher. When she began to snore, the cancer stick was moments from somersaulting to the carpet, until she heard Cutie Tudy's screeching voice outside. Her eyes flew open and flapped a few times, before resting on her sneaky, smiling face walking toward the building.

Cutie was arm in arm with her latest piece of candy, No Good Naylor, from up the block. Although he was easy on the eyes, he was a seventeen-year-old know-it-all who was one deed away from career criminal status. Cutie and her friend weren't the only ones who tried to steal Mooney's sleep that afternoon. Just fifteen minutes earlier two strange teenagers entered the premises, forcing her antennae to shoot up. Something was off with the duo, she was sure of it.

Mooney's eyes remained on Cutie and Naylor until they melted into the brick building and away from her prying eyes. Restless, she stood up slowly, tucked the sleeve of her robe in the pocket, and smashed her cigarette into the glass tray next to the table. She grabbed some dirty laundry from the back and the dishwashing liquid in the kitchen. Before stepping foot out of her quarters, she grabbed her keys and stuffed the hammer in her pocket. She picked up the .45 a week back after the rash of break-ins, robberies, and rapes in her complex. If anybody wanted a taste of what rested between her legs, it would cost them their lives.

It was said that Mooney moved as light as a cat, and the theory proved correct. Headed for the basement, her toes angled against the cold, hard steps like a ballerina. She continued to move toward the laundry room until she heard two voices. Since it was pitch-black downstairs, she placed the pillowcase down for a second, stuffed her hand inside of her pocket, and cocked her weapon without removing it from its holding place. When she was done, she picked up the pillowcase and continued in the direction of the sour-smelling laundry room.

A wave of anger crept over her as she moved into the darkness, especially considering two weeks earlier the tenants had a meeting with the property manager about a lockbox being placed around the light switch to prevent the creepy people from turning it off. This, after an eighty-seven-year-old woman was raped and left for dead just because she chose to wash her grandbabies' clothes. Since it was still as black as the bush on her pussy, she figured they didn't give a fuck.

"Come on, stop playing, Cutie," Naylor whispered in the shadows. "You know I won't tell nobody if you let me flip that button. So open your legs and stop fucking around. You so got me geeking."

Cutie sighed loudly. "I want to hook you up, but how I know you telling the truth?"

"Telling the truth 'bout what? I haven't lied to you since you gave me your number in front of your school."

She giggled. "I hear you, but you friends with my ex-boyfriend and stuff. I be seeing y'all together all the time shootin' dice out back."

"You already know I know the nigga, but I'd never do you like he did. He my boy and all, but he told everybody how sweet your box is." He paused. "To tell you the truth, that's why I'm here now. If you were mine, I'da never told nobody that shit."

"I knew there was a reason."

"I'm just being honest, Cutie. But it ain't like I want to just stick and quit."

"You promise you telling the truth? 'Cause I'ma cry my makeup off if you lying to me. I ain't no freak or nothing."

Yeah, right, Mooney thought.

"First of all you ain't no freak. And second of all, on everything I love, my mama included, I'm being real with you. I really want to be with you. Like more than I wanted to be with anybody."

This mothafucka wants the pussy bad, Mooney thought.

"Good, 'cause I really like you too. I told my friends and everything."

"Well, stop playing and let me feel that jelly right quick."

Cutie raised her jean skirt, opened her legs, and allowed him access into her body. His fingers pushed and prodded inside of her, scraping her labia along the way.

It stung a little, but she was so juvenile that wanting to please him was more important than her dignity, or her health for that matter; Naylor's hands hadn't seen soap or water in days.

He felt he was in there like swimwear, until Mooney whispered into the darkness, "Cutie, stop what you doing and come on over here. Now." She placed the pillowcase on the floor and it made a soft thud.

Naylor pulled his wet fingers out of her box and asked, "Who the fuck is that?"

Using the darkness to her favor, she said, "Don't worry about who I am. Worry about what I can do to you." She focused her attention back on the girl. "Cutie." She paused. "Come on over here. Don't make me wait much longer."

"I don't even know where you are!" She fussed, straining her eyes to clear up her vision.

"Just follow my voice. That's all you need to do."

"Ugh, I can't believe you doing this!" Cutie pulled her panties up and tried to push down her skirt, which hadn't budged an inch due to being so tight and tiny. It wasn't enough for her to give the boys in the neighborhood an idea of what she was working with; she had to put it all on display like a Macy's store mannequin. "This is so fucking embarrassing."

"No, this is embarrassing," Mooney responded as she flipped the light, revealing two boys across the way in the laundry room. Both held night-vision cameras in their hands. The plan was to put the video footage of Cutie getting it in on a Web site the three of them ran called Freaks On Blast. Had it not been for Mooney, she would've been a star.

"Oh my God! I can't believe you did this shit to me," she screamed at Naylor, hitting him on his collarbone with a bony fist. "You setted me up! You ain't tell me nobody was going to be down here! I hate you! I hate you!"

Naylor stood up and pushed Cutie away. She flew backward and bonked her head on the washing machine. When she was on the floor, legs up in the air, he focused on Mooney. He could've broken the old biddy's jaw if his arms were longer.

"I can't believe you setted me up," she repeated, rubbing her head.

Focusing his eyes back on Cutie, he said, "First off, ain't no such thing as *setted* you up. Second of all, you walked down here with me on your own. I didn't give you no piggy-back ride." He looked at his friends and said, "Come on, y'all. Let's bounce before I bust on these bitches." Naylor looked at Mooney and said, "You better hope I never see you again."

Mooney's voice was as cold as ice. "Now you know if you really feel that way we can make this the last time right now." Using her only hand, she pushed her gun firmly into his crotch, right above his nuts. Mooney wasn't up for killing minors, but if she had to go to jail, she was going to make it count. "So what you say, young man? You wanna die or live to breathe another day?"

Naylor looked at the gun and almost melted. "I'm g– going home," he stuttered.

"I think that be best."

When they walked up the stairs and out of sight, Mooney peered at Cutie in disgust. She knew the little girl was looking for love, but would have never thought she'd play herself in such a slutty fashion. "Where's your mother, Cutie?" She grabbed her pillowcase off of the floor and moved toward the washing machine and threw her rags inside. "Because I know she don't approve of the way you carrying yourself out here. Making movies and shit."

"Why you worried about it?" she asked in a snotty tone, crossing her arms over her chest. "I keep telling you that you not my mama."

"Trust me when I say I don't want to be." She focused on the mini miniskirt she sported even though Christmas was around the corner. "And it's obvious that you don't need to be watching yourself. Had it not been for me, you would've been famous." She shook her head.

Cutie hopped on top of the washer next to the one Mooney was using. Her white stained panties were on exhibit for anybody wanting a view. At the moment there was no one. "So what you gonna do now, tell on me or something?"

"First of all, close your funky legs." Mooney frowned.

She closed them and frowned. "Excuse me!"

Mooney shook her head. "Excuse yourself. And have I ever told on you about anything before?" Cutie didn't respond quick enough for her. "Ain't no need in you thinking too hard. You do a good enough job of telling on yourself as is."

"Well, this is different because you caught me with a boy. So are you gonna rat me out or not?"

"Depends," she said in a low voice.

"On what?"

"On if I ever catch you playing yourself like that again." She flipped the top on the dishwashing liquid and poured it inside.

Cutie felt like such the slut puppet. "How did you know I was even down here? And them too?"

"I know a lot." She smiled slyly. "You think sitting in the window all day makes me crazy. I say it makes me aware. I knew the moment I laid eyes on them before they came into this building that they were with him. They all have the same gait and, if you ask me, the same underhanded eyes."

"What's gait?"

"They moved the same. Walked the same. Stuff like that."

She sighed. "You know Naylor and his friends are going to retaliate against you, right?" Cutie warned. "They not the kinds of boys you mess with, Miss Mooney lady. I'm just saying."

Mooney took her weapon out of her pocket and aimed it at Cutie, who flinched. "If they do, then I got something for 'em." She tucked it back in her robe. "Plus I'm too old to be worried about some boy fool."

Now it was Cutie who felt sorry for her. "I'm serious. Naylor mean, real mean, and his friends are too."

Mooney laughed. "So what, you care about me now or something?"

Cutie frowned. "No! Ugh! I'm just letting you know that you should've minded your old-ass business. You can take the info or leave it. I don't care much."

Mooney grinned. She and the girl argued a lot, but there was a commonality between them, and if someone looked hard enough, they could even see love.

"After everything I've seen, there's no way I'm gonna let a couple of little boys scare me." She slammed the washing machine lid and leaned up against it. "And you shouldn't either."

Although Mooney was "Queen Cock Block," Cutie would be lying if she didn't say she was kind of happy that she saved her. She'd planned to do all of the freaky things she'd seen in the porno movies at her house. Not only that, but she missed Mooney. They hadn't been in each other's company in weeks, and there was something she wanted to know, but she didn't have an excuse to be around her until now. She was already getting shit from her friends because of the strange relationship developing between the odd couple.

After remaining silent, Cutie asked, "So you gonna finish telling me or what?"

"What's going on with your foster sister?" She reverted back to the topic. "How are you two getting along?"

Cutie frowned and pouted. "Damn, you act like you in love with her or something. Always asking me what's up with her. When you gonna start asking what's up with me? I got feelings too, you know."

"I do ask about you. All the time. Ask your mother."

Cutie tried to hide the smile, but it was exposed. "I never knew that."

"Well, I do. And I asked about your foster sister because the last thing I saw was you beating her over stealing your iPod. Which, by the way"—she pointed in her face—"you had in your pocket the entire time. Remember that?"

Embarrassed, Cutie said, "How could I forget? You never let me." She sighed. "I'm never home to see my foster sister. And Moms took a second job, and I'm always out the house. By the time I see her or my sister, they be 'sleep. And I like it that way." She kicked her legs back and forth on the washing machine, sending banging disturbances throughout the laundry room. "So you gonna finish telling me the story about Farah or what? Was she able to get out of the situation?"

"Which situation, little girl?"

She exhaled. It seemed as if Mooney enjoyed delaying the story just to annoy her. She was certain that

Mooney was aware that she wanted to know the fate of Farah Cotton and Slade Baker. "Farah killed Knox, her boyfriend's brother! The last thing you told me was that Slade's mother came in town and found Knox's phone under her bed. So what went on after that?"

"Let's just say things didn't go the way Farah intended, when Slade and his family showed up to her house to question why she had Knox's cell phone. Because, you must remember, the only reason she had it was because she killed him in her apartment, on the kitchen floor."

"Yeah, and then she drank his blood," Cutie added.

Mooney placed her hand in her robe and rested it on her gun when she heard a strange noise upstairs. "You're right. And Farah never for once thought that his death would be tied back to her in any way. Why would it? It's not like she ever met him before she killed him. And although she was dating his older brother, she didn't know what Knox looked like."

"Sometimes I have nightmares about Farah," Cutie admitted. "With the drinking blood thing."

"I know, it has kept me up late at night too. Originally she took to drinking blood to heal porphyria, you know, the blood disease she was born with. But later she started enjoying it."

"It seemed like a lot of things were going on in her apartment at Platinum Lofts," Cutie reflected. "With all the missing people she killed to drink their blood, she couldn't have gotten away with it. Right?"

"You're jumping way ahead now."

"What about Superman?" Her eyes widened. Truth be told she had a crush on him, although she never met him a day in her life. "Did he take her back?"

"She loved Slade. Well"—she sighed—"as much as anybody can love another person." Mooney gazed into the grimness of the laundry room. "The thing was she never realized how bad losing him would hurt, until she saw the look on his face that terrible day."

Chapter 1

Farah

"Slade, I've lost everything today. I don't want to lose you, too."

After leaving the hospital from visiting her friend Rhonda, who just lost her baby, Farah trudged into the house with a heavy heart. This was as a result of the shower she hosted at her house. The guilt wore her down, and she was having a terrible day. Things got worse when she walked into her room and saw her brother and sister there.

"Why are y'all in here?" She sat next to them and kicked her shoes off one by one. Then she flung her purse to the floor. "Any news on Chloe yet?" She was worried because the day prior, she had learned that Chloe was held for ransom with her boyfriend, Audio.

"No . . . I can't believe this shit," Mia said. "Our world is coming down hard!"

"Why is all of this happening? I can't deal with this bullshit right now," Shadow yelled. "Fuck!" Then he looked at Mia, and it was obvious they knew something Farah didn't. "We should tell her."

"What's wrong?" she asked, looking between them. "Stop playing games and tell me what's up! Please . . . I don't think I can take any more bad news."

"Mama's dead," Mia cried.

Farah was relieved that this was the reason for their dismay. "We went to tell her that Chloe was missing. She changed the locks so we couldn't get inside, so we called the police. I smelled something foul, but I didn't know what it was. When the police came, before they even got to her apartment, from the outside they knew what was up. She was dead. Sitting in front of a TV. Somebody slit her throat and shot her in the chest."

"Wait. Shot her in the chest?" She was confused. "Why . . . why they do both?"

"They didn't know she was shot at first, but when they took her to the hospital, and lifted the black gown she wore, they saw the bullet hole over her heart." Mia was breathing so heavily she had to fan herself.

At that moment Farah's mind floated. Prior to this new information, she thought she was the one who killed her mother. She murdered her mother because ever since Farah was a child, Brownie ridiculed her for having light skin. Brownie hated lighter-skinned women, believing they thought that they were better than she was. Her mindset was due in part to not appreciating her dark skin because of the persecution she experienced from her peers as a child. Even her own mother, Elise, believed her daughter was unattractive and should be grateful for anything and anybody who wanted to be with her, including her drunk and violent husband. Brownie's heart was always filled with hate, so she could never love Farah.

So when Farah went over to Brownie's house, she let herself in and raised the hijab covering her neck, to slice her throat. Now she was learning that someone raised the abaya, shot her, and pulled it back down to conceal the crime. But who?

Shadow popped up and marched toward the window. He leaned up against the wall and looked out through the pane to prevent himself from crying. "You should've seen her face, Farah. Oh my God! She didn't look anything like herself. The porphyria ate her up terribly! Our beautiful mother is gone."

Porphyria, a rare blood disease, caused havoc in their family. Farah, Mia, Shadow, and even their grandmother were stricken with it. Porphyria affected the nervous system and the skin, which impacted the way their bodies produced blood. But it was the physical effects that caused the family the most grief.

Farah didn't feel the same way about her mother's death. In her opinion, Brownie got everything she deserved. "I can't deal with her right now," she said. "I got to use all of my energy on Chloe."

Mia wiped her face and touched Farah's knee. "I understand you don't feel the same as we do." She looked at Shadow and back at her. "After everything she put you through, it's wrong for us to expect you to." She gave her a hug.

Farah gladly accepted. She loved her family, Ashur included, but Brownie she couldn't care less about.

"Grandma said she's coming over here in about an hour. You know she never comes out, but she wants to be there for us," Mia said.

That's all Farah needed was to see Elise's face right now. Farah was growing increasingly uncomfortable with everything and everybody.

"I almost forgot. Slade and them were over here earlier," Mia told Farah. "They wanted to talk here instead of at Markee's. They said they can't be sure if they can trust him yet."

It was unusual for Slade to come over to her house when she wasn't home, but she understood not being able to trust his cousin Markee. Markee worked for Randy, the same man who called in the ransom for Audio and Chloe. The real twist was that Randy was also Farah's ex-boyfriend. As it stood, her life was way messy.

"I never liked dude," Shadow said, referring to Markee. "He got a lot of shit with him if you ask me." He looked back out the window.

"Something happened while they were here though," Mia added. "I gave Slade my key to get back in, because we were going to the morgue to identify Ma's body."

As Farah replayed in her mind the tapes of what Mia just said, a frightful expression covered her face. Immediately she hopped off the bed and dropped to her knees. Shadow stood up straight and looked at his frantic sister in motion. Removing the box from under the bed with her stories, she was desperately seeking two things: her journal for the month, and Knox's phone.

When Mia saw her fling the books out of the box, she finally understood her horror. "Please tell me you didn't. Tell me you didn't write about what you did to Knox in your book." Farah looked at her without a response and Mia had her answer. "How could you be so fucking stupid?"

"I been writing in these books all my life! What am I supposed to do? Just stop?"

Shadow walked over to them. "Farah, after all these fucking years? What the fuck is in them books anyway?"

She held her head down. "Everything."

He leaned in. "*Everything?* Including the stuff we did that you knew about?"

"Yes."

He put his hands over his face and paced in place. "Get the fuck out of here! Who does that kind of shit anyway? Just call the police and make a fucking recording!"

The moment he said that, the front door slammed. Farah hopped off the floor, and they all walked into the living room to see who was there. Standing side by side in the middle of the living room were Slade, Killa, and Major.

Della Baker was sitting on the recliner. When Farah walked out, she said, "So this is Farah Cotton? The girl who stole my son's heart." Della looked at Slade and, using her cane, pulled herself up.

Mia and Shadow stood next to Farah.

"Yeah . . . that's her." It was obvious that he was avoiding eye contact with Farah.

She searched his eyes to see how he felt about her, but saw nothing.

"Earlier today, Farah, my son found something on the way to the bathroom," Della told her. "In your house."

Mia looked at Killa and rolled her eyes. When she was home earlier, he kept saying how he had to go to the bathroom. Now it all made sense. He made no fewer than ten trips within an hour, but she didn't think anything of it because Chloe was gone. "So you were snooping around?" she asked him. "In my house?"

Killa remained silent.

"I think we're asking the wrong questions, young lady," Della said. "How about we start by telling me how you got this?" She raised Knox's phone in the air. "Let's start there."

Farah rocked in place and her heart skipped beats. There she was, gazing at Knox's BlackBerry, the same phone she took from him after she sucked the blood out of his body and told him how sweet it was. Suddenly, she felt hot. She felt itchy, and she was certain a fresh bout of hives were coming along, which happened every time she stressed out. But she knew this would make her look guiltier. *Breathe, Farah. You can do this. Take your time. Breathe.*

"My nephew, Markee, told me that when he last saw Knox, he asked about a cute redbone at the end of the hall."

Farah shrugged. "There are plenty of cute redbones in this building. One of them used to live here."

"He led him to believe that he came to see you," she told her. "He seemed very interested when he told him that Slade dealt with you."

Farah felt dizzy. "I don't know . . . I don't know nothing about that. I never saw no Knox."

"You okay, young lady?" Della asked, taking two steps closer with the use of her cane. Della was a strong woman, and Farah got the impression that the wooden cane wasn't needed. If anything, judging by the way she clutched the handle, it would be used as a weapon. "Because you look like you seen a ghost."

"My sister is sick!" Mia jumped to the rescue. Her hefty body matched her disposition: angry. She would rip the woman apart if she had to, and she stood between them like a personal guard to express her intentions. "She not used to all of this excitement. And, to be honest, I don't much like how you coming at her."

Della stared Mia directly in the eyes. Nobody scared Mia, not even her own mother, but, for the first time ever, she felt fear.

"Let me tell you something. I've done my best to leave my heart on the doorstep. Know that if I didn't, everybody in here without a Baker name would be dead."

"So you gonna come into our house and threaten us?" Shadow roared. "You better watch how you coming at my sister." He stood next to Mia.

All of the Baker Boys stepped closer also, and Killa said, "And you better watch how you coming at my mother!"

"Everybody calm down," Della said, raising her hand. When everyone backed down a little, she addressed Mia. "Now that we measured everybody's dick size, let's talk about the matter at hand. Why would a phone get her excited if she didn't have anything to do with the disappearance of the man it belongs to?" She looked coldly into Mia's eyes.

"I think this is getting out of control," Farah said under her breath.

"It's been out of control," she corrected Farah. "And I haven't gotten a satisfactory answer. How did you get my son's phone?"

Farah knew keeping his phone was a risky move, and now she had to answer for it. "I gotta sit down for a second," she told everyone. "I've had a crazy day." She sat on the white sofa and the smell of leather slapped her in the nose.

"Do what you must, just as long as when you get up, you telling me something I want to hear."

Farah had to think quickly if she wanted to make it out of the situation alive. She knew the look in Della's eyes was official and she would not take lightly to someone lying to her face. The tension in the room was thick, and Farah found it difficult to breathe.

From the couch she took two quick breaths and said, "I got the phone from Eleanor McClendon's house. Knox was living there for a period, before he went missing." She swallowed a gulp of air and observed everyone. "When me and Slade went over to see about Knox, I saw it on the table. To be honest, I didn't know who the phone belonged to until now."

"Why you take it?" Killa asked in disbelief.

"Slade was questioning her about Knox and, to be honest, her responses seemed off to me. So I took it to go through it later . . . to see what we could find."

"Why didn't you tell me that before?" Slade gritted his teeth.

"Things moved so fast, Slade. And I forgot to tell you that I took it, but you gotta understand that I didn't know who it belonged to."

"Yeah, right," Killa said. Major put his hand on his shoulder to calm him down.

"I do love him," she said angrily, "and I would never have kept this from him had I known. Why would I keep something from you this important, Slade? I know how hard you've been trying to find him. I even tried to support you in that search. You know that."

Slade looked into her eyes, and an expression of hopefulness covered his face. He wanted to believe her, more than he wanted to be a Baker. After all, she was the love of his life. There wasn't a bitch he could name, dead or alive, who ever rocked his heart the way Farah Cotton did. But the question remained, was she telling the truth? And, if not, why?

"All I can say is that I'm sorry I didn't tell you, but I didn't know. And then with my mother dying, and my sister going missing, there wasn't enough time. Think about it. We went to Eleanor's yesterday, and today your brother and my sister are being held for ransom. When was there time to look through the phone? A phone was and is the last thing on my fucking mind. Slade, I've lost everything today. I don't want to lose you, too."

"Did you say your mother died?" Slade approached the couch and sat next to her. The leather moaned under his weight. He grabbed her hands and held them in his. He was all man. He was all hers. "When this happen, baby? And why didn't you tell me?"

His presence made her weak. And now that she knew he cared, she hunched downward and cried softly.

"We just found out our mother died today," Mia said, eyes still on Killa. In her opinion, had he not gone sneaking around in their apartment, none of this would've happened. "And she's right. Shit has been in motion ever since."

"Are you okay, Farah? Is there anything I can do for you?" He rubbed her arm.

Yes. Don't leave me. I'm going to be so bad if you leave me. "No, I'm fine. I just gotta catch my breath, that's all."

"Now everybody has the answer they were waiting on," Mia said to Della. "So, now that y'all have your answer, can you please leave so we can deal with our loss in private? All this investigation shit is making me sick, and it's not fair to me or my family."

"Not so fast," Della said, raising her cane slightly. "I want to see this Eleanor person." She looked at the way Slade held Farah's hand and was sick to her stomach. She saw his attachment, but she lived a long enough life in the South to know a snake when she saw one. "So where is this Eleanor person, Farah? We can clear all of this up right now."

"She's not too far from here," Slade advised, remembering how to get to her house. "We can ride up there now."

He moved to stand up, and she grabbed his hand. "No!" She paused. "Let me go find her first, since it was me who started this misunderstanding anyway."

"But you got too much on your mind right now," he responded. "Me and my brothers could roll over there."

"No doubt," Major said, eager to break this bitch's back if she was lying about Knox's whereabouts.

"Slade, please let me handle this. I'll go to where she is and try to find out if she knows something. Plus, if you and your brothers go, you'll scare her and she might run. You saw the look on her face when we went to her house."

He scratched his head and remembered how fearful she looked. "Yeah, she was a little off."

"See? So let me take care of this. It's the least I can do."

Before he could respond, there was a knock at the door. Farah knew immediately who it was before she even answered. Slowly she walked toward it anyway and gazed through the peephole. On the other side was her grandmother, Elise, ready to get all up in the business. And she was wearing her blue dress suit with the matching church hat, which meant one thing: she was coming to preach.

"It's Grandma," Farah said to Mia and Shadow.

"Shit," Shadow said, wiping his hand over his forehead.

Farah twisted the knob as she simultaneously tried to think of an excuse to get rid of her. Elise was an embarrassment, and although it was wrong, it was also true.

The moment the door opened, Elise's strong body odor threatened to knock everybody into the next decade. Although Elise washed her body every day with scalding hot water, she didn't use soap due to being stricken with porphyria, so her odor was always overpowering.

"Hey, Grandma," Farah whispered, blocking her entrance as if she were waiting for her to pay admission. "Now is not a good time. Can you come back later?"

Elise pushed past Farah, knocking her off her game. "It's always a good time for your grandmother." When she walked farther inside and observed the audience she said, "I didn't know you had company." She placed her tattered brown purse on the kitchen counter, along with her church crown. Then she approached the matriarch of the Baker family, Della, who was waiting in the living room with the others. She extended her rough, calloused hand. "My name is Elise Gill, and you are?"

With a firm shake she said, "Della Baker." She looked at her sons. "And these are my boys."

"Ma'am," each of the Baker Boys said, nodding one by one at Elise. Della and her boys tried to be respectful and keep straight faces, although Elise's odor was strong.

Elise scanned her grandchildren. "Well . . . somebody want to tell me what's going on?" Elise was inquisitive and knew something was off, based on the thickness of the tension in the room. "Are you all here because of my daughter passing today? Or is it another matter?"

"No," Della responded. "Unfortunately, we're here because *my* son is missing, although you and your family have my sincere condolences." She turned back to Farah. "Before your grandmother arrived, you were saying that you were going to visit Eleanor. Why don't you go ahead and do that now? And, if you don't mind, I want her brought back here. I have some questions I want to ask her personally."

"I understand," Farah said in a childlike voice. The woman gave her chills of the worst kind. "But what if she doesn't want to come back with me?"

"That's why I said I can go with you, Farah," Slade interrupted. "I can make her come with us."

"No, no." She extended her hands. "I know what to do. You and me both know she got a heroin habit. I'll bribe her back with me. It'll be fine."

"What is going on?" Elise questioned.

"Not right now, Grandma," Farah said.

"What about one of us going with you instead?" Shadow asked. "She don't have nothing against us. Plus, I don't want you handling this alone."

"I got it."

"Somebody want to tell me who the fuck is Eleanor?" Elise interrupted. "And where is Chloe?"

Everyone cleared their throats but Della.

"Chloe is hanging out," Farah said. "And Eleanor is nobody you need to be worried about."

Farah dipped into her bedroom, grabbed her coat, and headed back into the living room. She didn't want her grandmother anywhere near her business. Not to mention they had yet to drop the bomb that Chloe was being held for ransom. "Let me do what I have to and I'll be right back."

She swished past everyone and stole one last look at Slade. She observed his chocolate skin, his tall, built body, and even the scar on the right side of his neck. She was willing to do whatever she could to keep that man. Anything. And that included getting rid of the one person on earth who knew she was a liar.

On her way out the front door, a black kid with a grin on his face was staring at her. In his hand was a red box with a lid on it. He stuffed it into her hands and yelled, “Message!” before bolting down the hallway.

She started to run back into the house, remembering the promise Randy made just three days earlier. He said he would kill her, her family, and her father, Ashur. The box could’ve been a bomb or anything.

But when it fell on the grungy floor and the lid covering it toppled over, out flew a picture of Farah bent down in front of her white Benz. She was crouched over Knox’s bloodied body, with a hand placed firmly on his nose and mouth. *Who took this picture? Oh my God. Please don’t let this be happening right now.*

At first she thought one of her friends betrayed her, until she remembered Coconut, Rhonda, and Natasha were all in the car when she tried to kill Knox the first time. They could not have taken the picture personally. Then she thought about her ex-roommate, Lesa Carmine, and her friends Courtney and Lady. They had been in a war for months over who had a right to be in the apartment. But they didn’t know each other at that time, so she reasoned that it couldn’t be them.

The angle of the photo showed someone had to have taken the picture from the right, outside of the car. Possibly from the building. *Maybe it’s Eleanor,* she thought. *I definitely have to get my hands on that bitch now.*

She was just about to hurry and find her, until she heard the click-clack of Della’s cane from behind. When she turned around and looked up, she was staring down at her.

“What’s that in your hands?”

Chapter 2

Randy

". . . I'm gonna murder everything you love in life, including those precious cousins of yours."

Randy was leaned back in a chair in his backyard, smoking trees. It was the only seat in his house. He had packed and moved everything else into his new place across town. Why? Because the nigga had beef of the worst kind.

He pulled on the sweet smoke and it rolled up the back of his mouth and out into the air. It was cold as a mothafucka outside, but he didn't mind. Not only was one of his stash houses hit, leaving him with virtually no inventory, he had reason to believe that Slade and his brothers, along with his father, Willie Gregory, were to blame.

His heart told him not to call his father, but he needed to know if there was a possibility that they could make things right before things turned deadly. Besides, half of the reason his stash was robbed was his fault.

When Willie left the DC-based drug operation he started in his son's hands after being imprisoned, he was confident that Randy would turn it back over to him when he came home. Instead, Randy gave him a package, a small area, and a small team to run it. He was learning it was a big mistake.

He removed his cell phone from his pocket and dialed his father's number. It didn't take long for him to answer. "Dad, can I talk to you?"

"It depends on what we rapping about." His voice was strong and confident, and Randy knew he had everything to do with the robbery.

Trying to maintain his calm, he pulled again on the loud he was smoking. "What you mean?"

"Did you put a bounty on my head for fifty thousand dollars?" he asked. "After everything I did for you?"

Sure, Randy put the bounty on his head. When he learned that his stash houses were robbed, Willie was the first person he thought of. Why? Because some of Randy's men were still loyal to Willie and undoubtedly turned against him. So the question was not if he put a hit on his father's head, but who told? "I don't know what you mean."

"Sure you do. But just so you know, the bounty is reversed. The only difference is I'm paying one hundred thousand for your head. You see, son, you're worth much more to me dead. Rest easy, because you won't have too many peaceful nights left."

Randy stood up and the blunt fell out of his hand. If he knew one thing, it was that money motivated men to do some evil things. "So I guess we have nothing else to discuss?"

Willie responded by hanging up.

Randy stuffed his phone into his pocket and paced the ground. He didn't understand what was happening and why all of a sudden. He wanted to blame somebody, anybody, but the finger kept pointing in his direction. With his mother dead, he lost the only relative he had left in the world.

When Victor, aka The Vet, and Andrew, aka Lollipop, walked out back, he welcomed the interruption of his thoughts. He was hoping to get some good news.

"Sorry to bother you, Ran. Musty let us in and told us you were out back," Lollipop said.

Musty took Tornado's place as his bodyguard after Slade beat him to death with his bare hands in Farah's hallway. Musty was larger, stronger, and didn't speak much unless Randy told him to. He did a bang-up job of keeping the boss safe, and Randy could rest a little easier when he was in the building. So, without a doubt, although they both were on his squad, neither The Vet nor Lollipop would be inside his home unless Randy gave Musty the okay.

"You not bothering me," Randy told them. "Unless you not telling me what I want to hear. Where is the boy?" He scanned them, waiting for an answer. A bud from the loud he was smoking rolled across his tongue and he spit it out.

The Vet examined Lollipop and waited for a response too. He was the only person who could answer the question truthfully. Everyone else would be speculating because he was the last one with eyes on him.

After his stash houses were robbed, Randy put his goons out on the Baker Boys. The only one who could be located was Audio, and Lollipop said he had him. That was less than twelve hours ago; yet, he wasn't there.

The Vet had been in the murder, extortion, and kidnapping business for twenty years. Prior to working with Randy, he ran with Willie. That was, until Willie saw fit to fuck his wife when he got out of prison, which resulted in one of The Vet's children being fathered by him. The Vet, standing six foot three if he stood up straight, normally hunched. And instead of using the powerful voice he owned, he spoke in low, heavy whispers. But it didn't make him less deadly.

Lollipop was an albino who refused to let his hair stay its natural color, dirty brown. Instead he dyed it jet-black, and it always drew extra stares from passersby. He had a thing for young girls, and back in the day it was rumored that he'd give candy for sex to any cute face with pigtails. Sex. If they denied him, he took it and claimed it was consensual later. The girls always called it rape. The Vet told him on several occasions that if he ever got proof, he would put him out of his misery. For free. Besides, The Vet had three daughters, including the one Willie fathered, and he couldn't imagine a pervert like Lollipop violating them.

Lollipop had another flaw some might consider more disgusting: he lied constantly.

"Where is Audio Baker?" Randy asked in a stern voice. He threw the blunt out on the ground and stepped on it. "I was told he would be delivered to me today."

"I wasn't there, man," The Vet told him. "Remember you had me make sure the product we had left was delivered to the new stash house?" He paused. "If I was in charge of the kid, you'd be eating dinner over his body now."

Randy focused back on Lollipop. "I'm waiting."

"He went over a steep ditch and died."

Both Randy's and The Vet's jaws dropped. "Fuck you mean he went off of a ditch and died?" Randy was in a rage.

"I was following him down the highway. He was with some bitch, and the next thing I know, a car clipped them from behind and kept driving."

"You're saying they were involved in a hit-and-run?"

"Yes. And it was real icy outside. The next thing I know, the car started swerving and they went off of the side of the road." He spoke with his hands. "The highway was dark as hell, so at first I didn't know what happened. One minute I saw headlights and the next minute I didn't. It went down just like that."

Randy rubbed his throbbing temples. "Why in the fuck would you tell me you had him if you didn't? We put in calls asking for paper, and we don't even have the kid. How the fuck that make me look?"

"I know, boss. But when I told you I had him, I meant in my sights," Lollipop said.

The Vet shook his head because he was disgusted by him.

"The good thing is," Lollipop continued, "we don't have Audio, but the Bakers don't know that."

Randy was beyond irritated but realized he had a good point. "If they went off of the road, how do you know that they died?"

"I . . . looked," he stuttered.

Silence.

"Are you positive?" Randy asked him. "Are you saying you investigated his death personally? And that you got the fuck out of the car and checked?"

The Vet bit his tongue and remained in silence. If Randy asked his opinion, he would've told him that he believed Lollipop was a yellow-faced liar.

"On everything I love, that nigga is dead, Randy. You can rest good with that. At the end of the day, five of us know they went over the cliff, and two of us are dead.

Even if he was alive for a minute, which he wasn't, you would not be able to survive in these temperatures. It's freezing."

Randy knew something was off, but he also knew half of his story must've been true. He had people on guard around Platinum Lofts, and they all said the same thing: Audio Baker had not returned home. So, for now, he would lead Slade and them to believe that he still had Audio in his possession, until he got his money.

"If I find out you're lying and you fuck this up for me, I'm going to starve you to death. That means I'm gonna place your body in a building, strip you naked, and keep you alive until you die from no food and water. I want to be clear on that. Are we clear?" He paused to let his promise soak in.

"Yes," Lollipop replied in horror.

"Good. Both of you can go to the new shop and make sure we aren't hit again. We had another shipment delivered today, and I want shit to go smoothly. We won't have a situation like last time. Or I'll kill everybody, and start all over with a more responsible team."

Markee sat in his car for an hour eating donut after donut. He needed a major sugar rush if he was going to deal with his boss, Randy. When the last crumb was stuffed into his fleshy face, he flung his towel over his shoulder, pushed open the door of his Escalade, and trudged toward Randy's house. Before his knuckles could knock a second time on the door, he was pulled inside by three niggas with ugly faces and heavy guns.

He called himself fighting as they handled him roughly until Randy said, "You can let him go. You two go on to the shop. Me and Musty got this situation." Now free, Markee wiped the extra sweat off of his lip and stood in silence as The Vet and Lollipop exited the house.

"Come over here."

Slowly he approached and stood in front of Randy.

"My stash houses were robbed, Markee. And there ain't no need in you lying or telling me you don't know shit about it because I know it ain't true. So I want to hear it from your own lips. Were your cousins involved?"

"My cousins don't know nothing about no robberies. They not even here for all that shit, man. Knox was missing, and all they trying to do is get up with him so they can go back to Mississippi. The moment they find him, they gone. But I got to be honest. They not leaving without Audio, so if you have him like you say you do, you gotta let him go."

Randy hated Markee. Always had. And it wasn't because he wasn't loyal. It was quite the contrary. In his opinion, he was weak. "Does anybody know you came here?"

"I didn't tell nobody shit. I'm here on my own." The moment he told him that, he wished he could take it back. If he was alone, how would anybody find his body? "Is Audio okay, Randy?"

"He'll be okay if I get my money. A half a million. But if I don't get my paper, every last dime, I really can't make no promises."

"But my cousins are country niggas. They don't have that kind of money."

"You think I'm dumb?"

"No, I—"

"Yes, you do! But it's cool though. Most people do. Let's just say that I know that your cousins are working with my father and that they stole my shit. So even if they didn't have the money before, unless they don't know how to flip my product right, they should have paper now."

"If you hurt Audio"—Markee swallowed—"you gonna have a problem. I just want to go on record by telling you that." He wiped his face with the towel.

"Nigga, I don't give a fuck about you or your mothafucking cousins. Somebody stole from me and I want my shit. It's as simple as that. If I don't get my money, I'm coming at you and everybody else."

Markee passed gas, and the living room smelled of rotten meat. This was the main reason he didn't fuck with his cousins or want them in town. Before they arrived, he had a good thing with Randy. Money flowed. He kept bitches by the truckloads and had access to all the food he could eat. Now all that had changed. Even back in Mississippi his cousins were always getting into shit, and when the toilet was flushed, everybody was looking at him when it stunk.

"You know I'm loyal to you, Randy. If I even thought my cousins had anything to do with you being set up, I would deal with them myself. So trust me when I say they don't know nothing about no robbery. But you gotta let Audio go, man. His mother, Della, is in town, and she's not somebody you want to fuck with. She'll flip this city over trying to find him."

Randy laughed so hard his throat hurt. "Did you just say his mother was in town?"

Silence. "I'm not trying to make it sound like you're scared. I'm just being honest."

"You got five days exactly to find out who took my shit."

"But I don't know—"

"Five days, you fat mothafucka! And if you don't, I'm gonna murder everything you love in life, including those precious cousins of yours. Starting with Audio."

"I'll try my best to get on top of this, Randy. Just don't hurt him. You got my word that this is the only thing I'm thinking about."

"Your word was never good enough for me. Find out what's going on and tell me ASAP. In the meantime, bring Slade to me. We have business to discuss."

"Slade? But . . . he'll never meet with you."

"That's why you have to arrange the meeting without his knowing. Once I have my hands on him, I'll do the rest."

"Are you gonna hurt him?"

He smiled. "You don't give me enough credit, Markee. Would I do something like that?"

Markee walked back to his car with the weight of the Baker Boys on his shoulders. Before he reached his ride, he dropped to his knees and expelled all of the food he had in his stomach. This was the worst thing he could've imagined. He didn't want to betray his family, and yet he was sure that if he didn't, Randy would execute him in broad daylight.

His mind was so far gone that he didn't see Killa in his car, checking his every move. Killa left Farah's house earlier to watch Randy's house. Sure he could've run up in his crib and killed him, but he decided to play it smart. He knew for a fact that Audio was not in the house. Even Randy wouldn't be that dumb. But he was certain if he played possum long enough, Randy would lead him to his little brother.

Markee got into the car and sped off. He appeared to be in a hurry. Killa's only question was, what was Markee doing at Randy's? "Sneaky mothafucka, betraying your own people." He shook his head. "I got something for you though, and you not gonna like it either."

Chapter 3

Farah

". . . Do not trust him. I don't care what he tells you."

A cold air crept up Farah's spine as the mother of the person she killed stared down at the picture of her trying to take his life. Farah quickly stood up, placed the picture behind her back, and said, "It's none of your business, Ms. Baker."

Della gripped the head of her cane and leaned on it for support. "What did you just say to me, child?"

Although Farah really wanted to deliver her old ass, she had to remember that Della was the mother of a man she adored. She cleared her throat. "I meant, it's my picture and nothing you need to be worried about." She collected the lid and box off the floor. "I have to go now. I'll be back soon when I find Eleanor."

She sprinted down the hallway, and Della didn't take her eyes off the sneaky girl until she disappeared into the elevator. "That was a close fucking call," she said to herself.

Once inside the elevator, she bumped into Kindle and Raven, two freaked-out bitches who moved in with their brother and single mother last week. The first day she met them she saw them smack their mother in the back of the head when she didn't give them twenty dollars. And for that, she despised them. They both wore jeans so tight you could see the veins under their skin.

"Hi, Farah Cotton." Kindle waved with a sly smirk on her face.

"How come you always look like you've seen a ghost?" Raven added before they both stepped out on the floor and headed toward their apartment.

"I hate them bitches," she said to herself.

Luckily for them she had other shit to deal with. She pressed the button leading to downstairs and looked up at the ceiling. Since Della almost caught her with the picture of Knox in her hand, she used it as a moment to talk to the dead. "I know what you're trying to do, Knox. I love Slade, and no one will ever find out what I did to you. Do you hear me? Never!"

When the elevator rocked a little, like it was jammed, her eyes flew open. Now she wished she hadn't made the comment. It wasn't until the door unlatched and she was looking at the door leading outside that she was able to breathe a sigh of relief.

Too much was going on. First she had to find out where Eleanor was located and eliminate her before she ratted her out. Then she had to find the mystery boy who delivered the picture.

The moment she stepped outside and into the night air, she was approached.

"Farah, let me holla at you for a minute."

She knew exactly who he was. His voice was steady and immediately inserted fear into her. The voice belonged to Knight, Rhonda's fiancé and also the father of their dead baby.

She knew he would never believe her if she told him that the fight she got into with Shannon at Rhonda's baby shower, which resulted in her going into early labor, was not her fault. But, in her mind she was telling the truth.

Shannon thought it would be cute to roll in with Coconut and spray perfume in Farah's face, which temporarily blinded her. To make matters worse, Shannon had walked up to her and said, "'Bitch, that's why I got something you want, and his name was Slade Baker." Farah snapped, and when it was all said and done, she slapped Shannon so hard that her heel broke and Rhonda had to be rushed to the hospital.

And there Farah was, looking into the eyes of an angry, emotionally mutilated father. His brown leather coat was soiled with dried vomit, and he was visibly drunk. As despondent as he appeared, it didn't take away from his sleepy eyes and heavy sex appeal. She was just about to greet him when she noticed something else: he had a bottle of beer in his right hand and a gun in his left.

"You're just the bitch I wanted to see," he said, waving her his way with the barrel of the nine. "Come here, Farah. I gotta rap to you for a second."

Farah paused with fear. "Knight . . . what you doing here? Should you be in the hospital?"

"I'm where I should be. Right here."

She eyed the weapon again. "I . . . just . . ."

When he saw she was about to bounce, he caught up with her. Standing over her, he said, "What happened the other day? At the baby shower you threw for Rhonda?"

He was now in her breathing space, and the smell of beer and Burberry men's cologne made her nauseous. *Don't break out in hives, Farah. Don't break out in hives.* "What you talking about?"

"Bitch, you know what the fuck I'm talking about! How did she end up hitting her head on the edge of your living room table? They telling me you did that shit on purpose, and I'm not understanding if that's true or not."

"It's not true!"

"Why would you do something like that, Farah?" he asked, ignoring her denial. "I heard you were a sneaky bitch, but would have never thought you would go this far."

"I don't know what you're talking about, Knight." There was no reasoning with him, and she could tell he was about to get violent. "But I really gotta go somewhere right now. Can I talk to you—"

"Slut, anything you got to do ain't more important than what's happening now. There wasn't anything I wanted to be more than a father, and you took that from me! You took that from both of us." He laughed crazily. "Surely you can spare a few minutes to tell me why my life is changed because of you."

"Knight, please, give me a few hours and maybe we can grab some coffee and stuff like that." She looked at the gun. "Okay? But don't do anything right now that you'll regret later. I'm begging you."

"Who said I will regret it?"

"Knight, please."

"Give me one reason why I shouldn't pull the trigger." He raised the barrel of his gun and pointed it at her face. "All I want is one."

Farah wished somebody would come outside and save her now. Slade would be great, but her brother Shadow or her sister Mia would help too. But when she looked back at the building's door, it was evident that she was alone.

"You shouldn't pull the trigger, because I care about Rhonda," she wept. "And I never meant to hurt her."

Although the gun was still trained on her, he took a swig of beer with his other hand, and when he did, she shoved him backward and took off running. She heard the bottle of beer crash to the ground, and when she looked back, he was on the concrete too.

Luckily, his inebriation left her with time to fly for her life. Before he could rise to his feet, she was history. Now in her Benz and halfway down the street, she finally felt safe. Her car, which needed repairs, made loud clanking noises on the way down the street. At least it drove. Scanning her rearview mirror, she saw him run into the street and throw a piece of glass at her, but she was nowhere close.

All the stress made her thirsty. She wanted blood. Fresh blood. But now was not the time.

"Farah, you gotta do what you gotta to protect yourself. You see how people are trying to kill you," she said to herself. "It's you against the world."

When her phone rang, she started not to answer, until she saw the correctional center on the caller ID. It was Ashur, the man she knew as Daddy despite not being blood related. And also the man who, she was sure, had no idea that she was not his biological daughter, a secret her trifling-ass mother took to her grave.

"How you doing, Daddy?"

"I'm great, baby girl," he said cheerfully. "The real question is how is my red baby doing? I know good, so I'm not even worried about it."

She could tell by the sound of his voice that he was ignorant of what was happening to their family. *He doesn't know Mommy's dead,* she thought. *Or that Chloe's missing.* She knew one thing, and that was that she was not going to be the bearer of bad news. Besides, she had enough crosses to bear. "I'm fine, but I can't talk right now, Daddy. I just wanted to tell you that I love you."

"Okay, but before you hang up, I wanted to tell you that a friend of yours is in here with me. I think he said his name is Tank or something like that."

The brakes made a screeching noise because after hearing Tank's name, Farah pressed on her brakes so hard, she almost crashed into the car ahead of her. Randy told her that Tank was in jail with Ashur, but so much happened that she forgot to analyze exactly what it meant. At the end of the day, a man she wronged was in jail with a man she loved with everything.

"Daddy, listen to me, he is not a friend. Okay? Please be careful and do not trust him. I don't care what he tells you."

Silence.

When he didn't answer, she observed the cell to be sure the call hadn't dropped. "Daddy, are you there?"

"Yes, red baby," he said softly. "I got what you telling me." She could tell he was in an entirely different mood now.

"But I got to go, Daddy. I wish I could talk longer, but life is in a hurry over here. I love you." She hung up before he disputed. Three names were on her mind at the moment, and they were Eleanor, Chloe, and Slade. She was not trying to waste time thinking about Tank or Randy.

When she made it to Eleanor McClendon's complex she tried to come up with a plan to convince her to allow her into her apartment. The idea was to murder her in private. She was devising a plan of action when, surprisingly, she saw Eleanor exiting her building.

Eleanor's white skin was kissed with too much red blush, green eye shadow, and pink lipstick. She resembled a clown more than a woman of the night. Eleanor was clueless that Farah had her in her sights as she hustled down the block with her black raincoat wide open, revealing what was for sale to the lowest bidder.

"I finally got you now, bitch," Farah said, following her slowly in her car. "I'm sorry I gotta do this, but it's either me or you. I hope you understand." Whether she did or didn't was of no consequence to Farah; she was just talking shit.

Eleanor was in a world of her own, until she turned around and saw the eyes of a redbone veering in her direction. She felt off balance as she looked for something to hold on to for support. The day she'd dreaded ever since Farah and Slade infiltrated her place and forced what she knew about Knox's whereabouts out of her, had finally arrived. Farah wanted to kill her and she knew it.

The moment their eyes met, Farah slammed her car alongside the curb, jumped out, and charged in her direction.

Eleanor may have been old, but slow she wasn't. She caught wheels as she pushed toward the wind in an effort to save her life. Eleanor was already making promises to God if He let her survive. First she'd get clean and never press the stem of a needle into her pussy again, just to get high. Then she'd reach out to her son and apologize for all the things she'd done wrong to him. But first, for reasons she couldn't decipher, she had to deal with the fact that Farah Cotton was trying to catch her.

Farah hadn't expected Eleanor to be so quick when she first pursued her. She was already out of breath, but when she looked at the tail of Eleanor's raincoat flapping in the wind, she couldn't see any signs of her reducing speed. She was relentless, and Farah had to catch up quick if she wanted to win the race.

After a few blocks, Farah was finally gaining on her, until Eleanor dipped around a corner and ran directly into a cop and his partner. Since they were leaning on a fence, smoking cigarettes, it was obvious that they weren't DC's finest.

"Whoa, whoa, whoa," the black cop said, with his hands up in the air. "Normally we have to run after you, Eleanor. You must be some kind of scared if you turning yourself in to us," he joked.

"Somebody . . . somebody is trying to . . ." She was trying to catch her breath, but it was difficult. She leaned on the fence and kept looking behind herself in fear.

"Talk slower. We can barely understand you," the Spanish cop with him responded, as he dropped his cigarette and smashed it under his worn-out work boot. He eyed Farah suspiciously when she came into view. She stood behind Eleanor like an abusive boyfriend, waiting for the right moment to smack all the shit out of her.

When Eleanor didn't respond, the cop asked Farah, "Can we help you with something, young lady?"

"I . . . uh . . ." She tried to find something to do with her hands, but they fluttered about her like loose flags. "I'm lost and I saw you officers over here, so I . . . I came to get directions."

"Well, where are you going?" the Spanish cop asked. "Maybe we can help you get there."

"No, you can't," she screamed, way louder than she wanted. Both of the cops' hands hovered over their weapons. Something about her seemed dangerous. "I mean . . . I can find my own way now." She looked at Eleanor and tried to think of something she could say to get her to come with her, but Eleanor was shaking harder than a washer on the spin cycle.

"So let me get this straight. You not lost?" the Spanish cop reminded her before eyeing Eleanor's rocky stance.

"You know this girl, Clapper?" he asked, trying to do his job for the first time all day. "If something is up, you can tell us now." Although he didn't respect Eleanor's hustle, at least he knew where she was coming from, but the fine redbone before him he couldn't be sure of. Something in her eyes was pure evil.

"We're friends," Farah interjected. "I been knowing her for a long time and was coming over to talk to her about something private. She didn't know who I was at first and got scared. But she knows me now. Ain't that right, Eleanor?"

Silence.

"Is that true, Eleanor?" the black cop asked. "Because you can say the word and we can get this taken care of right now."

Eleanor looked behind her at Farah. She didn't want to spark up more shit than the neighborhood could stand, so she searched Farah's eyes. Searched them for the hope that she would leave her alone if she didn't tell the cops that she was gunning for her. In seconds, Farah nonverbally gave her the answer she needed.

Chapter 4

Slade

"Them niggas not gonna ask questions. They all about the killing."

Slade's head was heavy and his throat dry as he plodded toward the kitchen where Mia and Shadow were. Like everybody else, they were waiting for the verdict. Would Farah return with Eleanor or not?

The moment Slade walked up to them, Shadow grimaced. Shadow was eating an apple and upon seeing Slade's face, he tossed it in the trash.

Ignoring Shadow, he asked Mia, "Can I have something to drink?"

His country accent was all Shadow needed to get ignorant. "Yeah, if you go to your country-ass crib and get it. All the drinks over here are for family . . . and friends. Not traitors."

"I know you're upset, man, and I am too. But if you call me a traitor again, the way I feel right now, I'm not sure how I might react." Slade looked square into Shadow's eyes so he'd know he was serious.

"Shadow, why don't you go roll that thing up in my room," Mia said, trying to cool things off. Normally she was stingy with her smoke, but if she had to share a little to ease the tension, then she'd take one for the team.

Mia was thinking about unwanted repercussions. Shadow was on paper having just been released from prison, and she saw Slade kill a man with his bare hands. If they fought, either way you looked at it there would be a problem.

"Whatever the fuck," Shadow said softly, so that Elise wouldn't hear him cursing. "If you want a pull, come back there." He looked at Slade. "'Cause I ain't sharing."

Mia shook her head when he disappeared into the back of the apartment. Slade stood in front of her like he was waiting for something. "Your girlfriend not here. You can get yourself something out of the refrigerator if you thirsty."

Slade walked to the refrigerator and pulled it open. When he did, the handle came off in his hands. "Fuck," he yelled, holding the large silver grip. "I'm so sorry about this shit."

"Hold up. Did you just break the refrigerator?" Mia asked, astonished.

Slade, never really knowing his strength, said, "Yeah, sometimes I'm a little too rough for my own good." He set the handle on the counter and took out his wallet. "Plus I got a lot on my mind." He set $700 on the counter. "If that's not enough, let me know."

He went to the fridge in another attempt to open it, until Mia stood in front of him.

"I'll get it. You sit down." Before he took a seat on one of the flimsy bar chairs, she said, "On second thought, just stand." She opened the fridge on the side and handed him a bottle of water.

"I was hoping for something a little harder," he said, placing it on the counter.

She laughed and nodded at her grandmother, who was in the living room talking to Major, instead of Della, for whatever reason. "I don't pull out stuff when she's in the house. She nags too much."

"Wow, I guess I came up different. My mother prefers us to have a stiff one if we going through it." Slade looked exhausted.

"On second thought, I'll hook you up. Just tell me if my grandmother walks over here." Slade stood on guard. Using the counters to hide, she made him a stiff drink, lots of vodka. "Here you go."

"Thanks." He drank it all and then sipped on the water. "I needed that shit."

"When they leave, we have to talk about Chloe and Audio. I need whatever has to be done to be done, so we can get her back. Between her going missing and my mother getting murdered, I don't know how I'm still standing."

"I really am sorry to hear about your mother. You know what happened yet?"

"No." She sighed. "I don't know anything because we had to jump right into this. And I'm not going to lie, I'm mad at your brother about all of this. He had no right going through our shit."

"But look what he found," Slade said. "Knox's phone."

Mia couldn't deny that he made a good point. "Yeah, but Farah would've told you about the phone once she had a chance to look through it. All this shit came at a bad time, Slade. I think that's why my brother threw him out of the house earlier."

"Killa looked like he had someplace else to be anyway," Slade said, remembering how he kept looking at his phone and going back and forth over to Markee's house. "And try not to worry so much about Chloe because we all over that shit." He paused, looking into her eyes. "We gonna bring them both back safe." He shook his head. "I'm just worried about Farah."

"She's gonna be fine," Mia told him, "just as long as she has you when it's all said and done."

He looked at her. "Whether we're together or not, I'm going to always protect her," he responded. "But if she lies to me about anything, I'm not sure about the relationship. I hope you can understand that."

"She's not lying to you," Mia responded.

"Then we'll always be," he said.

When Elise yelled to Shadow in the bedroom and asked him to call Chloe to see where she was, Mia shook her head. "You know we can't even discuss Chloe right now because my grandmother will flip," she whispered. "She thinks Chloe is out in the streets. If she thought anything else, she would lose it."

"She'll be back home before she knows a thing."

Slade was about to go to the bathroom, until he saw his mother on the phone by the large window. He knew her all of his life, and could tell by the way her body stiffened that she was up to something.

Slade placed his water bottle on the table. "Excuse me, Mia." He ambled toward Della, until only she could hear him. "What you doing, Ma?"

Della placed the phone into her pocket and rested on her cane. "I don't want to lie to you, son,"—she looked into his eyes—"so don't make me."

"Please say you didn't call them." Slade shook his head. "You know how they are, Ma. Them niggas not gonna ask questions. They all about the killing."

She placed her hand on her son's. "Since y'all been here I've lost everything, Slade. I don't feel like being patient anymore. I want my babies home." She placed her hand on her chest and, for the first time in ages, she didn't appear strong. "And I want Knox and Audio home like yesterday. If I have to call on your cousins to make that happen, and they have to murder everybody in the process, then so be it."

When there was a knock at the door, everyone rushed to it, thinking it was Farah.

Chapter 5

Farah

"I'm the one who didn't like violence, remember?"

Farah stood outside of her own apartment, watching the door grow smaller and then larger repeatedly. Her mind was fucking with her. Her body shivered; her skin was wet with sweat and inflamed from the hives. From the outside of the door she could hear voices and imagined that everyone was saying bad things about her. She wanted them gone. Then again, she wanted a lot of things. She wanted her sister back. She wanted Slade to love her, and she wanted Eleanor dead. She was realizing she rarely got anything she wanted.

Before she left, her orders were simple: bring back Eleanor McClendon. She was so close to getting her hands on her that she could smell the dirt in her hair, but nobody wanted to hear how she almost succeeded. It was about the results.

Farah's mind went back to how she lost her. It was after she lied to the cops and said they were friends. Eleanor had looked into her deceitful eyes, turned back around to the cops, and asked, "Can you walk me home?" They obliged and the rest was history.

Farah smoothed the loose tentacles of her long hair, sighed, and opened the door. Immediately everyone rushed to her like a wave on a beach.

Della Baker led the pack, while everyone else stood behind her. "Where is she?" Her eyes peered over Farah's shoulders and landed on the closed door. "You said you were bringing her back. So what happened?"

There were so many people crowding Farah that she couldn't breathe. She searched the crowd for Slade. Where was he? She needed to see how much damage they'd done to his mind since she'd been gone, but she couldn't see him. She would be able to tell if only she could see his eyes. "I went over there"—Farah held her head down—"and Eleanor wasn't home."

They sighed and walked away. Everyone except Della.

When the crowd broke, Farah could finally see Slade leaned against the wall. His face was as blank as a white piece of paper. Emotionless. Bland. *Do you still love me?* she wondered.

"What you mean she wasn't home?" Della asked, breaking her stare. "Did you check around the neighborhood?"

Mia stepped next to Farah. "What you want my sister to do, pull the woman from her asshole? If she says she not there, it means she not there. Can't you see she's upset?"

"We all got emotions." Della looked around the apartment. "Look at the faces of everyone here. Everybody present has feelings. What makes hers any different?"

"I don't know what's going on with this Eleanor person," Elise said, pushing herself into the conversation, "but somebody better start telling me something."

"Grandma, not right now," Mia said softly.

"Yes, right now! What is going on in this apartment? And why is everyone deliberately holding things back from me?" Elise looked at Mia, Shadow, and Farah. "And where the fuck is Chloe? It's after midnight!"

Shadow stepped up. "Grandma, come with me to Farah's room. I want to put you up on some things. Okay?" When she didn't move he said, "Grams, please."

Reluctantly Elise disappeared with him, and Farah and Mia exhaled.

Focusing back on Della, Mia continued to take control. "My sister Chloe is gone and my mother just died. Not to mention no one has told my grandmother the details. The last thing we need right now is this shit."

There was slight arguing among everyone when, through the crowd, Farah saw Coconut sitting on her sofa and going through her phone like shit was still sweet between them. Like Coconut didn't come into her house with an archenemy yesterday to attend Rhonda's baby shower. What was the traitor doing in her house? Half of Farah's problems of the day were attributed to Coconut. Had Coconut never brought Shannon with her to the shower, resulting in Rhonda losing the baby, Knight would not have tried to take her life.

Mia, easily deciphering what caused Farah to turn a shade of blue, said, "Let me talk to my sister for a moment. In private."

"Make it quick. We have things to talk about." Della gave Farah one last look before slogging back over to the couch.

When Della walked away, Farah focused on her exfriend sitting on her sofa. Even though Farah hated her guts, there was no denying that Coconut was strikingly beautiful. Her golden-streaked hair fell over her shoulders and her legs were crossed, as she looked up at everyone from the sofa. They seemed to be entranced by what Coconut was saying. Was she telling them any of her personal business? Was she trying to fuck Slade? Or maybe she was there for Shannon to get Slade back.

Farah observed Slade, the way he focused on Coconut as she spoke. In Farah's opinion he was looking too hard at Coconut. Farah's wild thoughts kicked up another level when she considered how flushed she probably looked. *She's prettier than me. Much prettier. He's going to run off with her. Have a few babies. Maybe even buy a house and get married.*

"You are a sexy bitch," Slade said to Coconut. "I can't wait to make you my wife."

Farah was just about to step to them both when Mia grabbed Farah softly by her arm and whisked her into the kitchen. "What is up with you, Farah? You all bug-eyed and shit."

"Did you hear that?" She looked at Slade. "He said he couldn't wait to make her his wife."

Mia frowned and looked over at them. She saw a totally different picture. Slade looked like he was verging on suicide, and Coconut was talking to Della. If Mia had to be the judge, the last thing on Slade's mind was fucking with Coconut. "I don't know what you thought you heard, Farah, but he definitely didn't say none of that shit."

"He like her, don't he?" Her wild eyes rolled over them. "She's cuter than me." She looked at Mia. "Look at how clear her skin is." She looked down at her hands. "I look a mess."

"I don't know what the fuck is going on in your head right now, but it's the wrong time to be acting up. Keep your cool with this bitch, Farah."

When Farah looked out into the living room again, Coconut smiled at her, but it was softer than the looks she'd given her in the past. Was she not mad at her anymore? She smelled a snake.

"I don't like this shit," Farah told her.

"Me either," Mia admitted. "She got something up her sleeve, but I don't know what just yet."

"Well, why did y'all let her in? You know I can't stand that bitch. Plus earlier tonight, Knight approached me outside because of what happened to Rhonda at her baby shower. The last thing I need is her running her mouth about me."

Mia frowned. "What Knight wants with you?"

Farah sighed. "My life." She shook her head. "Has anyone heard from Chloe?"

"Not yet," she said softly. "And just so you know, I didn't let that sneaky bitch in here. Your grandmother did. In her mind it's once a friend, always a friend, no matter how hard they stab you in the face."

"This is not good." Farah shook her head. "She wants something."

"Outside of what you believe her reason is, why do you say that?"

Farah looked into her sister's eyes. There was something she didn't hide from her, just neglected to say. When she was ready she whispered, "She knows I hit Knox, Mia. She doesn't know his name, but she thinks I killed a man when I ran into him with my car. If it comes out today, I'm going to die. Did you see the look in that old bitch's eyes?" When they looked at Della she was staring in their direction. "She won't go away until she digs his body up from the grave."

Mia shook her head. "I'm not even going to worry about all that. Shadow and I don't make no mistake when it comes to hiding bodies."

"Where do you put them?"

"The less you know the better," Mia said. "Besides, I don't want you writing about it in them books of yours." She looked over her. "You are going to stop writing in journals, right?"

"Of course," she told her, scratching her skin.

"Farah, I'm serious!" She pointed in her face. "If Killa would've found the journal instead of the phone, it could've gone worse. Your diary writing days are over."

"I'm done, Mia. I promise."

"Good. And don't worry about them finding Knox. We've been burying mothafuckas since we were kids. If they find any bones, they won't belong to him."

"I hope you're right, because somebody snapped a picture of me and Knox and handed it to me," Farah murmured. "I didn't tell you this, but I met him before he came over the day I killed him. I accidently hit him with my car."

Mia's eyebrows rose.

"I got scared because he was all bruised and bloodied, and I was texting. I didn't want to go to jail," Farah cried. "So I . . . so I tried to kill him by placing my hand over his nose. It didn't work and he survived. My only problem is, I don't know who took the picture."

"You hit him with your car?" She gripped her by her arms and pulled her closer. "What the fuck are you talking about?"

"What's the big deal?"

"Farah, if someone examines that car, his DNA will be all over it. It's gonna lead right back to you."

She shrugged her off. "Well, that's not going to happen."

"How the fuck do you know?" Mia sighed.

"I just know, but that's not what I wanted to tell you. Earlier, when I left to find Eleanor and the kid handed me the picture, Della was behind me. She almost saw it." She started trembling. "If she would've seen that shit, I wouldn't be here right now!"

"That's why she was acting so weird when she came back inside." She looked at Farah's hands. "Where is the picture now?"

"In the trunk of my car," Farah said. "I haven't had a chance to get rid of it." She used an even lower voice.

Mia felt her stomach swell. "Farah, don't get me wrong. I understand you having to kill him when he showed up here, but why would you run into him and try to kill him when it was your fault?" She paused. "You got me worried about you."

"Worried about me?" Farah laughed. "I'm the one who didn't like violence, remember?" She pointed at herself. "I'm the one who wanted to live and love, but everybody in the house wouldn't allow me to. If anything, I'm a product of the shit that went on with Brownie as our mother."

Mia couldn't say shit. Farah pulled her card and it was the ace of spades. "We were all kids back then."

"I hear you, but worry about me *after* we get this bitch and everybody out of the house. Anyway, how long was she here?"

"She literally just got here before you did. She said something about wanting to talk to you, and when we said you weren't home, Grams said she could wait for you inside."

Farah looked at Coconut again and sighed. "Let me go see what this bitch wants." She approached the group.

"Are you ready to tell us about what happened with Eleanor?" Della asked. "We've been waiting for a minute."

"I thought I made myself clear. She wasn't home," Farah said. "Outside of that, there ain't much else I can say." She swallowed. "But give me some more time and I promise I'll find out where she is." Farah looked at Slade and then Coconut. "What are you doing here?"

"I have to talk to you about something, Farah. I didn't know you had company and I tried to call, but you didn't answer the phone, so I decided to come over."

"We can do it in private." Farah rushed toward the door and opened it. "Let's talk in the hallway."

Coconut grinned and stood up. "It was nice meeting everyone." She followed her into the hallway.

When the door was closed Farah asked, "What are you doing here?"

"I can't stop thinking about the baby shower yesterday, and I'm so sorry about everything that happened between us, Farah. I heard about Rhonda's baby, and I know for a fact it wasn't your fault. Not only that, word on the street is that somebody is holding Chloe for ransom. During times like these you need friends, and that's why I'm here. To offer my support."

Why is your skin so clear? Farah desired skin like hers. "Coconut, cut the shit. What do you really want?"

"I just told you. I know you're dealing with a lot alone, and I don't want you to go through it by yourself." Coconut grabbed Farah's hands. "I miss you. I really do."

Farah knew something was off, but with everything going on, she couldn't lie; having someone in her corner outside of her siblings didn't sound like a bad idea.

"Let's do this," Coconut said. "Come over my house later on tonight so we can talk."

"How I know you not here for Shannon? Or to get in my business? I know she wants Slade." She stepped back. "For all I know, all of this shit could be a setup." She looked down the empty hallway.

"You have to trust me, Farah. If you don't want the friendship, I'll understand. . . . A lot of shit has happened. Some of the things we did to each other can't be taken back. But if you come over later and we speak about it, maybe we can work on it. It's important enough for me to try. I hope it is for you too."

Farah muttered, "Okay."

Coconut pulled her toward her body and hugged her tightly. "I'm so happy you're going to try."

What do you really want, bitch? "Me too."

"I'll talk to you later." Coconut waved, smiled, and strutted down the hallway.

Farah watched her until she disappeared into the elevator. She was about to go back inside and deal with the nonsense in her living room, when suddenly everyone rushed out.

"We just found out where Chloe and Audio are," Shadow yelled, grabbing Farah's arm. "Come on. We heading out there now."

Chapter 6

An Hour Earlier

Audio Baker

"And every grimy thing I did in life I gotta answer for."

Audio and Chloe lay inside of Slade's truck in the bottom of a ditch. The freezing temperatures caused their toes and fingertips to burn, and they were in and out of consciousness. Blood covered everything visible, and both of them experienced unimaginable pain.

None of this would've happened had someone not clipped them from behind while Chloe was giving Audio a blowjob. Since they were certain no one knew where they were, in Audio's mind it was just a matter of time before they died.

Audio's mind wandered, but when he realized he hadn't heard his girlfriend's voice in a while, he grew worried. He turned his head slowly to the right, because his neck didn't feel connected anymore.

"Chloe, you all right?" he asked softly as he looked over at her. "Get up, baby. You can't go to sleep." When she didn't respond, with all the strength he could muster, he raised his arm and slapped her in the face. His hand slid off of Chloe's nose and fell to his side.

"Chloe, wake the fuck up!" When she didn't budge an inch, his heart bubbled. "Don't do this shit to me!" he demanded. "I need you, Chloe." He looked out at the darkness before him. "You can't do this!"

It seemed like an eternity, but finally she opened her eyes. A large piece of glass from the windshield pierced the flesh of her hip, and the torture reminded her that she was about to die. Blood ran down her sides and onto the floor at her feet. When she looked at his face, she wished he hadn't wakened her from death. "I wasn't in pain anymore. Why did you wake me?"

"You can't do that again, Chloe. You gotta stay up."

"We gonna die, aren't we?" She cried softly. "I don't want to die."

"Then don't say it again. You stronger than that shit, but you gotta stay up. Somebody gonna find us," he said to himself, although he doubted it was true.

She laughed, even though nothing was funny at the moment. "Who gonna find us? Nobody knew where we went, Audio. We've been out here all night and day and we are still alone, so don't tell me something just because it sounds good! I'm going to die, and you dying with me."

"I know my people, and they gonna come looking for us. Plus, I prayed on it."

Audio wasn't a religious man. He moved how he wanted, said what was on his mind, and took whatever he wanted. All that said, if there was one thing Southerners believed in, no matter how they carried on in life, it was that God existed. Unfortunately for him, the bitch he chose to share his life with came from a family of vultures and believed in the opposite. Audio and his brothers participated in nonviolent crimes, but the household Chloe was raised in saw violence daily.

"Since when are you so religious?" she asked, trying to move around for comfort. "We do a lot of stuff together, Audio, and I never heard you pray for anything but this pussy since I've known you."

"I can't believe you said *pray* and *pussy* in the same breath." At that moment, there was a small spot of hate in his heart for her. "And for your information, I believed in prayer all my life. Just 'cause you grew up in a fucked-up house don't mean I did. You gotta watch how you talk to me, Chloe. I'm a real nigga."

Chloe laughed again. "Whatever the fuck. You still haven't answered my question. How you gonna be religious when you smoke, drink, and get high all day? You no better than me." She touched her side, and her heart rocked when she felt glass sticking out of it. It pricked the tips of her fingers. "Fuck!" she screamed in pain.

"You all right?" He looked over at her.

"I'm fine, and don't try to skip the subject."

He didn't feel like discussing religion with her, since it was obvious she didn't respect it, but if talking about it would keep her mind off of her situation, he would take one for the team. "I said I believe in God, Chloe, but I never said I was religious. Religion ain't shit but a way of doing things. Going to church on Sundays. Praying every night . . . stuff like that. I don't need to do all of that to have a relationship with God. I talk to Him like he's one of my boys because He is." He leaned his head back on to the headrest.

"You still a grimy nigga."

Suddenly he wished Chloe would go silent. "And every grimy thing I did in life I gotta answer for. All my decisions are on me."

Chloe heard his frustration and started crying. He was her first love and the first man who ever clasped her heart without letting go. She fucked niggas here and there before meeting Audio, but never fell in love with anyone prior to that moment. If they were going to make it out alive, they needed one another.

"I'm sorry, Audio. I really am. I just want to get out of here so bad. I want to see my sisters again and my brother. I want to hug my mother and my grandmother." She was crying so heavily her chest rose and fell rapidly. "I don't want to die like this. My family won't be able to handle me not coming home."

"I know, babes, but if we don't have hope, we don't have shit. I just need you to stay strong, that's all." With a heavy sigh he said, "Try to relax, but whatever you do, don't go to sleep."

Another hour passed, and when Audio woke up, he was suddenly warm, and almost every area surrounding the car had an orange glow. When he looked over at Chloe, she looked peaceful and even wore a slight smile, but her eyes were closed. Why were her eyes closed? Like he had last time, he smacked her in the face, but this time she didn't respond. So he smacked her again, and again, and still got nothing.

When a cloud of grey smoke entered from the floorboard, he knew what was happening. They were about to die by fire. "Chloe! Wake the fuck up," he yelled. His heart rocked in his chest. "You gotta wake up! Please!" Audio maneuvered his body toward her so he could check her pulse, but he was so weak that he couldn't raise his hands again to feel her. Suddenly things looked extra fuzzy and he felt lightheaded. And although the scent of smoke was everywhere, he was no longer in pain, so he leaned back and looked out ahead of him. For the first time all night, he was at peace.

***

After having the fear of life pumped into him, Lollipop cruised down the street on the way to make sure Audio and Chloe hadn't been removed from their living grave. The smoke from the blunt he was pulling on filled the car and made him higher. He was feeling mighty good until he bent the corner and saw blue, white, and red lights everywhere in the distance.

When he saw the ambulance and the police cars flooding the area where Audio and Chloe went off the road, he knew it was over. The blunt dropped out of his hand and somersaulted toward his jeans. He knocked it off and slapped at the fire sparking on his clothing.

He was so afraid of being burned that he almost hit an oncoming car. Quickly he pulled his car over to the side of the road and put out the sparks. As he saw the paramedics working diligently to put Chloe and Audio into the ambulance, he took a few breaths and counted every cop car on the scene.

"One . . . two . . . three . . . four . . . five . . ." He stopped his count. "Fuck!" He contemplated killing them, but there were too many.

As he eyed the scene from afar, he hoped that what he told Randy about them being dead would hold weight, but only time would tell.

When Audio opened his heavy eyelids, he was in a strange bed, and his family was standing all around him. He never felt more love than he did in that moment. Shit was real, because if he was looking at them, it meant that he was alive and God came through.

Slade stood in the corner, arms crossed over his chest and a heavy look on his face. When Audio opened his eyes, Slade stood up straight and exhaled. He almost lost another brother, and he felt like it was his fault. They were in DC to survive and to keep their family together, yet they were falling apart. Slade stepped up to Audio, put his hand over his, and said, "Don't do that shit to us again. I'll be back." He stormed out.

"What's wrong with him?" Audio asked, watching the door.

"He's taking what happened to you hard, that's all," Della said softly. A blessed grin rested on her face. "As a matter of fact, we haven't seen him much lately. He's been working with Willie and putting money up for your hospital bills." She rubbed his hand. "But how are you, son?" Slow tears squirmed down her face. "In any pain?"

"I'm fine." He swallowed and his throat was dry. "But, Ma, what you doing here?" He tried to sit up straight, but every place on his body was tender. "What about Sheriff Kramer? If he finds out you're here, he's gonna have every cop in Mississippi here. It ain't safe. You know that." He looked at Killa and Major. "Why y'all let her come?"

Back in Mississippi, the Baker Boys committed minor crimes. When they kept getting into trouble, Della molded her sons and instructed them on how to get away with their illegal activities. None of her boys questioned how she knew so much about breaking the law, but under her leadership, they went from stealing cars and getting into fights to moving small amounts of weed in their town.

Their drug operation was getting off the ground until, one day, Sheriff Kramer solicited their help when a group of biker boys who called themselves the Killer

Bees came through. The Killer Bees committed crimes from rape to murder. A conversation took place with Kramer, the Baker Boys, and Della, and in the end he deputized the Baker Boys and dismissed all of their past infractions. Everyone, except Knox, thought shit was sweet. Instead of buying into the sheriff's plan just for a clean record, he taped all of their conversations with the recording device on his phone.

Within record time, Della was able to lead the Baker Boys in getting rid of the violent gang. Things were looking up, until an official officer killed another officer while aiming at the last member in the gang. Instead of accepting responsibility, the officer convinced Sherriff Kramer to blame the crime on Knox and his brothers, and to lie and say that the Baker Boys were committing vigilante justice without his knowledge. The sheriff agreed, despite all the Baker Boys had done for him.

There was one problem, which the sheriff became aware of later. Knox had the evidence to prove that he was a liar, and he made the mistake of telling him to his face. He sent everyone with a badge to find them, forcing the Baker Boys to have to split up to escape conviction. The destination was Washington, DC, where their cousin, Markee, resided. Slade drove with Audio in his truck, while Major and Killa hitchhiked. Knox opted to go alone, since he had the evidence needed to save their lives. He figured one black man looked less dangerous than five. Unfortunately, things didn't go as planned.

"We found Knox's phone, Audio," Killa said under his breath. "Knox had every conversation we ever had with the sheriff on that thing. We were able to prove that he was involved. We went back to Mississippi and everything, too."

"This is crazy." Audio placed both hands on the sides of his head. They'd been running so long that he thought it would always be his life.

"We got a few more things to take care of back home with the law, but for the most part, it's over," Major added. "It's not looking good for your boy Kramer though. They indicted him on all types of shit. We gonna be good, man."

Audio grinned. It was the best thing he'd heard in a long while. "So you serious?" His eyes widened. "No more running? They actually caught that mothafucka?"

"On everything we love, the shit is over," Killa said.

Slade walked back into the room, and Audio was relieved that he looked a little more relaxed. His family could finally be together, and they could head back down South. A smile spread across his face, until he scanned his brothers again. Slade, Major, and Killa were all in the building, but still something was off.

"So we still didn't find Knox?"

"It's a long story behind that shit, man." Slade leaned against the wall.

Audio's body seemed to deflate. "Does Markee know anything?"

Slade shook his head. "Markee has been on an extended vacation, and nobody has been able to find him. It's like he's hiding from something."

"I bet he is," Killa said, having firsthand knowledge that he met with Randy a while back.

"So what else is going on? I mean, nobody has seen or heard from Knox?"

"Like I said, it's a long story, Audio," Slade interrupted, "and when you better, we gonna give you the whole thing. Now is not the time."

"If you give him the story, make sure you tell him the part about Farah having something to do with this shit," Killa offered. "As a matter of fact, you can't even act like you gonna tell him why Knox is still not with us unless you talk about that bitch. I'm just saying."

Slade walked up to Killa and stood against him. He wanted to hurt him badly, but he was family. Fuck that . . . he was blood. "Don't put that out there unless you sure, Killa," his voice boomed. "I'm sick of y'all blaming her for shit she *might've* done." Slade looked at Killa and Major. "You niggas worse than the Pearly Twins down South with all this gossip shit. Unless you know it as a fact, I'd appreciate you not bringing her in this shit."

Major shook his head in disagreement. "I know that's your girl and all, and I kinda respect that shit, but in all honesty, things not looking too good for her. That's why Judge and Grant on their way now."

"Judge and Grant coming?" Audio asked in a shaky voice. He knew when they came to town it meant blood. They executed so many people and had so many people looking for them that only a select few had their number.

"And I said them coming here is unnecessary," Slade said.

"Now, I liked Farah for you at first," Killa said, "but the question wasn't answered to the best of her ability just yet. What was she doing with our brother's phone?"

"Farah had Knox's phone?" Audio inquired. He missed so much that he was totally confused.

"She told y'all why she had it, but ain't nobody listening," Slade defended. "Have any of y'all thought that maybe Randy had something to do with this shit?" He looked at his brothers and his mother. "Willie even said that his own son might be involved. He was the same nigga who called in the fake ransom on Audio."

"Wait, I had a ransom on my head?"

"And we taking that into consideration," Killa responded, ignoring Audio. "It just seems funny that can't nobody catch this Eleanor bitch."

"Well, get out there with me and help her," Slade said. "Instead all you want to do is play video games"—he looked at Killa—"while this nigga too busy surfing the Internet for his credit score." He paused. "Farah not in charge of this bitch, and he's not her brother. We are."

"Man, how much longer are you gonna take up for that slut? She's a fucking snake." Killa laughed in his face. "And as far as her not knowing about Knox, leave me alone in a room with her. I'll have her singing like a baby."

Audio saw a brown rock-like thing fly past Killa's face and land on his nose. Slade's blow was accurate and blood splattered everywhere . . . on the white sheets, floor, and even walls. He was about to go for another punch, until Della covered his hand with hers. "You got that one over on your brother, but you won't have another."

Slade dropped his hand and placed his hands over his face. He finally realized what just happened. Farah got into his mind and twisted things around. In the end, he chose her over his brothers, and it wouldn't happen again. "I'm sorry about that shit, man. I really am."

Killa held his bloody mouth. "Whatever, nigga."

"This is breaking my heart," Della interrupted. "My boys are fighting each other, while my youngest son is in the hospital bed." She looked at all of them. "Have we forgotten that just three weeks ago, he was fighting for his life?"

Audio's eyebrows rose. "I been here for three weeks?"

"Yes, son. And you almost ain't make it, but with God's blessing, you have a doctor who gives a fuck," Della told him honestly. "It's about family now, and I don't need y'all fighting. I got one son back, and I'm still working on the other. Now we gonna find out where Knox is, and I think the way we do that is by taking over Platinum Lofts and staying in Washington, DC." She focused on her oldest son. "Slade, whether you like it or not, Judge and Grant are en route and they bringing a lot of your cousins with them, too. I suggest you stay out of their way and let 'em do their work."

"We all can't stay at Markee's," Major said.

"I spoke to Vivian, the property manager at Platinum Lofts," Della continued. "We were able to rent a few apartments for a good price on a temporary basis. I guess because with all the missing people lately, folks are breaking their leases. I want us stationed at that building, and I want everybody to keep an eye on Farah Cotton at all times. Now ,I know you love the girl, and I'm not trying to get in the way of that. I just want you to understand that if she knows something she isn't telling us, we intend on finding out. When I first came in town, she had something in her hands when I walked into the hallway. Something she was trying to hide from me. I want to find out what that thing was."

There were so many emotions floating around that Audio felt selfish for wanting to ask his next question.

But if he didn't, he would worry. "So, what happened to Chloe?" He looked at his mother. "Is she okay?"

The expressions on their faces changed immediately. Truthfully she was hoping that he didn't care about the girl so much. Now she could tell by looking into his eyes that she was wrong. Yet another Cotton woman had gotten her hands on one of her sons. "Chloe didn't make it, son." Della walked up to him. "And I'm so sorry I had to be the one to tell you that."

Audio's eyes widened, and he had to tell himself to breathe. "How is . . . how is her family?"

"From what I've seen, not too good."

Chapter 7

Farah

"If you leave me, a lot of people will die."

The sheets wrapped Farah's body like a mummy. She felt comforted this way. Stiff. Motionless. She could smell something meaty cooking in the kitchen, and her stomach rolled. She was hungry; yet, she couldn't eat. She was disgusted; yet, she wanted to feel. Her skin was irritated, and sores dotted her body from a constant bout with hives. She knew she resembled a monster even if she hadn't seen her face in days.

Life was different now. One minute she and her family walked in to see Chloe in the hospital. She was bruised but alive. When they stepped out to get some food and returned, the doctor informed them that she lost oxygen to her brain and died. Farah, Shadow, and Mia tore the hospital up from top to bottom upon hearing the news. Even when threatened with prison, Shadow held the doctor up off of his feet and contemplated taking his life. It wasn't until Elise arrived and placed her hand on his shoulder that he came back to his senses.

"Shadow, if you go back to prison, you staying for life. Now, if you really want to kill this man, we can do that, but understand that I'm pulling the trigger instead of you. I'm not about to lose another grandchild," Elise told him.

When they went home, life for Farah was a mess. She missed Chloe running around the apartment singing, fussing, and violating her privacy. She missed her stealing her clothes and crawling into her bed on the nights she didn't want to be alone. Losing Chloe punched her at the core. Repeatedly. With no letup.

She unwrapped the sheets from around her body and tried to sleep. Besides, when she slept, she didn't have to think. She slammed her lids together until Mia walked into her room.

"It stinks like shit in here! Are you washing your ass at all anymore?" Mia asked.

"Thanks a lot for your encouragement, Mia." She rolled over and faced the wall. "If you can get the fuck out of my room, you won't have to worry about smelling it."

"You gotta get up and eat, Farah." Mia stood in the doorway defiantly.

The jeans that once hugged Mia's flesh were now loose and falling off her hipbones. She'd lost over thirty pounds since they buried Chloe and looked like a totally different person. Who would've known that under the cellulite and excess blubber was a curvy woman with a banging shape? Although losing weight was not her plan, it was the only positive thing that came as a result of her sister's death.

"You can't sleep all day, and I'm not going to let you keep doing this to yourself anymore. You still have family who cares about you, Farah."

Farah tried to suffocate herself by placing the pillow over her head. If Mia wanted to flop around DC like they never had a baby sister, that was on her. She preferred death. "Just leave me alone, Mia," her muffled voice called out from the pillow. "All I want to do is go back to sleep."

Before Mia could respond, Shadow hustled past her and yanked Farah out of the bed by her waist. Her fists and legs kicked wildly out in front of her, but he had her in a death grip. Once in the kitchen, he slammed her limp, stinky body into a chair at the table. Then he snatched a box of Cap'n Crunch off of the fridge and slapped it down in front of her, along with the milk and a bowl.

The smell of whatever meat was in the oven and the sweet cereal made her stomach churn.

He didn't consider if she was hungry or not; instead, he stabbed spoonful after spoonful inside her gaunt face. He didn't bother to wait for her to chew or not. He lost his baby sister and wasn't about to lose Farah too because she gave up on life. He didn't stop until she started crying and Crunch Berries leaped out of the sides of her mouth.

She cried hard and long. It was the first cry she participated in since the news that Chloe was dead. Seeing Farah's condition, Mia cried too.

"Now, I know it's fucked up," Shadow said, holding back his own tears. He wiped her face with the sleeve of his red sweatshirt. "You know I do! But I'm not about to lose you too, man. It ain't happening." He slapped his chest. "We all we got now that Ma gone and Dad is locked up! You gotta pick yourself up today, Farah. We gave you three weeks, but we not doing it no more. We even let you stay home and not go to the funeral, and held Grandma back when she tried to kick down the door to drag you there. But I'm done with this shit."

"I feel like this is all my fault," Farah sobbed, wiping her nose with her hand.

"What the fuck you talking about?" Shadow inquired, pushing the cereal out of the way. "This ain't nobody's fault! Nobody knew that she was going to jump in the truck with Audio and get into an accident. Can't nobody in here tell Chloe what to do, and we all knew that."

"I can't take this! I can't take it." She continued the pity party without any guests.

Shadow was fed up, and Mia wanted to slap her for the way she was performing. They missed Chloe too, but they also knew Farah was going about her grief in the wrong way.

"Listen, Chloe rode with a nigga she was feeling and paid for it with her life," Shadow said. "That shit don't have nothing to do with you, me, or Mia. Now, I need you to stop moping around the fucking house and wash your ass. You smell like one of them dirty bitches down the street." He stood up in full rage mode. "I'm sick of all this weak-ass shit around here." He pushed toward his room.

When the door slammed, Mia took a seat next to her sister. "One minute he acts like he loves me, and the next he goes crazy," Farah said as she wiped her tears.

"Shadow is taking it hard too, Farah, but he does love you, and every night he walks into your room when you're asleep just to make sure you're still alive. We both are worrying about you, but it's time to snap out of this shit and get your life together." She paused. "You gotta do it for yourself and for Chloe."

"I'm trying," Farah said under her breath. "I just don't know where to start."

"You can start with a bath," Mia suggested, and Farah laughed for the first time in weeks. "There go the smile I love from my sister." She rubbed her hand softly and observed her face. "Have you looked into the mirror? You have scabs everywhere on your body."

"I know. That's why I don't want to look." She swallowed.

"Do you remember the nigga Jean Hershey?" Mia asked. "Who went to school with me? With the water head and big eyes?"

Farah frowned. "Mia, I didn't go to school with you, so how would I know him?"

Mia rolled her eyes. "Anyway, he was on the news the other day," Mia explained. "Apparently when the kid Amico went missing, he was on duty as a manager for the movie theater. Miraculously the surveillance tape showing what happened that day is missing."

Farah was relieved that the tape couldn't be found, because even though Chloe killed him instead of her, Farah was still her sister and would most likely be linked to the crime in some way. "That's good for us, right?" Farah asked.

"I hope so, but I know this dude, Farah. He's hiding something. Bet money he got that tape either because he was doing something he wasn't supposed to at work, or he may be holding it for ransom."

Farah raised her eyebrows. "You think he's going to try to blackmail us?"

"I think if that was his plan, it would've been done already."

As long as the tape was gone, Farah couldn't care less what happened to it. Her mind was on other things. "Has Slade been by to check on me?"

"No." She removed her hand. "But it seems like every country nigga from down South live in this building now. They stake out the front, and I'm not sure, but something tells me they're looking at this door. Be careful when you leave out, Farah. Shit is serious."

Farah's head tightened. In her mind she would be seeing Chloe sooner than later if the Bakers had anything to do with it. "How you know they with Slade?"

"Because they been in and out of Markee's apartment and got accents thicker than my thighs used to be." Mia looked into her eyes. "Where is that picture? You got rid of it yet, Farah? Because, for all we know, they could be going through your car."

"Yeah, I tossed it out," she lied.

"Are you sure, Farah?"

"Yes." She looked at her hands. "Mia, I miss him so much."

"You don't need to." Mia frowned. "He been keeping time with different girls, and I'm only telling you so you can be prepared. They be young and dumb, but that's what it's been."

Farah felt lightheaded as a vision of him kissing a random bitch flashed in her mind. "Shannon been over his place too?"

"I don't think so," Mia said. "But, to be honest, I think he's just doing anything he can to keep his mind off of you. Or maybe he's chosen his family instead of being in a relationship with you. To be honest, Farah, he can't stay with you and stand by his family. He has to decide, and maybe he's made his decision. To tell you the truth, Farah, I don't know."

"He over me, Mia. I know it." She wanted to cry but held it down. "Were any of them prettier than me?"

Mia looked at her spotty face. She looked horrible, but the truth might send her back another month. "Now, who could be prettier than you, Farah Cotton?"

Farah trudged into the bathroom, walked up to the mirror, and placed her hands on the sink. For weeks she avoided mirrors on purpose, and now it was time to face her truth. Slowly her head rose, and when she saw the woman looking back at her, she crashed her fist into it. It had to be a mistake. This was the worst she ever looked. The mirror shattered under the weight of her blow as shards of glass sounded like bells falling into the porcelain sink. Not able to accept her new face, Farah plummeted to the floor and thrust herself into a crying fit.

With her knees against her chest, she rocked back and forth in a ball. "This can't be my life. This can't be my life." Porphyria, the blood disease she had been cursed with all her life, was causing her nothing but extreme stress, and she wanted it done with.

Hearing the noise, Mia and Shadow bogarted into the bathroom to check on her. "What the fuck happened?" he asked, observing the condition of her bloody, broken mirror. "Why did you do that shit?"

"Look at my fucking face!" She was rocking so hard that they thought she would roll out the door. "Look at my nose! I'm . . . I'm a monster. He'll never want me like this. He won't have anything to do with me."

"Farah, if you talking about Slade, things will be fine," Mia responded, wishing she'd never told her about the bitches. "You just gotta—"

"I need blood," she interrupted as she looked up at them with her red, swollen eyes. She looked so loony that they backed up for fear that she'd try to take blood.

"I need blood so I can be pretty and stuff. It works so good for me."

"Farah, you just got out of bed," Shadow said, sitting on the toilet. "You don't need to be killing nobody just because you *think* you need blood."

"I don't *think* I need it, I do," she screamed so loud it echoed long after she closed her mouth. "Look at me. Look at my face! Y'all don't have this disease the same way I do. You never did!"

"That's 'cause we take the medicine," Shadow said. "You don't want to take yours because you think it doesn't work."

"I took it for years and nothing I did worked for me but blood," Farah said, trying to get them to understand.

She had her first taste of blood almost six months ago, when her cousin Cosmo hooked her up with Grand Mike, a man who claimed he could cure her porphyria. With the hope of regaining her beauty, since her skin was badly damaged, she paid Grand Mike $1,600. In return for her money, he gave her vials of blood in a cooler. Farah drank the blood as prescribed and immediately felt better. She was no longer ill, and her skin cleared up miraculously.

Although Shadow, Mia, and Chloe felt she was feeling better because the blood had a placebo effect, Farah believed in its powers to heal.

"The medicine didn't work because you overreact, Farah," Shadow told her. "You have high anxiety. That's what Dr. Martin was trying to tell you, but you never listened! Let's call him to see what he can do for you."

Farah wanted to kill him for that comment. "That man will never touch me again. And if you call him, I'll run away and you'll never see me again. Do you understand?"

"Farah, stop being so—"

"Do you understand?"

"Whatever the fuck," he responded.

"I need blood," Farah continued. "And I need it now."

Silence.

Mia looked over to Shadow and saw he was beyond frustration. She said, "Farah, you have to contain your evil," Mia said. "Niggas is swarming the building looking for Knox, who we all know is dead. Let us not forget that Shadow had to help Chloe kill Amico in her room. We are hot right now. You are hot right now! Slow down."

When Chloe discovered that Farah drank blood and hid the vials in her closet, she destroyed them by the orders of her grandmother Elise. Farah was devastated when she learned her blood was gone, and hit Chloe for violating her privacy. Chloe was so overcome by grief for betraying her sister that she went out to get another victim, to take his blood. It didn't take her long when she met Amico Glasser at a movie theater.

With the promise of sex, Chloe lured Amico to her house. When she had Amico in her bed, she flipped the light switch off to conceal what she was trying to do. In the darkness, she pricked him with a needle to draw his blood. Instead of lying down and taking it, Amico fought for his life. Had Shadow not come home early from prison and walked into the room to save her, Chloe would've died that night.

"What about the nigga who dropped the pictures?" Shadow added. "We still don't know who that is."

"Exactly!" Mia jumped in. "So the last thing you need to be doing is killing folks and drinking blood."

"Not to mention you still haven't found this dopehead bitch. There are plenty other things to be done, Farah. Killing unnecessary people for blood should not even be on the agenda."

"Can you help me find her?" she asked, looking from him to her. "Eleanor."

"Farah, we been looking for this bitch for the past three weeks," Shadow admitted. "Now, either she disappeared, left town, or is already dead."

She wasn't relieved.

"No matter what, we won't stop looking for her, and when we do, we gonna put something in her head."

Farah grinned. "Okay, so now that I have your help, I can go out and take care of myself. I promise not to get caught." She looked up at them with wide eyes. "I've killed many and I've never gotten caught."

Mia and Shadow looked at each other in shock.

"Trust me. I'll be fine."

"I'm so tired of this Elizabeth Báthory shit." Shadow stood up.

"Who's that?" Farah inquired.

"Look it up," he said angrily as he exited.

"He'll get over it," she said, trying not to cry. She didn't want her brother to be angry with her and hoped eventually he would change. "He just needs some time."

Mia sighed. "Farah, it looks like you have your mind made up, so what you gonna do?" She sat on the toilet lid.

"I want to go see Slade. I need to see if he still loves me."

Mia shook her head. "That's a bad idea. But do what you have to do."

The only thing Farah wanted was to plead her love to Slade, in the hopes that he would take her back. So she took a bath, put on her prettiest red sweater dress, and drank half a bottle of vodka. Once dressed, she slathered makeup on her face. It was a half-assed job and she could still see splotches on her skin, but for now it would have to do. When she was as presentable as possible, she walked down the hallway toward Markee's.

On the way to his apartment, she saw a beautiful Asian girl and a black guy carrying a brown box. They smiled and waved at her, but she ignored them. Although she didn't give them the time of day, they continued to stare at her, until she walked up to Markee's apartment and knocked on the door. Something was off about them.

When the door finally opened, Audio examined her with a brown bottle of liquor in his hand. He could barely stand up, and the Hennessy orchestrated every move he made. "If you here, you must got information on my brother." His words slurred despite being slightly coherent. "If you don't, turn around and get the fuck outta here before I break your face."

Farah stepped back because Audio's eyes told her he meant business. "I don't know about you putting your hands on me, but since we talking about family, let's talk about the fact that you killed my sister, all because you couldn't drive a car. What about that, Audio? Huh?"

"Bitch, I will kill you if you ever come at me like that again!" He stepped out into the hallway. "I loved Chloe!" He pointed at himself with the hand gripping the bottle and liquor splashed everywhere. "And I never got a chance to tell her that shit before she was taken from me."

Farah's voice softened seeing the pain in his eyes. "And nobody ever questioned it before now, but you better give the same respect when it comes to Slade. I would never, *ever,* do anything that would hurt him or his brother." She lied so much that she really forgot she killed Knox and sucked his blood. "I can't even grieve for my sister because he's on my mind. I just want to talk to him."

Audio splashed the liquor into his mouth and walked backward into the apartment. The door remained open and five minutes later, Slade swaggered to the door. He wore the same blank expression he always did. Still he looked different. The black Chopard watch on his arm with the leather band made a statement . . . he was a dope boy.

I see you doing good from the robbery I helped set up, she thought. She remembered when he first dropped into DC and was broke. Now he made a come up, and it was partially because she helped them rob Randy by keeping him busy.

He looked her over, and she immediately felt self-conscious. "What do you want, Farah?"

"Can we talk?" She peered into the house and saw that everyone inside was staring in her direction. "In private?"

Della walked out of the kitchen, wearing a red apron and holding a knife in her hand. The way she held on to it made Farah shiver.

"It ain't much we need to talk about. I don't even know why you came around here."

He doesn't want to have anything else to do with me because of how I look.

"Slade, dinner is almost done," Della told him. "How about you say good-bye to your friend and have dinner with your family."

"Give me a second, Ma," he said, slightly annoyed by his mother's intrusion. He turned back to Farah. "I gotta go." He went to close the door and she blocked him.

"Please, Slade." She held the door. "I sucked your dick, fucked you raw, and you told me you loved me to my face." His eyes popped open and he looked back to see if his mother was still there. She was. "The least you can do is give me five minutes of your time. I deserve that much."

Not wanting the audience to hear their raunchy adventures, he rushed into the hallway and closed the door behind him. "Why would you come at me like that?" he whispered heavily. "With my mother inside the house?"

"Because I knew that was the only way you would close the door and talk to me. I'm sorry," she apologized. "How come you didn't see about me when I lost my sister?"

"I knew you were okay," he said in a low voice.

"How?"

"I asked your grandmother when she came by one day."

Although it wasn't the answer she wanted, it felt good that he at least cared.

"Is that all you wanted to know?"

"Who are them bitches who be at your house all the time?" she asked as if she still had the right. "The last thing I know was we were together."

"I'm not about to argue with you about what I do in my spare time, Farah."

"I want to be with you, Slade, and if we not together, the least you can do is tell me you are seeing other people."

"I'm seeing plenty of people." His words were cold, but his voice told her his heart felt something different. "You need to move on without me, Farah. I'm not good for you anymore."

"That's a lie!" She hit him in the chest. "And you know it!"

He walked into the hallway and leaned up against the wall. "Why are you doing this shit? Right now?" He paused. "Go home and be with your family."

"I spent three weeks with my family, but they're not the ones leaving me," Farah cried. "I'm worried about our relationship! What can I do but beg you, Slade? If there's any other way to let you know how much I love you, I'm willing to go there. Just say the word."

Silence.

Slade pushed off of the wall, stood over her, and looked into her eyes. "Farah, we over. I know it's fucked up, but it's best we split. It's for your safety."

There was nothing more in the world he wanted to do than be with her, but their relationship seemed to exacerbate the situation that Knox was still missing. He knew the things Judge and Grant were capable of. He could recount many stories where people who had beef with the Bakers went missing. At one point they were even considering putting them on Sheriff Kramer, but knew they needed him to stand trial for what he'd done. At the end of the day, Slade figured if they weren't together, she'd be out of harm's way and protected.

"It's over, Farah."

"I can't accept anything you're saying to me right now." She shook her head.

"You don't have a choice. Now, get the fuck out of here, because the next time I see you, all I'm trying to hear is that you found Eleanor."

"If you leave me, a lot of people will die."

His eyebrows rose. "What the fuck is that supposed to mean?"

"Just what I said." She looked up at him with a tearful stare. "Are you sure you want to be responsible for that?"

"Do whatever you need to do. Just stay from around here."

Thinking she was saying anything out of her mouth to convince him to stay, he responded by slamming the door in her face.

Whatever she did after that moment, whoever she killed, was all on him.

She wiped the last tears away and decided to be the best monster she could be. She was awful at love, but there was one thing in the world she was good at, and she decided to do it.

When Farah got into her car, she could tell right away that Mia and Shadow put some work into it when she turned the engine on, because it wasn't making the noise. Before pulling off, she remembered what Shadow said earlier in the bathroom about being tired of the Elizabeth Báthory shit. She decided to check the Internet from her cell to see who she was.

She remained in her car for thirty minutes, captivated by her story. She immediately felt a kinship with the former real-life countess from Hungary who reigned in the 1,500s. The only difference between them was that Báthory chose to bathe in the blood of her victims to maintain her beauty, while Farah chose to drink it.

Whether Shadow knew it or not, discovering that a person was alive who participated in the same kinds of crimes did nothing but validate her. What a sick combination.

Two cars behind her was a truck full of Baker cousins with Killa in the driver's seat. He was waiting for her to make a move, and now that she was on her feet, he would not let her out of his sights.

Chapter 8

Farah

"The night is young and so are we."

The cool night air made her feel powerful as she strolled into the Smoke Shop. The honeyed fragrance wasn't offensive, nor did it exacerbate her illness. In fact it was refreshing and made her horny. The stylish brown leather jacket clung to the waves of her breasts, and her cleavage puffed out at the top ever so slightly. There wasn't a man in sight who wasn't lusting after Farah Cotton.

"Damn, beautiful. You wearing that dress, aren't you?" a short man said, pimping toward her. Every tooth in his mouth was yellow or chipped, and not a thing was attractive about him.

Farah enjoyed blood, but she preferred her victims to be attractive. She couldn't imagine putting her lips anywhere near his dehydrated skin.

"Can I take you out? As a matter of fact, can I lick that pussy dry?"

She frowned when she smelled the scent of the rotten teeth in his mouth. "You can't do nothing for me but get up out my face." In need of separation, she strolled up to a black-and-silver hookah lamp. She wasn't looking to make a purchase, just looking the part.

"Damn, baby," Death Mouth continued, grabbing her softly by the elbow, "you can at least show some respect. I'm trying to show you how a real man can make you feel, and you giving me neck. What's up with that shit?"

She spun around and glared at him. "Look, nigga, I'm doing you a favor by carrying the fuck out of you. You don't know what kind of person I can be."

"So what is a pretty thing like you gonna do to me? Kill me?"

Silence.

He took the walk of shame out of the shop. Farah sighed.

"My man, come here for a second," Killa said when he saw Mr. Rotten Tooth exit the shop.

"Do I know you?" He frowned.

"Naw, but you might know him," he said, flashing a fifty dollar bill.

Broke and busted, he strolled over to Killa's black Suburban. "What's up?" he asked, looking at the four niggas in the truck.

"Is a bitch with the red dress inside there?" Killa asked him.

Irritated that she shot him down, he said, "Yeah, that slut up in there, acting like she too good for a nigga and shit."

"She look like she coming out anytime soon?"

"Naw, if you ask me she looks like she waiting for something or somebody."

Killa nodded. "Thanks, man." He dapped him up and gave him the bill. "We appreciate it."

When he walked away, Killa's cousin from Jersey said, "So what we gonna do now? Go up in there and kidnap the bitch?"

"No." Killa shook his head. "We gonna try to get up in her car first to see if we can find anything. And if that doesn't work, we'll push to plan B."

After bullshitting around the shop a little longer, it didn't take Farah long to spot a six foot tall sexy nigga. He took his brown gloves off and stuffed them inside the pockets of his black peacoat. His brown face was speckled with a few moles, and luckily for Farah, instead of the cigars, he was coming straight for her. She whipped her bone-straight hair over her shoulder and braced herself. Before he mumbled a word, she knew he would taste sweet. Trying to play a little hard to get, she picked up a pack of strawberry tobacco to give him a hard time.

Greeting her back instead of her face didn't spoil his confidence one bit. He strolled into her space, giving her nowhere to move but against him. From the shine of the hookah lamp to the right, she saw the reflection of his face. He was perfect. "You know you gonna be my wife, right?"

She whirled around to face him and beamed. "As bad as I look? You still want a girl like me?"

He looked her over. "In my opinion you are perfect."

"Don't say stuff you don't mean, because I take marriage very seriously." She touched her imperfect face. "Once you have me, you stuck with me for life."

He nodded, loving her already. "For life, huh?" He grinned. "As fine as you are, that's a chance I'm willing to take."

"You laying it on very thick, ain't you?" She surveyed the store. "I mean, ain't you supposed to be in here buying some cigars, or hookah stuff?" She waved the pack of strawberry tobacco. "You looking at me like I'm on the shelf."

"And you love it, too." He considered the curvature of her body. "Besides, when I see something I want, I jump at it. I'm not about wasting my time or yours." He paused and looked at her cleavage. "Is your boyfriend in here?" He looked around. "'Cause I know somebody's claiming you."

Thinking of Slade made her feel guilty, but he made his decision and she was going to do her. Besides, the man in front of her wouldn't be around long enough to cause serious problems anyway. "I'm single, so my only question to you is, what are you gonna do about it?"

"I have a few ideas," he admitted. "That is if you not too busy for a nigga today."

"I think I have a little time. But I have one question."

He nodded for her to proceed.

"Can I make you famous?"

He chuckled. "Hold up, what you mean about that?"

"The question requires a yes or no answer. Can I make you famous?"

Farah believed in giving her victims a right to decide before she killed them and took their blood. If they said no, she'd leave them to it, but if they said yes, it would mean their lives.

"As long as you let me take you out of here, you can make me anything you want. And that's on my mother," he told her.

That was one thing she loved about men. They always seemed to walk into the trap and lock the gate behind them. "Before we do all of that, you have to tell me your name."

"Floyd, but honestly, you can call me anything you want." He was on a roll, but she loved it. "What's your name, beautiful?"

"Farah Cotton."

"Now, that's a name." He took her hand into his.

She grinned. "Glad you like it. So where we going?"

"Wherever you allow me to take you."

"Lead the way," she said softly.

As Farah followed his white Honda, she noticed something was off in her car. Things were placed differently than they were before. And then her scalp seemed to tighten. Someone had been in her car.

"Oh my God! The picture! I left the picture in the trunk." She needed to check the trunk, but lust and blood were on her mind too.

Nervously, she followed Floyd, with plans to check her car the moment they parked. Looking out of her rearview mirror every so often, she was trying to be sure she wasn't being followed. Nothing appeared to be out of place, but her mind was so wrecked, she couldn't be sure.

After some time, what she did notice was how drastically the environments changed. One minute she was in a ritzy part of Maryland, and the next minute she was parking in one of the most violent areas of DC. She was no stranger to the hood, but it was unexpected for a man like him. Floyd looked like he played basketball overseas, but she wondered if he was a dope boy instead.

He parked his car and rushed toward her Benz to open the door. "You cool? Because you look out of it."

Farah popped the trunk, stepped out, and rushed toward it. It didn't take long to find what she was looking for. There, under the spare tire, was the picture of Knox. Looking behind her, she ripped it up into a million pieces and stuffed it inside her purse.

"It didn't work, mothafuckas!" she yelled into the night. "Do you hear me? It didn't work."

Floyd stepped back and asked, "Are you okay?"

Realizing she looked beyond crazy, she said, "Yes . . . uh . . . It's a long story." She didn't know who was in her car, or even how they got inside without popping the locks, but she grinned, realizing that she'd won.

"Well, you want to go inside and grab a drink?"

"Lead the way."

A little calmer, she observed the run-down apartment building before her. Green moss ran up and down the bricks, and it creeped her out. If there was anything she despised, bugs and grossness were it. "Yeah, I guess." She shrugged, rubbing her arms. "You live here?"

"For now." He grabbed her hand. "But come on in, sexy. Let me get you inside before you catch a cold."

Reluctantly she accompanied him up a set of dank-smelling steps and to a blue door. Although the hood was alive outside, the inside was on some VIP shit. A large, plush sofa sat against the wall, and a beautiful mahogany table sat in the middle of the living room. It smelled sweet and fresh, but not strong enough to worsen her illness.

Floyd removed his black peacoat and assisted her out of her leather. "Damn, you sexy as shit. And I love them shoes."

She grinned, wiggled her black steel-toed pump, and posed. "Glad I could make you happy already."

"I can't lie, you did that the moment I saw your face. And them hips."

"I love compliments, even though I see you keep looking at my spotty face."

"The last thing I'm thinking about is your face." He winked.

"So thank you," Farah told him.

He was so excited that for a moment, she felt sorry she was going to kill him.

"Don't thank me. I just love a bitch with a mean shoe game." He paused. "You drink merlot?"

"Sure." She dropped her purse on the table and fell onto his sofa. If she had to, she could certainly see living there. "As clean as this place is, you got to have a girlfriend."

"Why you say that?" He popped the cork on a bottle of wine. "Because I keep my place up?"

She raised her eyebrows.

"I'm gonna be real with you. You know I got somebody. Just like I know you do. You here now, so there ain't no need in playing no more games. We both ain't shit."

She giggled. "So all that shit in the store about me being wifey was game?"

"What you think?" He giggled. "And about my place being nice, even if I didn't have a bitch, I'd keep a fly place."

"And you don't have a problem bringing me here, knowing you got somebody in your life?" She was beginning not to like him, and it was always easier killing someone she disliked. "Because I know she wouldn't like what you're doing."

"We haven't done anything yet."

"You just like the rest of the niggas out there. Always want to fuck a bitch, play with her heart, and dump her when you get yours. One day niggas like you gonna be extinct, Slade. Just remember that shit."

He didn't know what caught him more off-guard: the name slip-up or what she said to him. "My name isn't Slade. I knew something was wrong with you after you yelled at nobody outside." Farah's crazy slid out, and now he was nervous.

"I meant Floyd."

"Who is Slade?" He paused. "Your man?"

"I said it was a mistake."

"Look, what I do with my bitch is my business, and what you do with your nigga is yours. All I want is to spend some time with you and maybe put a smile on your face. Is that gonna be enough for you or what?"

She shrugged. "I'm here, ain't I?"

"Good." He handed her a glass of wine and held on to his glass.

"So tell me about yourself," Farah said, sipping her drink. "Well, what you want me to know anyway."

"Okay, I'm an engineer and I love to fuck and have a good time," he said.

I can't wait to kill your ass. "Anything else?"

"You want more, huh?" He chuckled, "Well, I'm real close to my family."

"You got a big family?"

"Yeah." He sighed. "But my sister is dying of cancer and my mother is losing her mind because of it." Suddenly he wasn't cocky. "That's why I smoke so much weed, just to clear my mind. I stay at the Smoke Shop getting blunts and shit. I'm surprised I haven't seen you around there before."

Something about what he said put her on pause. "When you say you're close to your family, do you mean *really* close?"

"I'll put it like this, if it wasn't for my family, I'd be dead or in jail right now, so I take them very seriously. I talk to my family every day, and that's not an overstatement. I put nothing above them, including my girlfriend. That's one of the reasons we fight so much and I fuck around on her. She don't understand the bond I have with my family, and I can't understand why she don't get along with hers. If Chloe dies though, I'm gonna lose it."

"Your sister's name is Chloe?"

"Yeah. Why?"

Farah downed her glass of wine and stood up. "I'm out of here." She slammed the glass on the table, threw her jacket on, and snatched her purse. "It's been real, but I have things to do." It was easy to kill him when she believed he was selfish and thought only of himself, but now she discovered that he loved his family and that their sisters shared the same name. Because of it, she would spare him.

"Wait, where you going?" He approached her at the door and put his hand on it to prevent it from opening. "We haven't done nothing yet."

When she grabbed the doorknob, he yanked her by the elbow. "So you the type of bitch who like to play games? Come over a nigga's house, drink his wine, ask about his girlfriend, and bounce?" He frowned a little. "Wait, you know my girlfriend Candace or something? You one of her friends?"

"I'm trying to leave, Floyd. You really need to allow me."

"If you were in prison playing these games, you would already be on your knees with my nuts in your mouth."

Farah grinned. "You so stupid you don't even know when you've been spared." She shook her head. "I'm giving you back your life, Floyd, but if you don't get away from this door, you gonna find out what I really came for."

He stood at the door for a second until he recognized her glare. He'd been in jail long enough to know when a nigga was bluffing. She was not playing. He released her arm and she switched out of the door and on to her next victim.

She couldn't believe she wasted so much time at his house only for him to be ungrateful. She massaged her left temple and tried to calm down. *Hours wasted and no blood.* Before she renewed her search, she had to get out of the neighborhood.

She was strutting toward her car when someone yelled, "Can I holla at you for a minute?"

Farah took one look at the drug dealer in the souped-up silver Chrysler 300, rolled her eyes, and continued on her journey. "I'm not even interested." She waved as she wrestled for the keys in her purse. "So do me a favor and step the fuck off."

"Well fuck you then, you high yellow bitch! Want a nigga to kiss your ass and shit!"

Farah stopped in place, rotated, and faced the caller. She could tell by how little his head was in his car that he wasn't as big as Floyd. Despite his height, the one thing he had going was his looks. As a matter of fact, at a distance, he was inviting. So she twinkled and said, "On second thought, I *can* spare a few minutes." She approached his window and peered inside. The car was neat and clean. "I'm sorry about how I carried shit back there. I just broke up with my boyfriend and got a lot on my mind. I don't have a right to be taking it out on you though."

He smirked. "You were pretty cold." He was laying it on thicker than peanut butter. "But damn, why you let me unleash on you first? I wasn't even trying to come at you like that."

"It's not even that deep. Let's move past that shit." She looked up at the stars. "The night is young and so are we. Anyway, what's your name?" She leaned on his car.

"Glover, but my friends call me G."

"So, G, you got somewhere to be in the next fifteen minutes? After the day I just had, I really don't want to be alone."

His words flowed coolly out of his mouth, but his smile resembled a Cheshire cat. "I'm good if you are." He slapped his hands together and rubbed them like he was trying to warm up. "My mother gonna be gone all day. If you want, we can fuck at her crib. I don't have to check up with my weed man until later."

This nigga is perfect. He was cute enough to fuck, but irritating enough to soothe her conscience. "I'll go with you on one condition."

"As fine as you are, I'll give you anything but money."

Don't worry, nigga. I'm gonna take everything you got anyway. "You have to answer my question, can I make you famous?"

"You can make me anything you want! Believe that."

She grinned. "Well, lead the way."

***

Farah was sitting on top of Glover's dick, bucking her hips wildly. Sweat spilled off of her body and melted into the curly black hairs on his chest. His fingernails dug into the flesh of her yellow ass as he pushed into her wetness. She wasn't a pro by a long shot in the bedroom, but the last time she fucked Slade, he gave her enough jewels on how to move her waist. *If only you could see me now. You'd be proud,* she thought.

While on top of him, she leaned back so that her hands were on the bed while she pushed and wound against him. Her pussy syrup dripped all over his legs, and the bed was soaking wet. She fell into him, and her breasts pressed against his lips.

"Kiss them for me, baby." He removed his hands from her ass and gripped her left breast and sucked the nipple. "Work that tongue, G. Ummmm, just like that. That shit feels so good." If she closed her eyes tight enough, in her dreams he could've passed for Slade.

Although she was there for blood, she would be lying if she didn't say she was highly aroused by his fuck game. The nigga was brilliant, and in her opinion it was a shame that such good dick would go to waste.

Finished with her left titty, he moved to the right. When he licked them both clean, he placed his hands back on her cheeks and squeezed. "Damn, bitch, buck them hips just like that." He moaned. "I'm about to splash into this pussy."

Farah spun, pumped, and moved her waist as much as she could. Outside of fucking Slade, this was the best sex she ever had.

"You almost got me there, ma. Work it, work it!" As much as he pumped her up that she was handling business, he could've coached even the Redskins to victory. "Keep it just like that."

"You like what I'm doing, don't you?" This was the best reaction she ever got from a nigga outside of Slade.

"I love this shit, girl! You got me 'bout to juice up in that thing."

"Tell me you love this pussy." She was on the verge of an orgasm. "Talk to me nasty, or you not gonna get no more."

Farah getting up before he busted was not an option, so if he had to talk in tongues to keep beating that thang, then so be it. "I fucking love this fucking pussy, bitch. You a sexy red bitch, and I'm 'bout to let loose in this pussy."

The more shit he talked, the more she couldn't wait to taste his blood, so right when he was about to cum, she fell into his body, removed the razor blade that she had stuffed under his pillow when he wasn't looking, and dug into the jugular vein on his neck. To shield the pain, she bit into his neck and sucked the wound. Glover never felt anything so sexual in all of his life, so he had no idea that he was sliced. He was about to write it off as the best sex he ever had, until she rose up and her lips were bloody red.

"What the fuck?" He pushed her off of him and she tumbled to the floor. In panic mode, he held on to his neck and blood oozed through his fingers. "Why did you cut me?" He looked down at her. His blood was all over her breasts and belly. "Why would you do some shit like that?"

Farah scooted away and ended up with her back against the wall. Literally. "I was just tasting you, baby." She laughed, exposing her red teeth. "And you're so sweet."

Fuming mad, Glover dipped toward his dresser and grabbed his mother's 9 mm. Now armed, he dodged after her, ready to take her life.

***

At the moment, Farah's driving skills resembled a drunk's, but although she had wine earlier, she was as sober as a newborn baby. Her driving was impacted because of what had just happened. Glover almost switched shit on her and took her out of this world, instead of the other way around. She still couldn't believe she was alive. She clutched the steering wheel so hard her fingernails were imprinted on it.

When G pushed her to the floor and approached her with the gun, had it not been for the steel heel on her shoe, which she used to stab him in his groin area, she would've been murdered. After she stabbed him repeatedly everywhere her shoe would land, he lost so much blood that she was able to wrestle the gun out of his hand and put a bullet in his head. When she was done, she cleaned the place up as much as possible.

Starved, she strolled into the IHOP restaurant to order pancakes with cheese. When her order was complete and she was on her way out, she smacked into Rhonda, who was walking inside. At first she was going to pretend she didn't see her, but Rhonda blocked her path and stared directly into her eyes.

This is all I need right now. "Hi, Rhonda." Farah sounded dry.

"I'm sorry to hear about what happened to Chloe." Her expression was bland and emotionless. "She was always real cool with me and I liked *her* a lot." She looked her over. "So, how are you holding up? You look good."

"I'm not as good as I look." Farah observed Rhonda's hands and the way she was carrying herself. Something felt off. "Knight came up to me the day my sister died. He kind of blamed me for everything that happened with the baby and it fucked my head up. You know it wasn't done on purpose, right?"

"He told me what happened." She ignored her question and stepped closer to Farah, who backed up. "But if you alive, it means you're okay. Thank God for small favors, right?"

"I'm alive, but it wasn't without a fight, Rhonda. He had a gun and everything. Had I not pushed him down, I would be dead."

"I don't care what you would have done to him, Farah. Me and Knight are not together anymore."

"What?" She frowned. "Why?"

"Because he doesn't want to be with a woman who can't hold a baby."

"That's so fucked up on his part!" She reached out to touch her arm, but Rhonda snatched it away. "I liked Knight for you. We all did."

"Well, he didn't feel the same way." Her creepy expression made Farah uncomfortable.

"How come it looks like you're still mad at me?"

"You get anything in the mail lately?" Rhonda asked with a grin. "Anything at all?"

The hair on the back of Farah's neck rose. The first thing she thought about was the picture she had ripped up in her purse. Although she didn't get it in the mail, she received it all the same. "Why you say that?"

Rhonda smiled and walked past Farah to the counter.

"Rhonda, why did you say that?"

"No reason." She grinned. "And if you talk to Slade again, tell him I said hi."

Chapter 9

Slade

"Nigga, I don't give a fuck if we blood or not. Don't ever tell me I'm not doing what I can to protect my brothers."

Slade sat at a flimsy square gray card table inside of a gym with Major, Killa, Willie, and some of Willie's men. Willie owned the gym because of the openness , which made it difficult to place microphones if the Feds were after him. The smell of dirty boxing gloves and unwashed floors hovered in the air, but nobody seemed to mind. Audio was outside chain-smoking because he hadn't come to grips that he and Chloe were done. Truthfully his absence was appreciated, because these days, Audio never knew what to say out of his mouth.

After the main objectives were covered, Willie decided to talk about what else was on his mind. "You're not going back to Mississippi, Slade." He looked him square in the eyes. "I hope you know that."

The last time somebody told him he wasn't going home it was Willie's son, Randy, and suddenly Slade could see the family resemblance. Slade looked at his brothers in disbelief. "What you mean, I'm not going back?" He frowned and placed his clenched fist on the table. "I thought we made our arrangement clear when we shook hands. DC not for me or my brothers."

He covered his face with a soft smile. "Let me clear up my position. What I'm saying is that I'm going to make you an offer you can't refuse." He looked at Major and Killa. "All of you. Once you see the paper I'm putting on the table, you won't want to ever go back, except on holidays." He chuckled.

Slade eased up a little, although he was still tense. The money had been great since he'd been in Washington, DC. It allowed him to be able to rent his own place in Platinum Lofts, pay his brother's hospital bill, and buy a new ride. Not to mention, with having paper, the search for Knox was constantly funded. But it didn't make him like DC any more. His only objective was reconnecting family and returning to Mississippi.

"Me and my brothers appreciate everything you've done for us. We do, but you need to prepare yourself for the fact that we are out the moment we find our brother. DC may be good for you, but for us it's bad luck," Slade said in a low voice. "Not to mention, our cousin Markee has been missing for months. It's not like him to up and roll out without talking to anybody in the family. Something ain't right."

"And ain't no amount of money you can offer up can get us to change our minds," Killa added, ready to board the next thing smoking out of the city. "If you ask me, we losing more than we've gained."

Willie's expression was tight because he was so used to throwing money around to grant his wishes that he couldn't understand rejection. "I'm sorry about your family members. I really am. But unlike the respect I have for Knox, when I first met him, I can't say Markee is of the same breed."

Slade frowned and sat closer to the table. "Anybody with a Baker name is of the same breed." He sat back in his chair. "Even if he wasn't, it ain't your call."

"You're right, and I didn't mean it that way. I'm just saying that we do great together, so whether or not you reconnect with your family, I don't see why we should end the relationship. Can you honestly say that you've made as much money ever before in your life as you have with me?"

"I can honestly say that none of this shit matters," Slade explained. "Like my brother said, family does. Not to mention, there are a lot of niggas I need to get away from out here before I catch a case."

Willie waved his hand for a bottle of Scotch to be brought to the table. "Are you referring to Randy? If you are, you need to know he's not moving the same. He's afraid, son. The one hundred thousand dollars I placed on his head has him stuck. He moved out of his house and everything. And because I met with the connect and made an exclusive deal, he can't cop from him anymore."

"I went by his house the other day and saw he moved," one of his men said.

"So you see, son, it's all good. He won't be coming out of his hole for a while."

"You can't trust shit Randy does or says," Major responded. "I'm still not understanding why he would say he had a ransom on my brother's head when he didn't."

"If I know him like I know I do, it was probably the plan to kidnap your brother." He looked at the Baker Boys seriously. "But his team doesn't respect him, so maybe something went afoul. What I want to express to you boys is that we work good together, and if taking my own son out will make you feel safer, then . . ."

Slade sat up straight. "Get this straight: it ain't a nigga alive who can make me feel unsafe, or safer. I'm going back home because there's nothing here for me anymore. Case closed."

Killa and Major knew he was referring to Farah despite never saying the words, but they both knew their brother and could bear witness to the fact that Slade had never been this destroyed before. All of the money and all of the bitches he had in his life couldn't stop his heart from beating for her.

"I understand what you're saying," Willie said, sliding the glasses of Scotch toward each of them. They weren't the type of niggas to sip Scotch, but they accepted the glasses anyway. "You have to respect a man with goals. I just know that my business ventures have increased with you boys around, and if there's something I can do to change your minds, I won't stop until I find it."

Something in his voice told Slade that, in the future, there would be problems with him when it was time to bounce. Besides, any man who would kill his own son could never be trusted. For now, while he was making paper, it was best to stay cordial.

"And I can respect your diligence, Willie, but the answer will always be no."

They were just about to down their drinks when an albino with coal-black hair strutted inside the gym with a navy blue gym bag over his shoulder. Willie's men immediately rushed him, knocking him to the floor. His bag was yanked from his grasp and the contents were searched. When the only things they found were some boxing gloves, a towel, and a mouth guard, everyone breathed a little easier.

Now that things were safe, Willie strolled up to him, his brown tailored suit hanging effortlessly off of his frame. He grabbed him up by the top of the shirt and his men gripped him by the arms. "How did you get in here?"

"The door was unlocked." He moved to point at the door, but Willie's men thought he was making a crazy move and punched him in the gut. The man doubled over before his men stood him up straight again.

"I asked you, how did you get in here?" Willie repeated.

"I'm telling you, man, the door was unlocked."

"So you calling me a liar?" He frowned, stepping closer.

"On everything I love," he said in a weak voice, "the door was unlocked when I walked in here. I wouldn't even fuck around with you like that."

Willie was just about to give the order to kill him, when one of his men whispered something in his ear. It was then that he remembered that Audio went outside to chain-smoke, leaving all of then vulnerable. The kid was getting on his fucking nerves and, truthfully, he didn't see his benefit. In his world, he got rid of things that were useless. "Didn't you see the sign that the gym was closed?"

"I come here every Saturday night, man." He paused. "If it was there, I probably overlooked it." He looked around at everyone. "I would've never stepped in here unless I thought it was open for business. All I wanted to do was hit the bag a few times."

Willie looked over his light skin, black cotton sweatpants, and matching shirt. He looked harmless enough. Although Willie was prepared to give him the nod of approval, Slade saw something different in his eyes.

"Get out of here while you're still able. We busy right now." Willie shooed him with a wave of his hand.

Lollipop grabbed his gloves from the floor when Slade asked, "You box?" Everyone looked at Slade.

Lollipop stopped what he was doing, eyed him suspiciously, and said, "I do all right."

Slade stood up and approached. "How about me and you go a few rounds?" Killa and Major followed him. Slade stopped inches away from Lollipop. "You got gloves I can borrow, Willie?"

"Yeah," he responded skeptically, "we got some in the back." Willie waved his hand, sending one of his men on the search.

"I thought y'all were having a meeting," Lollipop interjected. "I'm not trying to break that up." He picked up his mouth guard and towel and seemed in a hurry to go back out.

"It ain't a problem. We rounding up anyway." Slade removed his watch and handed it to Major. "You look a little out of it. You sure you came to hit the bag?"

Lollipop nodded.

"Okay, let's go at it then."

This was not the plan. Lollipop was instructed to go to the meeting, see who was present, and report back to Randy. Originally he knew it was a bad idea to show up at the gym, for fear he'd be recognized, but now things seemed much more serious. He heard about how Slade murdered one of Randy's men with his bare hands. He wasn't trying to be his next victim. But after much time and discussion on Randy's part, he reluctantly gave in. "I should have a few minutes to go one round."

Slade grabbed the gloves and wrap from one of Willie's men, and Major and Killa put them on his fists. When they were secure, he slammed them together and hopped inside the small ring next to them. When he looked down, Lollipop hadn't moved an inch. "You coming in or what?"

Lollipop could feel his balls in his throat. Something about Slade told him it was a bad idea, but he couldn't back out now. He didn't even know if the gloves he had would fit, because they belonged to Randy. After one of Willie's men slipped them on, he felt they were too tight, but jumped into the ring anyway. "I'm with it."

Slade smiled, slammed his gloves together, and grinned. "Good, let's do it." He hopped around the ring a few times before throwing a jab geared for Lollipop's jaw. Quick on his feet, he got out of the way just in time. "I see you know how to dodge a punch. Let's see if you know how to take one." Using a more calculated move, Slade slammed his glove into his jaw as lightly as possible. His objective wasn't to kill him, at least not right now. He wanted to hurt him to see what he was made of. Still, his lightest blow sent Lollipop flying against the ropes.

Lollipop shook his head and tried to toss away the pain. His only objective now was to make it out of the ring alive. "I ain't hardly feel shit." He rubbed his throbbing jaw. "But I see you a—"

His sentence was broken because Slade stole him in the face again, forcing Lollipop's lips to slap together as he fell to the floor. This time Lollipop couldn't recall where he was or his first name. For a second he lay in the ring, face up, trying to decipher if he was a man or his cousin Melinda from Virginia.

"You all right, man?" Willie grinned from the outside. "Because you can stop anytime you want." Although the show wasn't planned, he had to admit it was great entertainment. "This shit ain't mandatory."

Lollipop turned over and crawled to the ropes. With the little strength he had left, he pulled himself up, loosely dangling from the sides. Finally on his feet, he turned around and faced Slade. Unlike his present condition, Slade looked unscathed. "I'm fine," he said to everyone. "Give me a second."

"You sure?" Slade asked with slight remorse. Originally he was looking to take his frustrations out on someone, considering all of the fucked-up things going on in his life, so when Lollipop came in with the gloves, he figured he'd be a worthy adversary. Now he felt sorry for the man. "Because we can end this now."

"I said I'm fine." He smashed his gloves together and approached. "Stop wasting time, nigga. Come on!"

Originally Slade was thinking of the best excuse to let him off of the hook; that was, before the left side of his face was met with a crushing blow. The punch took him so much off-guard that he fell into the ropes and lost time. When Slade stood back on his feet, he grinned. Maybe he was a worthy opponent after all. Now he would show no mercy. Before Lollipop could understand the damage he caused, he was struck in the chin with an uppercut that sent him flying out of the ring. He flapped his legs and arms until he landed at Willie's crocodile-shoe feet.

"Dammmnnnnn!" Major cheered. "You just space-shuttled this nigga!"

Willie laughed heartily, looking down at him. "I think you've had enough," he told Lollipop. "You should be going about your way now." He helped him to his feet, and one of his men stuffed Lollipop's bag into his chest. He gripped it with his glove-covered hands and tried to stop swaying. "Come back when it's not so busy and get some practice. Because you need it."

"When you do come back, make sure Slade isn't here." One of Willie's men laughed.

Lollipop held tightly to his things, looked at Slade once more, and angrily stomped off.

"I don't know, Slade," Willie said, approaching the ring. "Something tells me you have a new enemy."

Killa removed one of his gloves and Slade said, "Tell him to get in line."

After the boxing match, Slade and his brothers exited the gym, with Willie and his men following them. The Baker Boys were about to approach the truck when Slade scanned the outside surroundings. "Where is Audio?" His head swiveled from right to left quickly. "Fucking with that dude in the ring, I forgot that he never came back."

Killa stepped away from his brothers, and from where he stood, looked up and down the dark streets. "I don't know. He told us he was coming out here to smoke a cigarette." He zeroed in on a building on the side of the gym. "Maybe he—"

"Wait, there he goes right there." Major pointed up the street.

Slade glanced up the block and saw his brother on the side of the building, talking to some chick. He was furious for a number of reasons. First of all, he should've come back to the meeting a long time ago. Secondly, the way his body swerved, he could tell he was busted. "Audio, get the fuck over here, man! We 'bout to bounce!"

The girl and Audio looked at them. Audio raised a finger and replied, "Give me a second."

"Your time is up, nigga. Leave that bitch alone and come now," Killa yelled. The girl frowned and placed a fist on her hip.

"Y'all good?" Willie asked, although he wanted to offer his opinion on Audio's recklessness. He thought it was unprofessional and dangerous that he would hang in the shadows when they had beef. He decided against it, knowing it would be bad for business.

"Yeah, we fine." Slade gave him some dap. "We'll get up with you later."

"A'ight, be easy." Willie and his crew climbed into his Navigator and left the scene.

Slade refocused his attention on Audio, who was now wobbling toward his brothers. He shook his head, although he understood why he was in a bad way since Chloe was killed. "Go help him, Killa," Slade said in disgust. "Before this nigga falls on his face."

Killa and Major offered their shoulders for support as they walked him toward the truck. They were almost there when, through Slade's peripheral vision, he could see a car pulling up slowly. When he turned around, he witnessed a black Dodge Caravan slither up the block. When the tinted windows rolled down, three weapons were aimed in their direction. Bullets with their names on them spit from the guns, and Slade saw a glimpse of Lollipop's face as he led the gunfire. He knew something was off with that nigga the moment he saw his face, and he let him slide. Now his brothers might have to pay with their lives.

The Baker Boys dropped to the ground, and Slade released the .45 tucked in his waist. When he looked toward his brothers to see if they were okay, he saw Killa had already released his hammer and was firing so many bullets at the assassin that the windows were completely destroyed. Together, Slade, Killa, and Major lit the car up like a California wildfire. Holes splattered into the interior of the car as it flew away from the scene.

When they were gone Slade ran up to his brothers and checked them over. "Y'all okay? Anybody hit?"

"Naw, we good," Killa responded, looking at Major, who was too stuck to respond. "I wonder who the fuck that was." He looked down the street.

"I know who it is," Slade responded, deciding to keep Lollipop's identity to himself for the moment. "And when we catch this nigga, he's gonna wish he landed." He focused on Audio, who, although still drunk, was a little more lucid. "If you don't get this drunk shit under control, you on the first thing back to Mississippi, nigga." He stabbed his finger into Audio's chest. "I'm not fucking around with you no more! You ain't the only one who lost somebody. Get over yourself."

"I'm sorry, man," he said, rubbing his hand over his face. "I know you're right."

"Looks like they landed anyway!" Major said, looking up the street.

When Slade saw the girl Audio was with lying in her own blood, he shook his head. "Damn!"

Slade slammed Markee's apartment door shut and stomped inside, angry that he hadn't found Eleanor. If he wasn't chasing Audio to make sure he didn't kill himself, he was searching for her. Nobody had seen her on the streets or in the dope houses. Slade even blessed a few dope boys with some money to let him know if she showed up. . . . Nothing.

He threw his coat on the couch and walked to the kitchen to grab a bottle of water. When he turned around, he saw his mother, Major, Killa, Audio, and two people he hadn't seen since he'd left Mississippi: his cousins Judge and Grant. He was so focused on Eleanor when he first entered that he didn't see anybody in the apartment.

When he saw the looks on his family's faces, he asked, "What's going on?" He focused back on his cousins Judge and Grant. "And what are they doing here, Ma? I thought we agreed that you would at least give me a chance to bring things under control first. We don't need outside help."

"First off, we're not outside help," Judge said, approaching him from the kitchen. "We're family, and I think we're getting off to a wrong start." He grinned. "Slade, I haven't seen you in months, man. The least you can do is give me some love." He opened his arms, but Slade didn't accept.

Judge and Grant Baker were both certified killers, and they were anything but practical. When people called them to eliminate a problem, the research should have already been done, which meant they were there for the bottom line, to dispose of the problem.

Judge stood six foot five and he was all meat. Although Slade could kill a man with his bare hands, just looking at Judge would force an opponent to change his mind. He was as chocolate as Slade and the rest of the Bakers, but as ugly as a rhino, and he couldn't give a fuck about what you thought about his appearance. He had a beautiful wife whom he adored and kept at an undisclosed location. At the end of each job, he returned to her, and they carried on as if blood was not shed. As long as he had her, everything and everybody else was trivial.

Grant, on the other hand, stood five foot five, and although he was the shorter of the two, he was the one you had to worry about. He made the decisions and Judge enforced them. Grant always wore a stiff smile on his face to hide his sinister intentions, and the fact that he loved killing was undisputed. So it was obvious why Slade was worried about seeing them. If they were in town, it meant one thing: Farah was going to die.

"Ma, can you tell me why you call Judge and Grant?" Slade asked. "You know we were handling the situation. I told you that when you first told me you were reaching out to them!"

"I want to tell you why I made a decision to call them, baby, but first, were you able to find Eleanor?" Della stood in the middle of the floor and balanced herself on her cane. When he didn't answer she continued, "Were you able to find her or not, son?"

He stepped closer to his mother. In a low voice he said, "Ma, why you doing this? I'm so close to finding her, and I told you all I needed was a little time. Not to mention the entire Baker family is already in the building. We didn't need them."

"Close to finding her and finding her are two different things. Aren't they, son?"

Slade threw his weight into the sofa, placed his hand over his face, and eyed Judge and Grant. They were there to murder somebody he loved, without even considering that she may not be involved. This was the last thing he needed at the moment. It wasn't that he didn't fuck with his cousins, because he loved them. The problem came in choosing between the Baker name and Farah Cotton.

"What happened today?" Della asked. "When you went to search for her?"

"I went by her place, but she don't live there no more." He wiped his hands over his face again and dropped them into his lap.

"How you know she moved?" Della asked, sitting next to him.

"I paid the property manager a few bucks to let me inside her place. Everything she owns is gone, except for some things she had in the refrigerator." He exhaled. "No way she still lives there."

"I'm wondering why she would move," she continued.

"I don't know." He shrugged. "But the more this chick hides, the more I believe Farah. She's hiding something."

"What you talking about?" Killa asked. "Markee was the last person to see Knox, and he said she was good people. As a matter of fact, he threatened to hit him if he disrespected her."

"I know all that, but if she didn't have nothing do with Knox's disappearance, why leave? The dope boys said they haven't even seen her in days. I know she not clean, so where she copping from? She's a certified dopehead and can't go too long without a hit. And when she tries to find one, I'll be there waiting."

"What about Willie?" Killa asked. "He used to be cool with her. If I'm not mistaken, she used to sell weed for him. Does he know anything?"

"I talked to him about her the other day," Della said. "Even he hasn't been able to find her."

"Okay, so where else could she be then?" Grant asked. His voice was calm, but his body was tense.

"We have no clue," Major responded.

"Well, let me and Judge try a hand at it, man. You've done a lot, and we don't want you thinking you're alone in this shit." He stepped closer. "All we need to know is if she has any family in the area, who was the last person who saw her, and stuff like that. Since she's dodging you, maybe she's more likely to talk to us instead."

"She doesn't know anything more than she's said already," Slade responded. "Trust me." He looked at Judge and Grant. "Let me handle this. Besides, Knox is my brother."

Irritated, Grant stepped back. "Let you handle it like you handled protecting Audio? Because, from what I understand, he almost got killed the other night fucking with you." He paused. "Oh, I get it. Maybe you want to handle it like you protected Knox. To make matters worse, nobody has seen or heard from Markee. I don't know, man, but something tells me that the way you doing things ain't working no more."

"We didn't come all the way out here to be fucking around," Judge muttered. He was so tall that his voice bounced off the ceiling.

"He's right," Grant added. "We came to find Knox, and if you want to find your brother like you say you do, then you should appreciate our help."

Grant didn't have a chance to defend himself. By the time his last syllable was uttered, he was slumped to the floor and looking up at the ceiling. Judge was about to approach when Killa, Major, and Audio stopped his movements by blocking him like a wall. Slade stood over Grant and gave him his undivided attention.

"Nigga, I don't give a fuck if we blood or not. Don't ever tell me I'm not doing what I can to protect my brothers," Slade said. "You better watch your mouth before I break your jaw and you won't be able to use it to pop that shit no more."

"Slade, what has gotten into you lately?" Della asked, witnessing her son lose it all.

"Ma, I don't have time for this shit."

She smacked him so hard his neck twisted. "I think you need a reminder on who the fuck I am. Don't let this cane fool you." Della tossed it across the room. "It only lengthens my reach, not limits it. At the end of the day, I'm your mothafucking mother!"

Slade felt awful for talking to his mother so recklessly, and he made plans to apologize every day when it was all said and done. "I'm sorry, Ma. I really am. I didn't mean to come at you like that," he said under his breath. "I just wanted you to—"

"Slade, you been in DC too long, son. Too long. And you're making clouded decisions. It's becoming clearer that the girl is a bad influence after all."

Judge helped Grant off the floor, and Grant rubbed his bloody mouth and said, "Della, don't worry about it. That was on me. Slade is deep into this shit, and I came out of the mouth wrong." He looked at his cousin. "I'm sorry about the Knox and Audio comment, man, but it ain't like you don't know who we are and what we came to do. We did cleanup work for y'all on things we taking to our graves."

Slade frowned. "So why you bringing it up now?"

"Because I think you need a reminder." He wiped his mouth. "Look, I promise we won't hurt your girl. I just want her to answer some questions for us, and after that, we out. Cool?"

"I won't have her hurt." Slade looked at all of them. "I need you all to know this."

"Even if she's responsible for Knox's disappearance?" Grant asked.

"On my life, if she had anything to do with his disappearance, I will kill her myself."

"We on the same page, then," Grant said. "But we still need to talk to her."

As much as Slade hated to admit it, he knew they weren't going anywhere without talking to Farah. "I'll let you talk to Farah. Just let me speak to her first."

Della shook her head. Seeing her son this weak for the girl made her stomach churn. "Slade, they came all the way up from—"

"Don't worry about it, Della," Grant said softly. "I'll give him that time. After all, from what I've been told, he really cares about the girl." He focused on Slade. "Just as long as you know I'm not going anywhere until I speak with her. Can we agree on that?"

"I guess I don't have a choice." This shit was making Slade's head ache. "Where are y'all staying anyway?"

"We got an apartment here in Platinum Lofts."

Slade saw blue.

"You ain't know? It's a takeover until we can find Knox, man. Shit is beyond serious now. It's deadly."

Chapter 10

Judge and Grant

". . . it's just a guess right now, but we have to start somewhere."

Although Grant agreed not to speak to Farah before Slade, he didn't say anything about not questioning other people in the building. After some research, they discovered that Vivian James, the property manager, was missing her son. It was just a hunch, but if Grant learned anything in his many years in the disposal business, it was that hunches paid off. They decided to pay her a visit.

From the outside of the door, they could hear Vivian speaking to someone inside. For a minute they remained silent, trying to hear anything useful. After a while, they knocked on the door, and Vivian opened it with a smile on her face. "Hello there." She looked at both of them. In her opinion they had the kindest eyes. "Are you boys okay? I mean, the apartment is fine, isn't it?"

"Yes, ma'am." Grant grinned. "Everything is perfect. We were actually hoping we could talk to you about something private."

She opened the door wider. "Sure. Come on inside."

Once they entered, the first thing Grant noticed was three very attractive women sitting on the sofa. They were talking among themselves and didn't seem to know that they were even inside the apartment. Then he saw the pictures of a chubby kid all over the walls, and it was evident that whoever he was, Vivian loved him very much. "I didn't know you had company." He nodded toward the living room. "If this is a bad time, we could come back later."

She waved him off. "Don't worry about it. They were actually just about to leave."

"No need," Grant said softly. "If we can step to the side for a minute, this will be quick."

"Sure," she said softly as they moved closer to the kitchen. As always, Judge stood behind his brother and remained silent. "What can I do for you boys?"

"Well, ma'am," Grant continued, "we were wondering if you could tell us anything about Farah Cotton."

Her face went gray and the pleasantries were over. "Uh . . . why are you asking?"

"Because someone very dear to us is missing. Actually, he's been missing for a while now, and we believe that she may have had something to do with it. Of course we can't prove it, and it's just a guess right now, but we have to start somewhere. Can you tell us anything useful about her?"

She sighed and appeared saddened. "Actually, I can do better than that." She turned to the sofa. "Girls, come over here for a second."

The three women strolled toward them, although hesitant. Judge's huge presence usually left a nervous impression on the people he encountered.

"This is Lady and Courtney," she said, pointing to two women in tight jeans. "And this is a young lady you'll definitely want to talk to."

She resembled Farah Cotton so much in the pictures that he saw, that for a second, Grant grew offensive.

"Her name is Lesa Carmine, and she was Farah's old roommate."

Grant looked at Judge and they both grinned. This was the big break they were waiting for. "What can you tell us about Farah Cotton?"

Lesa was nervous and looked at Vivian.

"It's okay, honey," Vivian said as she rubbed her shoulder gently. "Tell them what they want to know. It's for the best."

She looked at Judge and then Grant. "I can tell you a lot. For starters, you need to know that she considers herself . . . well . . . she considers herself to be a vampire."

Chapter 11

Farah

"... if you gonna kill me, do it already."

After a long night, Farah strolled into her apartment and immediately noticed everything was peaceful. She was grateful because it would give her some time to think about her sister. Although she occupied her time with trying to find Eleanor, the pursuit of blood, and the fact that she was no longer with Slade, in the end all she thought about was Chloe.

She tossed her purse on the kitchen counter and placed a cup of coffee in the microwave. She contemplated calling Slade again, but knew it was useless considering her other attempts ended in vain. *He's probably with some young bitch with a cute face and fat ass*. The idea made her sick at the stomach. She ran to the bathroom, released her guts, and wiped her mouth off with the back of her hand. Staring in the mirror she noticed her skin was not as beautiful and she needed more blood.

To get a little more comfortable, she trudged into her ex-roommate Lesa's room. Farah put her out after she failed to pay rent and discovered that she drank blood. Although it had been months since she'd been gone, no one had bothered to properly clean it. The room wasn't the freshest because of all the nasty shit they did to get her out of the house, including Shadow pissing over her bathroom floors. It was the one place she knew her siblings wouldn't bother her. Once inside, she changed into the brown velour tracksuit she kept in the closet, and examined her figure in the mirror on the door. Her body was still tight, and despite a few sores on her yellow skin, she looked slightly bronzed.

Before leaving the room, she grabbed from under the bed the metal lockbox she purchased some time back. She bought it after Shadow and Mia threatened her life if she didn't stop writing down in her journal the illegal things she did. She entered the code and pulled out her recent book, which was made of red leather. Although she knew she shouldn't keep them, something about writing every day relaxed her mind.

Flopping on the edge of the bed, she opened the journal and a list floated in her lap. When she picked it up, she saw the names of those she believed to be responsible for sending the picture of her trying to kill Knox. They were Eleanor McClendon, Lesa Carmine, Nadia Gibson, and her friend Rhonda. Her reasons for thinking they could be involved varied.

Eleanor probably wanted her arrested so she wouldn't hunt her down and kill her. Besides, her apartment was right next to the scene of the accident. Then there was Lesa. Although she could see easily why Lesa would want her head, considering how they ripped her clothes, poisoned her drink, and threw her out on the streets, she didn't know her at the time the picture was taken. Nadia also had motive, considering she denied her application as a roommate when she applied to live with her, but she didn't know her at the time the picture was taken either.

Finally there was Rhonda. Although Rhonda was in the car at the time of the accident and could not possibly have taken the picture from that angle, she did mention the picture at the restaurant.

With no more answers to who was trying to ruin her life than when she started, she locked her journals back up and left the room. With her coffee out of the microwave, she strolled back into the living room. She was about to sit down when there was a knock at the door. *I knew this shit was too good to be true.* She placed her coffee down and yelled, "I don't know who you are, but whoever it is, can you please go away? I don't feel like company right now." She slumped into the sofa and grabbed her coffee cup.

Knock. Knock. Knock.

Fuck! She focused on the door in frustration. "Who is it?" she screamed, placing her cup down and sliding out of her shoes.

"It's Vivian James. Open the door, Farah. We have to talk."

If there was one person she hated more than anything in the world, it was the property manager, Vivian. For one she never wanted Farah to live in the apartment to begin with, even when she shared it with her boyfriend Zone, before she pushed him out of the window. For two Vivian had suspicions that Farah had something to do with her son being missing, but since she couldn't prove it, she took to stalking her instead.

From the couch she said, "Vivian, I'm kind of busy right now." She focused on the door, hoping she'd walk away. "Can you come back later?"

"This is about business." She paused. "I need you to open the door now, Farah. It can't wait."

Farah trudged toward the door and flung it open. "What's so fucking important that it couldn't wait, Vivian?" She looked out into the hallway. "Is the building on fire or something?"

Vivian was about to give the sassy-mouth tenant a piece of her mind, until she spotted something dried and burgundy on her chin. "What's that stuff on your face? It looks like . . . blood."

Goosebumps rose on Farah's skin and she spit on her finger, rubbed her chin, and said, "I . . . I ate some candy or something earlier." She appeared nervous and her lips trembled. "Now, I know that's not what you wanted with me. So what's up?"

She exhaled and shook her head. "*Okay,* as you know I've tried to honor the fact that your sister died. Unfortunately, I'm not going to be able to do that much longer."

"What the fuck do you mean you tried to honor the fact that Chloe died? Bitch, she's not here anymore. There's nothing to honor about that."

Vivian stepped back. "You know what I mean."

"I don't know what the fuck you talking about. How about you explain yourself?"

Vivian took two deep breaths. "Maybe that was the wrong choice of words, and I'm sorry if you took it the wrong way. It's just that . . . well . . . unfortunately you aren't the only one who has lost someone, and recently at that. Let us not forget that my son is still missing and I still don't know where he is." She gave her a knowing look. An accusatory look. "My loving son is out there and anything could be happening to him right now, so trust me when I say I know what you're going through."

"And I told you I didn't have anything to do with that, Vivian," she lied. "If I knew anything about your son, I would've told you. You're forgetting one thing, my sister was killed and your son could still be out there somewhere. With all that said, what do you want with me right now?"

Vivian shook her head. "Farah, where is your rent for the month? It's beyond late, and I can't wait for it any longer."

She sighed. "What are you talking about?"

"I'm talking about the rent is due the first of the month." She looked at the yellow chart in her hand. "And we're beyond that period right now. Every month I have to collect personally with you. You're the only one who can't seem to understand the importance of paying on time."

"I doubt that very seriously. I know for a fact that before Lucia and them moved, they paid when they wanted. Anyway, how come everybody but me gets a fifteen-day grace period?"

"Because you have been known to take the grace period and some more, Farah. And just when the paperwork goes in to have you evicted, you come up with the money. It's always an excuse with you. 'I can't pay my rent now because I have a hair appointment,' 'I can't pay my rent now because I gotta pay my light bill.' It's annoying at best." She paused. "And to be honest, since Zone was murdered—"

"Zone wasn't murdered," she interrupted. "My man fell out of the window in this building due to it not being up to code, remember? Because of that shit his family was paid millions. So if you gonna tell the story, tell it right."

"You know what? Sometimes I think you escaped from Crescent Falls."

Farah tilted her head. She didn't know what Crescent Falls was. "What is that?"

"It doesn't matter." She laughed. "Because the bottom line is this, since you lived here alone, you've had nothing but weird people in and out of this apartment. I've let the leasing company know, but they don't seem to care right now. But I do, and you should be aware that I am keeping my eyes on you."

"I'm not allowed to have company? If that's the case, why am I paying rent? I mean, if you clocking who comes in and out of my apartment, shouldn't you be paying my bills for me?"

"Don't be ridiculous."

"No, you don't be ridiculous! I said I'll pay the rent, and for real, unless you can do something now, all you can do is wait. Now, is there anything else? Because my coffee is getting cold."

"Nothing for now, Farah. I'm just here to let you know that I'm watching you, and from what I learned recently, some other people are too." She grinned.

Farah's eyebrows pulled together. "What does that mean?"

Vivian wore a look of satisfaction. "Don't mind me. Oh . . . I almost forgot to tell you that Lesa and her friends said hi."

Farah tried to remain calm, although her body trembled. "So you talk to her now?"

"Sometimes, but they have such vivid imaginations. Can you believe that they told me you drink blood?" She shook her head. "Young people these days will say anything."

It's settled. Lesa and them bitches she rolls with gotta go. "I'm not worried about shit you saying, because everything you speak is lies."

"I guess we'll find out. Just know that the countdown has started for your rent. I won't wait a day past the fifteenth to file for an eviction. That much I promise."

When she left, Farah slammed and kicked the door. "Dumb-ass bitch! Always in my fucking business! I'm not going to take you fucking with me much longer. Be careful. Be really careful."

She paced around the kitchen until the house phone rang. Her temples thumped and she wanted to do something to make her feel better. The last thing she wanted was to speak on the phone. Still, she snatched it off the wall and said, "Whoever this is, now is not the time."

"Farah, how are you?" Randy asked calmly. "It's been a long time."

Scared, she stumbled back into the stove. She hadn't heard his voice since she went to his house the day Slade and his father set him up and robbed his stash houses. Even then they had a few choice words, and she hoped that she wouldn't hear from him again. She was wrong.

"What do you want with me, Randy?" She stood up straight and looked at the tiles on the floor. "I'm kind of busy right now."

"Come on, is that some way to treat somebody who looked out for you since you were too young to fuck? Who gave you money for your rent, apartment, and clothes? Who put you in your first car?" He chuckled. "And looked out for you when that punk-ass nigga you fucked with couldn't afford to take care of you? Come on, Farah, I deserve more respect than that."

She opened the refrigerator and grabbed a beer. *Fuck coffee.* "I don't have time for this shit right now, Randy," she said, although she knew he didn't care.

"My sister died, I don't feel good, and I'm really tired. So if you gonna kill me, do it already, but please don't call my fucking house again."

"You talk to me like I didn't understand your sister died already. Don't you understand that that's the only reason you still alive? I deserve a little more credit than that, bitch."

While he was talking, it dawned on her that he could have sent the picture. Since she'd known him, he'd done everything in his power to stalk her. Maybe this was his way of fucking with her mind. "Randy, can I ask you something?"

"What?"

"Did you send that shit to my house?"

Silence.

"Randy, did you send a picture to my house? If you did, it's fucked up that you trying to ruin me like that. All I ever did was love you."

He laughed. "You always got some shit going on, don't you? No matter what, you just can't just live a normal life."

"Whatever, Randy."

He laughed. "I just wanted you to know that you're still on my radar. You and that nigga you deal with."

"And my father too?" She paused.

"Hey, whatever Tank does to that man while he's in jail is on him."

"You should know Ashur is stronger than you know." She tried to convince herself. "If anything, I'm afraid for Tank."

"If that's true, I guess we'll see. I just hope you're having a good time with life, Farah, because it won't be yours much longer."

Farah was preparing to respond when someone in the background on Randy's end said, "Welcome to Serenity Meadows! How can we help you?"

"Hello?" Farah said into the phone. "Hello."

When she looked at the phone, Randy was gone. But why? Farah snatched her purse off the counter and stomped toward her bedroom. The only thing she was interested in at the moment was relaxing and taking a nap, but when she opened the door to her room, she wanted to jump out of her skin when she saw Shadow in her bed with Kindle and Raven, two girls from down the hall.

Kindle's hair was wrapped around Shadow's fist as he pumped into her from behind, while her cousin Raven was face up, under Shadow's nut sack as she licked his balls.

Farah couldn't stand either of them, mainly because they were loud, ridiculous, and always fighting in the hallway. Although someone would probably say the same thing about her, she would dispute it to the fullest.

"Hold up. What the fuck are y'all doing in my house?" she screamed. That was one of the things she hated about her apartment. There had been many times when she thought she was alone and almost got caught talking on the phone about private matters. "And why didn't you go in your room, Shadow?" She stepped farther into the room and was angry when she stepped on one of their panties with her bare foot. "Yuck!" She kicked it away.

"My bad, Farah," Shadow said, covering up his dick with the edge of the sheet, leaving the girls naked. "I heard you out there, so I tried to keep the girls quiet. We almost done. Check back in a minute."

"You not answering my question." She placed her hands on her hips. "How come you in my room? What's wrong with yours?"

"Because my room ain't got no TV, and your ex-roommate's room stinks." He grinned as if shit was funny. "Don't worry. We about to bounce."

"You know what, I want both of these bitches out of my house in the next fifteen minutes. If they not gone, I'm gonna start swinging."

"Wait, who the fuck is you talking to?" Raven said, covering her body with Farah's robe. "You don't have to be all wild and shit just because this your house."

"Shawty, you don't know my sister," Shadow said, snatching the robe from her. "On second thought, get your shit and get the fuck out, both of y'all bitches. I already bust anyway."

When she remembered she had asked him to get something for her, she said, "Did you at least get the medicine I asked you for?"

He looked at her strangely. She guessed he didn't want her to say it in front of them. "Yeah, it's in my room. On my dresser. I don't know what you want with it, but be careful."

Farah stormed out of her room, grabbed the meds, and called the one person she thought she wouldn't talk to in a while.

Coconut's new apartment had Farah jealous the moment she stepped inside. The latest technology, from flat-screen TVs to expensive surround systems, was everywhere. The couch was made of expensive cream leather, and the carpet was nice and plush. There was even a picture of Coconut and Jake on the wall like they were a married couple, and she wanted to throw up at how happy they looked. It seemed like everything around her reminded her that Slade dumped her and she felt worthless.

Originally Coconut and Farah were supposed to share an apartment together in Platinum Lofts, but Jake, Coconut's boyfriend, decided that he wanted her to himself. And since Jake was a dope boy with heavy money and Farah was always broke, there was no competition. As far as Farah knew, Jake didn't fuck with her, so she was surprised she was allowed into their house. Something was off.

A few drinks later, Farah was relaxed and surprised because Jake seemed to be really cool. His tall, lanky body resembled a ball player's physique, and his dope boy swag made him even more appealing. It was easy to see why Coconut chose him.

They were sitting in the living room watching TV when Coconut said, "So you been holding up okay? With Chloe being gone and all? Because I know even though y'all fought so much, she loved you and you loved her."

Farah sighed. "I'm holding up as best I can." She focused back on the movie and grabbed her drink. "I just got a lot I'm trying to sort out. A lot of shit is catching up with me."

"What you mean?"

"It's a long story, but I do appreciate you having me over." Farah's mind floated to Eleanor. "Hey, you remember that white lady Eleanor? I think you call her The Clapper?"

"Yeah, I get my weed from her. Why?"

Farah tried to remain calm. Coconut told her that she copped weed from her before, but it totally slipped her mind. "Uh . . . do you still see her?"

"Yeah, I saw her earlier today." She reached in the ashtray and pulled out the blunt they just smoked. "You just helped me smoke her shit. She got the best."

"Where she gets it?"

"I think she get it from Willie, Randy's father." She shrugged. "But who knows."

Farah was breathing so heavily she was hyperventilating. "Uh . . . when is . . . I mean, when you gonna see her again?"

Coconut looked at her worriedly. "I'm not sure. She told me she'll get in contact with me because she has to get out of town. Sounded pretty scared for some reason." She touched her hand. "Are you okay? Because you look flushed."

"I'm fine," she lied, trying to calm down. "But thanks anyway." Farah didn't want to press the issue, but she had to revisit the Eleanor topic soon. Asking too much might send Coconut's antennae through the roof. "I still can't believe Shadow had them bitches from down the hall in my bed, girl. I almost murdered all three of them! What the fuck type shit was that?"

Coconut laughed. "Girl, he did just come home from jail, you know." She laughed. "I'm surprised his fine ass hadn't kicked the freak party off a long time ago." She shook her head. Secretly she was crushing on Shadow, but had no intention of letting him know.

As the girls were in mid-conversation, Jake walked back into the living room, holding a beer. "Farah, you ever talked to my man Park again?"

Park was Farah's ex-boyfriend, who she met in high school. In fact, she and Coconut met Jake and Park at the same time, but Farah couldn't get with him after a while because he was too weird in the bedroom. For instance, he got off when she stuck her finger up his ass and coughed on his dick. In the end, she always felt weird around him, so she decided to leave him alone.

Although she licked the tip of his dick a few times, she never fucked him, and to be honest, she never regretted it either. Not to mention she always thought he wanted Coconut instead of her.

"You know I wasn't really feeling Park like that, Jake." She laughed. "That nigga was way too weird for me. Why you ask anyway?"

"Because he asks about you all the time." He sat close to Coconut and rubbed her knee. "He said the other day that he didn't like the way you carried him. Said you started fucking with his cousin or some shit like that."

"Who is his cousin?" Farah asked.

"Randy." When he saw the expression on her face he said, "Wait . . . you didn't know that shit?"

Farah turned blue. "No. I mean, me and Randy were together, but he's not the kind of nigga who likes to talk about other dudes, so it never came up." Farah scratched her head. "I really didn't know that shit."

"Yeah, that's his cousin." He paused. "Don't worry about it though. Park is married to some broad he met from Jersey, so he couldn't have been that mad. Plus we were kids back then." He rubbed Coconut's knee harder. "On another note, I been telling Coconut y'all don't need to be beefing, so I'm glad y'all put the drama behind you."

Jake was cool, but he was starting to give Farah the ills. Why did he care if she spoke to Coconut or not? "So when is the wedding day?" Farah asked, nodding at the picture. "I see y'all playing house and can't keep your hands off each other."

"Girl, when I'm able to satisfy him all the way around the board." She paused and looked into his eyes. "Well, at least that's what he keeps telling me."

He nudged her leg. "Stop playing. You know how I feel about you."

"I hear you," Coconut responded. "I still want the ring though." She looked into his eyes and he looked away. "Why you ask when we're getting married?"

"Because it's time to make it official. Y'all been together forever and virtually married now. Plus I see your love."

"We beyond love at this point. It's way deeper than that," Coconut told her. "We got an understanding that works for both of us." She kissed Jake on the lips and Farah grew hot between the legs. They appeared seconds away from creating a porno.

"No doubt," Jake said. "I been telling my shorty I never fucked with a female like her before. I just want to make sure she's willing to do any and everything she can to satisfy me."

"Haven't I given you everything you've asked, Jake?" She looked over at him. "When I wanted to move in with Farah, you begged me to get a place with you. Didn't I leave? And when you wanted *that thing,* didn't I arrange it? I've given you everything . . . but . . . this."

Farah didn't like not knowing the secret they were obviously not trying to tell her. "What's going on? Everything cool between y'all?"

"She can tell you better than I can." Jake stood up and kissed Coconut on the forehead. "So I'ma let her do that and go grab another beer."

Jake quickly dismissed himself and pimped into the kitchen. Farah looked at him as he peered into the refrigerator. "Girl, what is up with him?" she whispered.

"And what is he asking you to do that you're obviously uncomfortable with?"

"It's a long story, Farah, and I really need your help right now, but I'm not sure how you're going to take it. The last thing I need you to be is mad at me, since we're cool again."

Farah rubbed her leg. "What's up? Stop fucking around. Spit it out!"

"That's kinda what I wanted to talk to you about when I showed up at your place that day."

Farah knew there was a real reason and hoped it didn't have anything to do with Slade like she originally thought. "It ain't about Slade, is it? I mean, you not gonna tell me you like him or some shit like that, are you? I saw how you were looking at him that day, and I wasn't feeling it."

Coconut frowned. "I don't know what you talking about, Farah." She laughed. "Don't get me wrong, Slade is fine and all, but he ain't my type."

Farah exhaled. "Oh . . . Well, what's up?"

"I'm really feeling Jake, girl. To the point where if the nigga dumped me, I might lose my mind and my lifestyle. You see all this shit I got." She flashed her rings and pointed at her Birkin bag on the loveseat. "This nigga is official, and I've known him all my life."

"Coconut, you telling me things I already know. Remember, I've been knowing you forever. But how do I play into all of this?"

She took two quick breaths. "Well, the thing is, he had a fantasy of fucking with me and one of my friends. We talked about it in the past, but I wasn't ready to deal with it back then. Eventually he left it alone until now."

Farah's skin warmed. "And . . ."

"And he chose you."

Farah backed away and frowned. It wasn't like she couldn't get with the freaky shit. As a matter of fact, it made her feel good when she explored her wild side. To take it a step further, Coconut and Farah kissed each other's boxes on a regular, so it wasn't a thing. But they never talked about what they did behind closed doors to anyone else, and they certainly never considered bringing in a third party. They preferred to blame alcohol for their promiscuous activities.

"You told him we went there with each other before?" she whispered, looking behind her to see where he was. His back faced their direction, so she focused back on Coconut. "What if the shit gets out and he tells somebody else?"

Coconut pushed her playfully on the leg. "Yes, I told him, and Jake's way cool about that kind of shit. As a matter of fact, he's turned on by it. Normally we bring in an outsider, but recently he shared with me that he wanted to see what it would be like to be with you." Coconut wore a smile, but she looked like she was breaking down inside.

"How do you feel about that? Honestly? Because you look like you ain't feeling the shit."

"I want him to feel like he can have everything with me. Like he don't have to cheat because our bedroom is open to any of his fantasies. You know bitches out there would jump at a chance to be with Jake. Including some of my friends." She eyed Farah.

"Don't look at me, because before today, I didn't even fuck with Jake."

"I know it's not you," she reassured her. "I didn't want to tell you, but Shannon went at him the other day when we were over Rhonda's house."

Farah furrowed her brows. "You were at Rhonda's after she lost the baby?"

"Yes, and I'm not fucking with that bitch no more either, Farah. Something is way off about her. Do you know she lied about her entire pregnancy?"

"What you talking about? Her stomach was as big as a globe."

"Jake is cool with Knight, and it came out the other day." She paused. "Apparently Rhonda went to the doctor's months before the baby was due, and was told that her baby was dead inside of her body. They said she needed to undergo emergency surgery to remove the fetus. She could've died leaving the baby in her body. Instead of letting them do the surgery, she ran out. She was so scared she was going to lose Knight when he found out, that she decided to lie. Knight found out by one of the doctors the other day."

"When did she know the baby was dead inside of her?"

"For two months, Farah. The bitch was sick. They saying Rhonda walking around DC right now talking to herself and all kinds of shit like that. You better be careful though. She kept talking about you for some reason."

"I already saw her." Farah recalled her eyes. "She approached me when I went to grab something to eat. She didn't look right then, but I had no idea." She shook her head. "I actually felt responsible for her losing the baby. Now I want to kill this bitch!"

"I blamed you at first too. Who would've known she could do something so crazy? Still, be careful. You never know what somebody like her might do."

I'm gonna get that bitch way before she get me. Especially now.

"Anyway, you gonna do it? What I asked you about Jake?" She put her hands together like she was praying. "Please, Farah, do this for me. I need this. You gotta know I wouldn't ask if it wasn't so serious."

Her decision wasn't rocket science. Jake was fine, she loved Coconut, and she was bored out of her mind. She had so much negative shit going on in her life that she didn't have a problem with having a little fun. But, there was one thing. Her piggy bank was bare. She didn't have a cent to her name, and her property manager was threatening to throw her out if she didn't come up with the rent. So if they wanted her to be a part of their threesome, it was going to cost.

"I'll do it. On one condition."

Coconut jumped up and down in place. "Girl, you don't even know what this means to me!" She grinned as if she had just asked her to be a bridesmaid instead of share her boyfriend's bed. "He gonna finally realize that there ain't shit I won't do for him. I owe you big time for this shit."

Tell me about it. "Hold up, Coconut, we not finished talking business yet."

"Business?"

"Yes, because if I get down like that for y'all, what's in it for me?" She paused. "I mean, Jake gets his rocks off and you get to keep the man you always wanted. But what about me?"

Coconut backed up a little to look at her friend seriously. "Are you playing?" She frowned. "You want us to pay you?"

"The question is are *you* serious?" Farah combatted. She just lost her sister, she didn't have a man, and she killed for blood. She was starting not to care much about what other people thought about her. "It's cool for you to ask me to be a part of your little situation, but it's not cool for me to ask y'all to look out? Times are hard for me, Coconut. I mean, don't be so selfish."

"I'm not saying it like that. It's just that—"

"Let's be fair, Coconut," Jake interrupted, joining the conversation. "If she wants some paper, it ain't like we can't make that happen." He looked at Farah and licked his lips. He wore all over his face what he had planned for her. "But if I'm gonna look after you like that, I expect a little more in return. I'm into some shit you might not be down with, but if we paying, I want my money's worth."

Farah thought briefly about Randy's sadistic ass. When she was with him, she was pissed on, bitten, beaten, and made to feel less than. There was nothing he could do outside of breaking her skin and/or killing her that would make her go away. She needed the money, and to be honest, she looked forward to the experience.

"If you looking after me and blessing my pockets, there ain't shit I wouldn't do for you."

Coconut saw the look in her eyes and grew worried. She recalled conversations she had with Lesa about Farah's shiesty behavior. "Farah, what ever happened to Lesa? Your old roommate?"

"From what I understand, she's doing okay. For now."

Chapter 12

Farah

"If you got an hour and a lunch break, I can show you exactly what I'm talking about."

Farah cruised down the darkening streets with the sounds of Keyshia Cole blasting from her stereo. An open bottle of wine sat tucked in her purse in the passenger seat, while she sipped on the rest from her cream-colored coffee cup. She had a lot on her mind and a lot on her list to take care of that evening. She looked forward to a time when she no longer had to look over her shoulders or worry about people out to get her.

When she pulled up in front of a small brick house, she sat outside for a minute and took it all in. Huge green trees lined the front, and decorations from holidays past still donned the door. She wondered what it would be like to live in a house like this . . . as a child. Did the person she was looking for always feel safe? And loved? The thought made her envious and at the same time ready for war. So she downed everything in her cup, took a deep breath, and grabbed her purse. Before exiting the car, she surveyed her surroundings to be sure the coast was clear. When it was, she eased out of her car and approached the house.

The moment the door opened, Lesa stumbled back when she saw Farah's face. The blue cashmere sweater Lesa sported lit up her eyes and made her even more beautiful.

"How you been, Lesa?" Farah tried to stare inside from where she stood. "How does it feel to live back with your mother? You two getting along better, I hope."

"I . . . uh . . ."

Farah laughed. "I can't believe this. When was the last time you were at a loss for words? Especially considering the word on the street is that you can't keep my name out of your mouth."

"F . . . Farah, what are you doing here? How did you know where I lived?"

"As long as you on the East Coast, Lesa, I'm gonna always be able to find you," she responded, leaving out how she searched the Net for her mother's information. "Now, I asked you a fucking question. Why do you got a problem with keeping my name in your mouth? Don't you know what happens to snitches? Or do I have to remind you?"

Lesa looked off balance when she saw Farah reaching into her purse. Afraid for her life, she ran into her house, screaming her lungs out. Farah was right on her heels, ready to finish what she started, until she glanced at the mirror on the wall. In it she saw a uniformed officer sitting on the sofa. When the person turned, she saw it was Nadia Gibson and the joke was on her. This was the last person on earth she wanted or needed to see.

Farah backed out slowly at first, before flying out of the house at lightning speed. On her way down the steps, she tripped and fell, sending the wine bottle she planned to crack over Lesa's head crashing to the ground. Wine covered everything and glass crunched under her boots as she made it to her car. Nervous about being arrested, she softly bumped the car in front of her as she wiggled out of the parking space and back into traffic. From the rearview mirror, she could see Nadia waving at her with an evil grin on her face.

Although Farah considered this a defeat, she wasn't ready to claim it as a win for the officer either. She would do whatever she could to silence anybody trying to ruin her life, including a hating-ass cop.

Farah arrived at the blood drive bright and early the next day, eager to do her thing. Normally she preferred to move in the darkness, but the night before had proven to be unsatisfactory. She couldn't get her hands on Lesa and her search for Eleanor had once again ended in vain. It was time to do something she loved: hunt for blood.

When her phone rang and she saw it was an unknown number, she figured it was her father. It had been a while since she'd spoken to him, and she wondered how he was doing since hearing the news. She felt like a coward for not telling him Chloe was missing and Brownie was dead, but at the moment she couldn't handle his reaction. "Hello, Daddy. How are you holding up?"

"Baby girl, I'm not good."

Farah's stomach rumbled.

"You can't even imagine what it's like to lose a child and the love of your life at the same time." He paused and took a deep breath.

"I'm so sorry, Daddy," Farah said, observing a truck behind her from the rearview mirror. "I wish you didn't have to be alone."

"Don't worry too much about me. The good thing about my situation is I'm in the right place to take out my frustrations, and I wanted you to know that it may be a long time before I talk to you again."

"What . . . Why?" she yelled.

"Let's just say that problem you told me about the last time you talked to me was taken care of. He won't be doing anything to anybody else ever."

Farah's heart rate increased. "You talking about . . . You . . . kill—"

"Don't say it over the phone. Just know that it's not a problem anymore and that I don't want you out there worrying about me. If they pin it on me, I might be in solitary for a long time, and I just wanted you to know in case you don't hear from me. Tell Shadow and Mia to be easy, and that I love them too. Bye, baby girl."

He ended the call, and for a second Farah sat in silence. Part of her was relieved that Tank was dead and could not harm him, but the other part blamed herself because had she not tried to rob Tank, he would not be in jail trying to take his life. She hated Randy and hoped at some point he got exactly what he deserved. In fact, she prayed on it.

The truck she was worried about was still behind her, so she turned around and it pulled off. "Are you following me?"

When the vehicle was out of sight, she observed the building hosting the blood drive. She decided to select her next victim there, figuring anybody donating would most likely have a clean bill of health. The blue sweater dress she wore presented her ass in 3D, and she looked so edible that only a gay man could deny her. Once inside of the building, she strolled to the counter, grabbed an application, and scanned the room for donors.

After completing her paperwork, she sat in the lobby and waited for her fake name to be called. Although she had no intention of giving blood, she had to at least look the part. Bad prospect after bad prospect crawled inside, and she was starting to believe the blood drive was a useless idea. After an hour of waiting and ignoring her name when it was yelled, she was about to leave. That was until she finally saw her prospect. He was tall, handsome, and chocolate, just like she liked. He walked in with a swag about himself that said he was the only man in the room. Farah had to have him. The only problem was he wasn't sitting anywhere near her.

Quick on her feet, she strutted toward the bathroom to stall. She hoped the seat she'd chosen earlier would be taken, which would give her an excuse to find another one, next to her potential victim. When she walked out of the restroom, she saw her plan worked when she eyed some girl going through her fake Gucci in her seat.

Beaming, Farah whipped her hair over her shoulder and switched toward her prize. Her hair moved effortlessly with every step she made, and she was sure there wasn't a soft dick in the house. When she made it across the room, she wiggled into the seat next to him and said, "How long do you think we have to wait? It seems like I've been here all day." She paused only to breathe. "I sure could find something else better to do with my time."

He was totally involved with a text on his phone and said, "Not sure. I just got here myself." But when he finally observed her, he grinned as he scanned her from top to bottom. His eyes said it all . . . he loved what he saw. There was a quiet shyness about him that turned her on, and to her mind, he was the perfect catch.

"Why you looking at me like that?" she asked.

"No reason," he lied. "Anyway, usually when I come, it doesn't take this long." He looked over at the counter. "I think you can reschedule if you have to. They need you, not the other way around."

She crossed her legs. "You do this all the time? Donate blood?"

"Whenever I can," he admitted. "I feel like I'm doing my part by giving blood. You know?"

She felt like she'd hit the jackpot. Finding someone who felt like he was doing something in life because he donated blood was a goldmine. "What do you mean?"

He sat back in his plastic white seat. "My sister died when I was in the military serving in Iraq. She was in a car accident caused by a drunk driver. She lost a lot of blood, and even though it didn't save her, I donate out of memory. What made you donate?"

"I just love blood."

"That's different."

"Different is good. At least that's what I think." She paused. "Can I ask you a question?"

"Sweetheart, as sexy as you are, you can ask me anything you want. And that's on everything."

Her next question was serious because if he said no, she would leave him alone and he would inevitably save his own life. "Can I make you famous?"

He laughed heartily. "That's an odd question. How does one make one famous?"

She put her hand over his crotch and rubbed lightly. His eyes popped open and he hoped no one was looking. When he looked across the room, the employee who handled the paperwork was staring dead in their direction. “If you got an hour and a lunch break, I can show you exactly what I’m talking about.”

“I think my schedule just cleared up.”

When Farah followed him to a nice house in Virginia, she was impressed. Since it was midafternoon on a weekday, there wasn’t a car on the street. She figured most people were at work and that was even better. But when she followed him inside, she was disappointed that the decor didn’t match her first impression. There wasn’t much furniture, and it looked like someone had just moved in.

“This your house?” she asked as she followed him.

“No, not exactly. Well, I’m renting a room.” They walked toward the back.

“Did you say you’re renting a room?” she asked, disgusted. “How old are you, if you don’t mind me asking?”

He turned around and grinned at her. “Old enough to satisfy your every need.” He took a key out of his pocket and placed it in a gold doorknob. “Is that enough for you? Besides, you’re gonna make me famous, right?”

Silence.

Once inside the room, she saw how dreary it was, and she wanted to roll over and die. Everything was juvenile. There were posters all over the walls of models in swimsuits, the bed was twin-sized, and the sheets were on the floor. To make matters worse, his clothes were thrown everywhere, and it smelled like he hadn't taken the trash out in a year.

"Can I use your bathroom right quick?" She stepped on a plastic water bottle and it crackled under the weight of her shoe. "I want to freshen up."

"Uh . . . sure. It's out there." He removed his wallet and keys and threw them on the dresser. "But don't keep me waiting too long. You got me ready to see how you gonna make me famous. It was the only thing I could think of on the way over here."

"I bet it was." She frowned, trying not to touch anything. "Anyway, does somebody live in this house with you? It seems so empty."

"I have some more roommates, but they not home at this hour. Most of them go to work and college. But since I can never be sure because I don't know they schedule, knock on the bathroom door first. I wouldn't want you walking in on something you don't want to see." He laughed.

Irritated, she plodded down the hallway and couldn't get over the feeling of wanting to smash his face in and run. When she reached another door, she knew it was the bathroom because of the sign that read, ALL RESIDENTS, PLEASE KNOCK BEFORE ENTERING. *Is this a house or group home?*

She slogged into the bathroom. Once inside, she threw cold water on her face and stared at her face in the mirror. Although her skin was clearer, it was obvious that she needed more blood, so she had to calm herself down to follow the plan. When she thought he was a sexy, shy, horny bum, it was sweet, but now she was so turned off that she contemplated leaving. She reasoned that Elizabeth Báthory would not allow a messy room to stop her from achieving her goal, and neither would she.

She checked her purse for the meds Shadow got for her, and then after giving herself the energy she needed to go back, she walked to his room. When she opened the door, he was in the bed, toes spread, with his extra-long brown dick in his hands. Now she couldn't wait to kill his ass.

"Get over here. Got me waiting all day and shit." He jerked himself so hard the muscles of his arms buckled. "I know that pussy stinks so good, don't it, baby? I hope you ain't wash it up too much, because I like to smell a juicy pussy."

"What you doing?" She frowned from the door. "When you take your clothes off so quick?"

"The moment you left. Now stop fucking around. I'm waiting on you," he said with his tongue hanging out the side of his mouth.

Farah threw her purse on the table next to the door and it landed on the floor. She started to pick it up but thought, *Fuck it . . . When in Rome, be as nasty as everyone else.* Slowly she eased out of her clothing and stood in front of him for a minute to drive him crazy. She couldn't lie. As much as she loved blood, there was something about tasting the goods before she killed them that just did it for her.

"I'm trying to have a little fun with you too, but can I have something to drink first? I want to be right for you, baby. I hope you don't mind."

"You want a drink right now?" he asked with an attitude. It was obvious that the only thing he wanted to do was fuck. "I was all ready to dig into them walls. I'm not even thinking about getting anything to drink."

"And you can have these walls, but you gotta get me something to drink first. And to be honest, it feels like you have the heat on hell in here."

"I hope you not fucking around with me, Farah." He scooted out of the bed with his swollen dick pointed in her direction. "Otherwise we came here for nothing."

"I'm not fucking with you. At least not yet anyway." She giggled.

Silence.

He stomped out of the bedroom furiously. While he was within the house, she removed a small pill from her purse. After the close call she had with the dude she killed with her shoe, she decided it was better to have her victims limp and weak than aware and strong.

A few minutes later, he returned with two Cokes. "This all we got." He raised them in the air. "I can give you water, but it'll be from the faucet."

He handed her one and placed the other down. "No, this is fine, but can you get me a glass of ice too?" She placed her hand over the can. "This is not as cold as I like my drinks. I need some ice."

He sulked. "Dang, why can't you just drink the shit? It's cold enough. You ain't in the gym or nothing."

"It may be cold enough to quench your thirst, but it ain't doing shit for me. Please just get me some ice. When you get back, this pussy will be waiting on you; although the longer you procrastinate, the more easily I'm turned off. It ain't nothing for me to go home and play with my own pussy instead."

Hearing this, he scurried to the kitchen and she plopped the pill into his soda. She shook it a few times so it would dissolve. When he returned, she poured her soda over the ice and performed like there was nothing wrong. Apparently he was extra thirsty, because he drank his until he swallowed the last drop. All she could do was smile, realizing that in a moment she would have what she came for.

When he was done, he jumped in the bed and fussed with a condom on his dresser. "Now we can stop the games and get to it," he told her, stroking his dick again. "Get over here."

"Whatever you want, baby."

Farah climbed on top of him and kissed him softly on the lips. He pulled her on top of his dick and pushed into her gushiness. When he tapped her jelly walls and could go no farther, he moved to the left and then the right. He filled her up, and her pussy syrup poured all over him.

"Fuck this pussy, baby." She nibbled on his ear. "Just like that. Work that shit."

"You like this shit, don't you?" he asked, already knowing the answer. "Tell me how much you like this dick." He slapped her ass and spread her cheeks as he continued to plow inside of her. "Damn, you feel so good."

Farah continued to bash her pussy into him as he met her thrust for thrust. When she first entered his crib, she wasn't feeling him one bit, but now that she saw how good he could fuck, she decided to enjoy herself and go with the flow. It was funny; she always knew how to pick them.

"If I would've known you would've been this good," he said softly, "I would've left with you the moment I saw you walk out of the bathroom." He was feeling suddenly lightheaded.

She wasn't interested in anything he had to say anymore. She thumped her pussy against his dick five more times, and when the time was right, came all over him. Her body shivered as she gripped his shoulders and dug her fingernails into his flesh. "Mmmmmmm, that shit feels so good."

When he felt her gush and heard her moan, he pushed all the way into her and filled her up with nut. It was the best sex he'd had in a long time. "Damn, you felt so fucking good!" He barely had enough energy to move and figured she wore him out.

Farah kissed him softly on the neck. "Thank you, honey. You not so bad yourself."

He laughed, stroking her meaty ass cheeks. "You a cool mothafucka too."

"What you talking about?" she asked, wiggling her waist over him again.

"I ain't never have no bitch ask me if they could make me famous before." His hands slid off of her body. He was exhausted and could no longer hold them up. "What you mean by that shit?"

She kissed him again and then she fell into his chest. "You really want to know?"

He chuckled. "Yeah. . . . What you gonna do? Tape me and sell them?"

"I wouldn't dream of doing anything like that, baby. I meant this." She sliced into his jugular vein and sucked his blood. Her teeth dug into his flesh, and she tried to drink everything that pumped through his veins. He was weakened and couldn't defend himself. Suddenly, his life flashed before his eyes.

Before long, he wasn't moving at all. She sucked and sucked until the roof of her mouth ached and her gut was full. There was something about the kill that made her feel invincible. She could almost feel her skin brighten up.

Standing over him, she admired her work. In her opinion he looked much more beautiful dead. His eyes were closed, and blood rested all over his chest and neck. Who needed Slade when she was queen of her world? The way she lived life allowed her to play God. She only wished she had someone she could share her experiences with. Someone like her.

Shadow and Mia wanted no part of her lifestyle, and she couldn't dare tell anyone else, for fear she would be caught. For now she would have to keep her secrets to herself. She was still thinking that when she heard someone come into the house.

"I wonder if she knows some nigga just walked in the house," Grant said to Judge as they watched the house Farah had been inside for an hour. They were in a gray rental car used to follow her every move.

"Who knows?" Judge shrugged. "Maybe she's about to get into some crazy threesome. What I wonder is what is she doing at a blood drive?"

"Maybe she really does believe she's some kind of vampire," Grant told him.

When Farah crawled out of the window with a sweater dress and her shoes and jacket under her arm, they sat up straight. "Hold up. Do you see that shit?" Grant asked, pointing at the window.

"This bitch is loony," Judge responded, shaking his head. "Something is really off about her."

"And why is her face covered in . . ."

"Blood," Grant responded, looking at his brother.

"I don't know what's going on with this bitch, but it ain't good," Judge said under his breath.

"The question is, should we tell Slade, or keep this shit to ourselves?"

Chapter 13

Nadia Gibson

“If you give her some time, she’ll hang herself.”

“I’m sorry about leaving you so early, Joe. I had a meeting regarding this Farah Cotton bitch that I didn’t want to miss,” Nadia said, sitting in her police cruiser outside a motel. She looked over at the small plastic Baggie to her right, the real reason for her speedy exit. “I hope you’re not mad with me.”

“Why would I be mad? I mean, I was wondering where you were, but I figured it was work related. My only problem is that I didn’t get a chance to dig into that pussy before you left. Last night was right. When you off that shit you can go nonstop.” He paused. “Anyway, I was calling you on something else. Did you get a chance to look at the paper?”

Nadia raised the wrinkled paper in her lap. Of course she read it. She looked at it ten times that morning, going over detail after detail. The main story was the six men who were all murdered with a slice of the jugular vein. The worst part was, they didn’t have a suspect. Nadia had spoken with Lesa and her friends. She was aware that Farah was a self-proclaimed vampire, but without any proof, they couldn’t attribute the crimes to her.

"Unfortunately I read it." She sighed. "Do you really think Farah is involved in these too?"

"I don't know. That's what you have to find out," he said seriously. "And later tonight, when you're done, I want you back over here and in my bed so we can have part two."

She giggled. "What about coming into the office today?" she asked him. "I was kind of hoping to stay out and question a few people in the field."

"Do what you have to do. After all, that's one of the benefits of fucking the boss."

When they ended the call, she leaned back into her seat and turned up the slow jams playing in the background. Her mind was all over the place, and it was time to get it right. In her mind, the police car she captained gave her the right to do anything she wanted, including snorting coke behind the driver's seat. She opened the small plastic bag, poured a small hill on the corner of her hand, and inhaled. When she was done, she wiped her nose and leaned back.

"What the fuck am I doing?" she asked herself out loud. "Why can't I stop this shit?"

No one responded, and she didn't want an authentic answer anyway. Besides, she fucked better, talked slicker, and seemed emboldened by the magic dust. She'd been on and off the drug for six months. Every attempt to stay clean ended in her fucking some nigga she met in the club, only to be kicked out the next morning.

It wasn't until she started fucking Captain Joe Walton that she had some normalcy in her life. He accepted the fact that she snorted coke, provided her with a place to sleep, and, because he was her boss, he covered her absences at work, which meant she would always be employed. No, she didn't love Joe, but for coke she would do what she had to do.

When all the powder in her nose was gone, she eased out of her patrol car and knocked on the hotel room where Beverly Glasser had told her to meet her. She moved anxiously in place and knocked again heavily when there was no answer. "Where the fuck is this bitch at?" she asked herself.

"If you talking about this bitch," Beverly said as she opened the door, "I was working." She went about cleaning the room, leaving the door ajar.

Nadia was flustered. Although she was in charge of the case, Beverly always made her feel like a child, and she never quite knew what to say to her. "I'm sorry. I didn't know you heard me. I wasn't talking about you anyway." She rubbed her clammy hands together.

"Sure you weren't, Nadia. And I own this hotel, not just work in it." Beverly was an older woman with black-and-gray hair and a serious face. Her light blue uniform clung against her hefty body, and the gold name badge protruded from her breast. Whenever she moved, it was obvious that she meant business. "Don't just stand out there. Come on inside."

Nadia ambled inside, closed the door, and leaned against it, but the magic powder had her so busybodied that she couldn't stay still for long. Instead she shuffled and looked extremely uncomfortable.

Beverly scanned her and shook her head. "So what have you found out about my son?" She tossed a naked pillow on the floor. "By this point, you had plenty of time to hear something, so I don't want any more excuses." She tucked the sheet under the edge of the bed. "Tell me something good."

"I can't give you any information before I have it, Beverly." Her hand hovered over the handle of her gun, not because she was threatened, but to fake power. "Not to mention she's had a death in her family recently and her family is guarding her closely."

Beverly stopped in place. "So everyone who loses a family member gets away with murder?"

Nadia remained silent.

"Don't play with me, Officer." She pointed a finger in her face. "I don't know if I told you, but I don't like games."

"And I'm not trying to play you. It's just that we should be a little more sensitive at this moment. If you give her some time, she'll hang herself. Just the other day I was interviewing her ex-roommate, Lesa, and her friends, and Farah came over to the house. I don't know what she was there to do, but she got away from the scene before I could ask. Trust me, we will get this Farah Cotton."

Beverly laughed. "You have two faces." She pointed at her. "At first I thought I liked one of them, because I felt I knew where you were coming from, but now I'm not so sure about that. You see, you remind me of a tree, you change with the seasons, and that makes you unstable."

"What is that supposed to mean?"

"It means that I'm tired of your mood swings and your fucking excuses! What that bitch is going through doesn't make my heart ache any less. My son is missing, and you lead me to believe that Farah had something to do with it, and I want her to pay!" She threw the comforter on the bed.

"I know what you're saying, ma'am, and it's like I told you. We're investigating this case, but everything we do doesn't include getting in Farah's face every five minutes. I actually visited the movie theater the other day to get the videotape from the evening your son went missing. Suspiciously, they don't know where it is. The manager, Jean Hershey, is a first-class asshole. He claims that on the day Amico went missing at the movie theater, they weren't taping. I thought he was hiding something, so we got a search warrant. We couldn't find the tape, so we are working overtime on this matter."

Beverly stopped making the bed, wiped her hands on her dress, and said, "Sit down."

Nadia looked at the light pink comforter in disgust and said, "I'm fine over here. Thanks anyway."

Beverly said, "I'm not in the business of saying what I want done more than once, so I'm asking that you not make me." High and half out of her mind, Nadia took a seat, although her leg moved rapidly under her body. "Good. Now, I know that you have been doing this for years, but I also know you got a drug problem. You've had it for a while, but you didn't think I would find out. But when it comes to my son, I find out everything."

"I don't even know what you're talking about." Nadia tried to look out into space to avoid eye contact, but it didn't work.

"If lying to yourself makes it easier, so be it. I will say this, I'm not gonna tell them people you work for that you got a problem. As a matter of fact, it makes me feel better having something over you."

Nadia grew angry. If there was one thing she hated, it was being blackmailed. "Just because I'm on drugs doesn't mean I can't do my job."

Beverly laughed.

"I'm serious. You've been trying to handle this investigation since I first told you I was on the case, and it's making my job difficult."

"Making your job difficult?" she repeated with a glare. "Making your job difficult?" She huffed. "Bitch, I lost my only son!" Beverly walked up to her and slapped her face. "Don't tell me what the fuck you can do. Just do it." She pointed at her. "I'm tired of you dragging your feet, and if I have to put a fire to it, that's exactly what I intend on doing!" She walked away and sat on the edge of the bed. "Do you know how it feels to have your heart tell you that your son is dead, even though you can't put him to rest?"

"N . . . no," she stuttered.

"Exactly, but I do." Tears rolled down her cheeks. "Now, I'm not under any illusions that my son is alive. I've made peace with that weeks ago, but it doesn't stop me from wanting to know what happened."

"Beverly—"

"Shut the fuck up and listen to what the fuck I'm saying. I want that bitch investigated, and I want an eye kept on her at all times. If you follow her long enough, she'll give us exactly what we need. I'm sure of it." She stood back up. "In fact, I found out that she's been rolling with some high yellow bitch and her boyfriend."

"If you're referring to Lesa Carmine," she started, still feeling her cheek on fire, "she left town after Farah showed up at her house. She just looks like her."

"This young lady looks different. She had blond streaks in her hair and could pass for white. Keep an eye on them, all of them, and pretty soon something will come up."

Chapter 14

Slade

"If you would go so far as to denounce your family, you were never a Baker anyway."

The Baker Boys walked Audio up to the check-in counter at the Baltimore/Washington International Airport. Since Chloe died, Audio couldn't bring himself to a place of closure, so they thought it best that he leave and go back to Mississippi.

Right before Audio checked in, he turned around and faced his brothers. "I don't know why y'all doing this," he said. Even at the moment, he reeked of vodka. "We still haven't found Knox. I thought that was the plan. None of us was leaving without our brother, and we were all going home together." He looked at Major and Killa. "Let me help y'all. Please."

"You gotta go, man," Slade interjected. His heart was heavy when he heard the sadness in his voice, but nothing about what he said would change the decision. "I know you want to stay, but we can't take the risk of something happening to you. Aunt V gonna take care of you and help you get over this thing."

"I'm not talking to you," he yelled in his face. "All you care about is yourself and that bitch." He pointed his finger into his chest. "If you gave a fuck about me you wouldn't be doing none of this shit."

Hearing how his brother felt about him ripped his heart open. Of course he cared about him. He loved him more than he could explain, but the way he was carrying on in DC would get either himself or the entire family killed.

"Audio, you know I care about you." He placed his hand on the back of his head and pulled him toward him. Their foreheads touched. "You my kid brother. It's just—"

"Get the fuck off me!" he yelled, pushing him into Killa. "If something happens to me back home, it's gonna be your fault!"

"Audio, you going too far," Killa said combatively. "Now, you been down here for months drunk and almost got yourself killed! We understand you loved Chloe. I feel you on that shit. But us sending you back on that plane is on you, not us."

"If y'all send me on that plane, I'm no longer a Baker! You hear what I'm saying?" He looked at all of them.

Slade's head was slumped and his shoulders were hunched, until he heard his words. Hearing his statement made him as hard as stone. "If you would go so far as to denounce your family, you were never a Baker anyway."

Silence.

"I guess you right," Audio yelled, storming away.

Slade stood in the middle of the airport and watched his kid brother until he was out of view.

"Come on, man," Killa said in a low voice. "You gotta see your peoples before Judge and Grant. I don't know what's up with them, but they been following her like crazy. The other day I heard them talking about something they saw. When I walked in the room, they got quiet."

Slade didn't move. He couldn't move. He was fucked up by what Audio said and wondered if there was truth to his statement. Yes, he was wrapped up in thoughts about Farah, but as far as they knew, he didn't fuck with her anymore. He didn't call her, didn't visit her or ask about her. He even started keeping time with someone regular to make the days go by.

"Go see Farah, Slade," Major added. "Audio gonna get over that shit."

"I hope so."

Slade paced the area outside of Farah's door for five minutes. He hadn't seen her in months and had a feeling she was with someone new. He just hoped he'd never see them together. When he gathered enough confidence, he knocked on her door and waited.

When the door crept open and he saw how beautiful Farah was, his heart melted. The long black gown she wore clung to her curves, and he was enamored all over again. Why was she so fucking sexy? Why couldn't he have her? Why couldn't he love her like his heart begged? And then he remembered: she could possibly have had something to do with his missing brother. "Can I come in for a minute? I want to talk to you."

She remained standing at the door, preventing him from entering. Her body trembled, although her eyes were stern. "What do you want with me, Slade? We have nothing to talk about."

He sighed and tried to find the right words to say to her. He could be a bully when his heart was involved, and he knew that. But this was about business, not pleasure. "You gonna make me talk to you out here?"

She folded her arms into her chest.

"Come on, Farah. The least we can do is talk in private."

"You made it plain how you want our relationship to be, so I'm not going to try to change your mind anymore. I moved on, Slade. I'm good over here."

"Farah, I understand we over. That's not what I'm here to talk to you about."

Her head hung because his words cut deep. Prior to that moment, it was only a *possibility* that they would never be together again . . . now it was a fact. "If you don't want to talk about us, what do you want?"

He stepped closer and stuffed his hands in his pockets. "I'm here because I want to talk to you about Knox. Have you found anything about Eleanor yet?"

She sighed and shook her head. "I told you all I know about the situation. Don't you think I want her found too? I don't want this shit over my head for the rest of my life, Slade. I know what you're thinking."

"You couldn't begin to know what I'm thinking."

"Yes, I do. You're thinking that I had something to do with his disappearance, and it doesn't make sense to me. And I finally know that there's nothing I can do to change your mind. Not to mention the fact that every time I turn around one of your family members is staring at me."

"What the fuck is that supposed to mean?"

She pointed down the hall at Judge. "Man, can you please go in the apartment?" Slade told him. "I'm talking to her right now."

"Grant told me to keep my eyes on her door."

"Well, what Grant gonna do if I punch you in the face?"

He hurried away, leaving them alone.

"You see what I'm saying? I've never seen this many country niggas in all my life."

He frowned upon hearing her comment.

"So they gotta be here for me. Am I right or wrong?"

"Farah, can I come in? Please. I'm not trying to talk to you about this shit in the hallway. You owe me that at least."

She reluctantly opened the door and walked inside. He followed, closing the door behind him. "You right about my people being in town to find out what's up with Knox." He stuffed his hands into his pockets. "And they gonna be questioning you too. I'm here to try to prevent that."

"I knew that shit." She fell into her sofa. "So what they gonna do, hurt me? Kill me? You gonna let them get me, Slade?"

"Don't say that shit. You know how I feel about you." He paced in place. "I wish you would've told me you had my brother's phone. I could've defended you better, but the way shit played out, I found out the moment they did."

"You should've defended me whether I had his phone or not, Slade. You promised to take care of me. You promised to love me forever." She shook her head. "To quote you correctly, the first day we fucked you said, 'I told myself if I ever fell in love again, that I would never abandon her when she needed me the most.' Well, I needed you the most and you failed me. Are you a man of your word or a liar?"

Slade's jaw clenched. Everything she said aimed right at his heart. "Farah, don't do this shit to me."

"Don't do what?" She stood up and approached him. "Don't love you? Don't believe that you are a man of your word?" She shook her head. "You don't know who I was willing to be just to be with you, Slade. You don't know what I was willing to give up. I never loved a human being more than I loved you, and I doubt I ever will."

"What do you mean what you were willing to give up?"

"I've done some things I can't take back. Some things I dream about most nights. But to be with you, I was willing to change it all."

Slade looked over her and frowned. She was evil, he was sure, but why was he still drawn to her? "Did any of those things have to do with my brother being missing?"

Farah backed up and slapped him before rushing to the door. "Get the fuck out!" She opened the door. "Now!"

"Farah, I'm sorry—"

"Fuck sorry! I want you out of my house, Slade." When he didn't move she said, "Don't make me call the police. I know how much you hate them."

Slade trudged to the door. He didn't want to leave and he hated that they were parting on those terms. "I'm sorry for making you a promise I couldn't keep. I love you, Farah, but I can't choose you over my family. I hope you understand that." He walked out, leaving her alone.

Slade entered Markee's apartment before going to his own. It was months later, and Markee still hadn't returned. The moment he walked inside and saw Major and Killa pacing the living room floor, he knew something was up.

Frightened, he rushed up to them and asked, "What the fuck is going on? Somebody fucking with you?"

"Man, the nigga Randy and the same bum-ass nigga we saw at the gym shot at us!" Killa yelled. "I want this nigga's head, Slade! Like yesterday."

"Fuck you mean they shot at y'all?"

"We were taking Ma grocery shopping for Sunday dinner. We hadn't even gotten there yet, when all of a sudden some niggas in a white van pulled up and started blasting at the car. Had it not been for Major handling the wheel and getting us out safe, we would be dead right now."

Slade was so angry he was swerving in place. He told his mother that she needed to stay close to Platinum Lofts, but she never listened. He knew it wasn't her fault that she was shot at, but putting herself in harm's way was all the way foul. "Where is Ma now?" He looked toward the back of the apartment.

"Willie took her to get a weapon."

At first Slade wasn't feeling the fact that they were spending a lot of time together. He didn't want him trying to manipulate Della into convincing them to stay. It didn't take him long to remember that she was her own woman and could spot bullshit a mile away. "He got three niggas with him, too, so she should be good."

Slade walked away from his brothers and leaned up against the wall. He thought about all of the things he was going to do to Randy and the man he knew as the albino when he got his hands on them. "On everything I love, I'm killing both of them niggas with my bare hands. That's a promise."

Chapter 15

Farah

"I'm not much on talking to strangers."

Dressed in an all-black cat suit with a cute red jacket, Farah stood in front of the mirror and observed her frame. She was certainly dressed for murder. She was just about to leave when her phone rang.

"What's up, Coconut?" she asked, skimming through her purse. "I don't have a lot of time to talk to you right now. I'm on my way out the door."

"Okay, I was just calling you to give you some information." Coconut sighed. "If you're so busy that you don't have time, never mind."

Farah hung up and was heading out the door when curiosity got the better of her, so she turned back around and called Coconut back. "I got a few minutes. What were you going to tell me?"

"I wanted to tell you that I'm supposed to be meeting Eleanor tomorrow. She called and asked if I needed anything. You want me to hook the meeting up?"

Farah's temples thumped. This was the moment she was waiting for. Trying to remain calm again, she said, "Uh yeah . . . that'll work. When do you think you can do it?"

"Anytime," Coconut replied. "But did you want me to pick something up for you instead? You can pay me back later if you want."

"Naw, I want to buy my own. Just call me when you on your way to see her."

"You got it." Coconut paused. "Before you go, Jake wanna know if we seeing each other later."

Farah rolled her eyes. "Tell him it's cool with me, but I really gotta go now. I'll talk to you later."

Coconut's call saved her a trip later on in the week. With her schedule clear, she could indulge in her favorite pastime: the quest for blood. With a smile on her face, the moment she stepped out of the building a man wearing a red jacket and a beautiful Asian girl approached her. Both of them were extremely attractive and she always wondered if they were together or not. She'd seen them many times, and they always appeared fixated on her.

"You're Farah Cotton right?" the girl said. It was a windy day, so her long brown hair whipped around her neck like a scarf.

"Who's asking?" Farah responded, prepared to gut her like a fish if need be. "I'm not much on talking to strangers."

The girl giggled. "There's no need to be violent." she smiled. "Unless you're having fun anyway." She looked at the man. "I'm Mayoni, and this is my boyfriend, Carlton. We moved here a few months back and have been dying to meet you, but every time we try to talk to you, you're always coming and going."

After dealing with Coconut and her boyfriend, she automatically assumed it was ménage à trois related. "Why y'all wanna meet me?"

"You want the truth?" Carlton inquired, with a light grin on his face.

"I wouldn't ask if I didn't."

"We wanted to meet you because we have a lot in common," Mayoni replied. "And since the world is so small, we figured we'd introduce ourselves."

"Well, I don't want any friends, so I prefer if you just come out with it."

"Okay," he responded, "we wanted to meet you because we're vampires too. And not the kind of vampires you see on TV or no shit like that. We're consenting adults who enjoy blood and pain. Just . . . like . . . you."

Farah's face flushed. Who were they and why did they assume they knew so much about her? "That sounds like a personal problem to me."

"We not coming at you crazy or nothing, so there's no need for you to be on the defensive," Carlton continued. "We just wanted you to have people you could relate to because we know how it is to be alone."

"First off, I don't know what you're talking about, but even if I did, why are you so interested in what I do? You don't even know me." She looked between them. She preferred to do things sneakily in the night and wasn't into an audience. The only reason she didn't stomp off was because she was interested in who they were.

"We know more about you than you think," Mayoni advised.

"I doubt that very seriously." Farah rubbed her face, feeling a breakout coming along.

"We know that if you keep doing things the way you have been, you're going to end up in jail," Mayoni added. "We know that the car right there has been following you wherever you go."

Farah turned around and saw a gray rental car in the distance. The people in it ducked, but she could still see their heads.

"Who are they?" Farah asked them.

"We don't know," Mayoni said. "But they're definitely fans and have been following you for a while."

Farah frowned. "What is this all about?"

"Come with us," Mayoni persisted. "Let us show you something, and if you don't like what you see, we won't ever bother you again."

"What about the car?" She looked behind her.

"We know how to shake them," Carlton replied. "Just follow us."

Farah was following Mayoni and Carlton until suddenly they pulled into a gas station along with a white car. "What are you doing now?" she asked as she parked behind them. When she turned around, she exhaled when she didn't see the gray car. She didn't know who was in it, but she had a feeling it was Baker related.

Mayoni and Carlton exited their car and approached the white one, which had been behind them the entire time. *Do they have a follower too?* She observed Carlton walk up to the driver's window while Mayoni walked to the passenger side. There was only one person in the car. When Farah saw Officer Nadia's face in the left side mirror, she was about to pull off. The only reason she didn't was for fear of being spotted. Things were getting weirder by the hour.

Carlton bent down, looked into the window, and said something Farah couldn't hear. Before long, Nadia sped away from the scene as if her life depended on it.

Mayoni and Carlton looked at her car, smiled, and said, "Come on. We're almost there."

Without even telling Farah what happened, they got back in their car and she followed them to the destination. Even if she wanted to turn back she couldn't. She had to know what Nadia wanted and what she said.

After driving quite some time, she ended up in front of a large, beautiful brick mansion outside of Maryland, in a rural area. The closest house near the mansion was about fifteen miles away. *What am I doing here?* She parked her car behind the couple's black Escalade and sat for a moment. Part of her wanted to run, and the other part told her they were the answer to her boredom.

Mayoni and Carlton eased out of the truck and looked at Farah. When she hadn't moved, they knocked on her car window. "You coming?"

Reluctantly she got out and stood in front of the home. "First, can you tell me what that was back at the gas station?" She looked at both of them.

"That's Officer Nadia. She's been following you too," Mayoni said.

"What . . . ? For how long?"

"I'm not sure," Carlton said. "But we know her face."

"So she saw me?"

"Yes."

Farah turned white. "Well . . . did she say anything?"

"Nadia is a cokehead. We let her know it, and promised to ruin her career if we ever caught her following you again."

"Are you serious?" Farah responded, with her jaw hung.

"We don't play like that," Carlton said.

"This way," Mayoni said, grabbing her softly by the hand. When Farah didn't move she said, "Trust us. We got you."

After considering that she didn't have anything to lose and that they hipped her on to two cars that could've followed her as she committed murder, she decided to go with them. She followed them through the large mahogany doors and into a gothic-like foyer. Cherry wood and black dominated everything, including the furniture. When they approached another door, Mayoni said, "We know you're going to love this."

When she touched Carlton on the shoulder, he pushed open the doors and inside was a plethora of beautiful people. A quick count ended at fifteen. Most were black, and they ranged from light skin all the way to dark chocolate. They seemed united, and everyone was dressed in black with a tinge of red. For instance, the women either wore red shoes or red lipstick, while the men wore red iced-out rosaries. They were drinking from red wine glasses, and soft music played in the background. The ambiance captivated her immediately, and everyone seemed mystical. On the far end of the room was a wall, which was covered by black velvet curtains. It resembled a covered movie screen.

"What is this?" she asked them, looking at everyone in attendance. She couldn't help but acknowledge the tingling sensation pulsing between her legs. The irony was, she was dressed perfectly for the occasion. "Is this a party or something?"

"Not really. It's almost time for a show." When she said that, someone activated a button on the wall, which opened the curtains.

Behind them was a glass wall. When she stepped closer, a woman sitting on a red-and-black chair, wearing nothing but a red sequined bathing suit, looked out into the crowd. Her chocolate skin glistened under the one light in the room, and her beauty was intoxicating. She seemed nervous but prepared, and Farah was glued to the scene.

Seconds later, a dude with long, neat dreads running down his back entered the room from the right. He stepped up to her and ran his hands down her long brown hair. At first she flinched, but when he continued to stroke her skin, she ultimately relaxed.

Farah examined her mannerisms. Her arms and ankles were tied lightly to the chair with black scarfs. Was she a victim or a willing participant? Farah wanted to know.

When he flicked a golden blade and ran it along the side of her arm, Farah felt the heat in the room turn up as everyone watched with anticipation. The woman wasn't out cold or drugged like Farah preferred her victims. She seemed to be anticipating what would happen next.

After what Farah considered foreplay, he sliced the flesh on her shoulder. The woman licked her lips and smiled at him.

"Again," she said as her voice amplified from the speakers in the room.

He sliced her again and she squirmed. "Do it again."

Over and over he sliced her, and Farah was overly stimulated. She didn't know who the man was, but she was drawn to him immediately. She hadn't had that level of attraction since she met Slade Baker in the hallway of her building.

"Who is he?" she whispered to Mayoni.

Mayoni grinned, enjoying the way Farah's eyes lit up. "His name is Bones. Why? You like what you see?"

She nodded slowly. "A lot."

Focusing back on the scene, she saw Bones lower his upper body and suck the puddles of blood that popped up on her skin.

Just when she thought she'd seen everything, the door to the glass room opened and a beautiful light-skinned woman with long brown hair strolled up to them. She dropped to her knees, moved the woman's bathing suit to the side, and slithered her tongue into her pussy. Bones continued to slice into her flesh, while other bloodsuckers tasted her sweetness. The scene was so sexual that, at this point, Farah was soaking wet.

"Everybody here has been tested for HIV and other diseases," Mayoni said to Farah. "So you never have to worry about getting anything here but pleasure."

Farah focused on Mayoni and Carlton intensely. There was something else to this. She knew it. "How do you find the . . ."

"Are you talking about the women? Who get sliced?"

"Yes."

"We call them Givers. Or Slaves," Mayoni responded. "It's whatever they prefer."

"So how do you find the Givers?"

"There are more people out there than you realize who enjoy pain," Carlton added, touching Farah softly on the arm. "It's really easy. And the best part is, our Givers are willing and able to do whatever you desire. This eliminates your risk of being caught."

"We're like you, and we want you to join us," Mayoni said.

Farah's eyes moved rapidly. She focused on their expressions, then at the spectators, and then at the scene behind the curtains. Something in her heart said it was a setup. She was so jumpy due to the new world she was experiencing that she ran out of the room and then the house.

They quickly followed, and Mayoni yelled, "Where are you going, Farah?"

"Don't leave like this! Let us explain!" Carlton added.

When Farah didn't bother to stop, Mayoni said, "Why are you so afraid?"

Needing some air, she stopped where she was and leaned on her car. She pointed at the house. "I don't understand any of this. I'm so confused. I mean . . . why? How? Are you trying to tell me that everyone in there is a . . . vampire?"

They approached her, and Mayoni responded softly, "If you ask doctors, they'll say we have Renfield's Syndrome, but among ourselves, we simply say we are lovers of blood and pain. We're not hurting anything or anybody, so for real, we hate tags."

"But when you met me in front of the building, you called yourself vampires."

"Because we knew you could relate to that," Carlton interrupted.

"Well, what do you want with me?" She looked at the house. "You seem to have enough people who are with that shit back there."

"We told you earlier," Carlton added. "We want you to join us. That's why we took our time and approached you when we felt the time was right. We don't have these events every day, so this is special. You don't have to be alone."

"Whether you want to believe us or not, you are one of us, Farah." Mayoni touched her on the arm. "And there's no turning back now."

***

After the wild evening Farah had, all she wanted was to go in the house, but the first people she saw when she exited the elevator leading to her floor were Judge and Grant. They faced her door, and chills ran up her spine. There was no way on earth she was walking into that fire, so she backed into the elevator and left the scene.

Chapter 16

Lollipop

"Niggas make slip-ups all the time, and I made one."

The windows were wide open as The Vet cruised down the road with Lollipop in the passenger seat. They were on the way to meet Randy at an undisclosed location. After a group of Randy's men, with Lollipop in the lead, attempted to murder the Baker Boys and were spotted, Randy went deeper into hiding. At the moment the only thing on his mind was talking to Lollipop about his reckless behavior.

Cloud-shaped puffs of smoke filled the truck, and two half-empty cups of Hennessy rested in the cup holders. Choosing to support Randy was proving to be more than it was worth for both men.

"I can't believe how fat that bitch was," Lollipop said, pulling on the sweet blunt between his fingertips. "Bet money if we put her near Coco, she would make her ass look like a sandwich. That bitch got the kind of ass you can eat off. It's all real, too, none of that fake shit them bitches be pumping into their cheeks."

"First off, are you talking about Coco? Ice-T's wife?" The Vet looked over at him as he steered the vehicle smoothly.

Lollipop blew out a puff of smoke. “Who the fuck you think I’m talking about?”

“Nigga, that bitch you talking about back there is fifteen years old, which means she’s a child and incapable of being sexy in any kind of way. Second of all, she’s black, so even if she was a woman, which she isn’t, there’s still no resemblance.” He eyed him. “You so busy thinking about stupid shit that you don’t have your head in business. Because of you them niggas spotted us and been firing the few corners Randy had left. Do you understand what that means?” He paused. “Randy ain’t able to do business at all. Nothing is coming in, nigga.”

Lollipop set the blunt in the ashtray and grabbed his cup of Hennessy. “My head is in business. Niggas make slip-ups all the time, and I made one, but it ain’t ’cause of me Randy not making paper. With or without the slip-up, he’s at war with the Bakers.” He sipped his drink. “But what I really want to know is this: Do you have a problem with me or something? Because lately you been coming at me sideways.”

The Vet shook his head. “If you just realizing that I got a problem with you, there really is no hope for you.” He laughed. “I been had a problem with you, nigga.”

“What did I do?”

“For starters you’re sloppy and a fucking child molester. I don’t trust people like you.”

“I never t . . . touched a kid once in my life.” He squirmed in his seat. “You shouldn’t believe everything you hear, man.”

The Vet laughed, although he could feel his blood boiling under the surface of his skin. Here he was getting all worked up by someone he didn’t even respect. “Let’s just say you have your ideas and I have mine.”

Lollipop was fixing to spread his lips to say something sideways when The Vet's cell phone rang. He observed the number.

"I think you got the wrong—"

"Hold that shit you about to say," The Vet said. He threw his hand up in Lollipop's face. "I gotta take this call." He focused his attention on the phone and answered. "What's up?"

"We waiting on you to deliver that package. Where is it?" asked Musty, one of Randy's men. "It's like you taking all day."

"It's under control," The Vet said, looking over at Lollipop. "And it shouldn't be much longer."

"Well, hurry up. Randy trying to see that nigga like yesterday."

"I can't work no faster with you in my ear." He frowned, not taking lightly to people telling him what to do. "We en route though."

"I get that. . . . Oh, before you leave, I wanted to tell you that when we had my daughter's party yesterday, the nigga Lollipop had your little girl hemmed up in the corner crying. I don't know what it was about, but it didn't look too good."

The Vet was so taken aback that he almost hit the car in front of him.

"What the fuck, man!" Lollipop yelled. "You almost killed me. I know you on that call, but don't forget you not alone in this bitch. Be careful."

The Vet was about to steal him in the jaw, but Musty's voice brought him back to reality. "Everything cool over there, man? You ain't about to do something that can wait, are you?"

The Vet took control of the car and gave Lollipop a look that shook his soul. Focusing back on the call he said through clenched teeth, "Why you just telling me this shit now?"

"Number one, I handled the situation immediately. The moment I saw what was going on, I asked him why she was crying. I had the nigga off his feet on the wall, V. As a matter of fact, I didn't let him down until Elena promised me that he didn't hurt her. Beyond that there wasn't much I could do because the nigga swore to God and all the moons that he wasn't fucking with her."

"Why wait until now to say something?" His fingers squeezed the steering wheel so tight it left indentations in it.

"Because I haven't talked to you until now to put you on to what happened. I figured you could use a little inspiration anyway to bring him to us." When silence met him, Musty said, "You okay, man?"

"I'ma holla at you later." He hung up and looked over at Lollipop, who felt the tension.

"You all right, man?" Lollipop asked, moving closer to the window.

The Vet remained silent.

"Who was that on the phone? Randy?"

"What happened yesterday at Musty's son's party?" He drove so slowly his speed was under the limit. "I'm hearing some things I want clarification on."

Lollipop's facial expression immediately looked guilty. "Aw, man, I hope this not about me disciplining little Elena." He laughed. "The kids were playing too rough, and I went over there to say something to her. She probably took it the wrong way. You know how kids are when they have too much sugar and shit like that."

"Since when do you feel like you can discipline my kids? Or anybody's kids, for that matter? You don't even have kids of your own."

He swallowed everything but his tongue. "V, I know you not mad about that shit, man. For real, it ain't even that deep. If I thought it was more I would've put you on to it right away, but you were kicking it with Musty and them and I honestly forgot to say something."

The Vet continued down the street in silence. Besides, he wasn't going to get anything near the truth from Lollipop. He was a liar and couldn't be honest if someone spoke it for him. Instead of holding trivial conversations, he detoured and continued down the street in the opposite direction. When he finally parked, they were in front of the Platinum Lofts apartments.

Lollipop looked around the dark streets. "Wait . . . why are we here?" He searched out of his windows. "Don't them niggas live in this building?"

"Yeah, but I gotta take care of something right quick."

Lollipop moved to exit the car. "I'm going with you."

"No, you not. Stay here. It'll only take a minute."

"You gonna be quick, right?"

He didn't respond.

"V, you coming back, right?" Lollipop asked.

The Vet eased out of the car without responding, leaving Lollipop alone. The silence he received from The Vet on the way over there tugged at him, mainly because he knew he was dead wrong in more ways than one.

The truth was, Lollipop was totally in the wrong when he hugged little Elena too tightly at the party. When she sobbed and threatened to tell her father, he said he would sneak in her room every night and beat her until she was dead. When Musty walked up on the scene and caught him, at first he thought he heard too much. When it turned out he was only reacting to what he saw, he was slightly relieved. Now he knew it was foolish to assume so.

When The Vet hadn't returned, Lollipop turned his head to the right, only to see an angry face staring at him. When he turned to the left, he saw the same thing. Every direction he turned revealed a member of the Baker family.

"Oh, no . . . please . . . please don't." His neck snapped from left to right as he scanned all of the glares, hoping to see The Vet. His fear went to another level when he looked ahead and saw Slade grinning at him.

Chapter 17

Farah

"I've been nervous all day just thinking about how things will go down."

Farah stood in front of the mirror with her short one-piece black dress and observed her figure. She puckered her lips, which she saturated with red lipstick. She was ready. Ready to be among her own. Among people like her. Vampires. In Washington, DC. Before she could participate in any events, they had sent her to one of their doctors, and she was given the clean bill of health. She was actually happy they did it, because at least she knew her status.

When her phone rang, she broke her stare. She'd been waiting for a call back from Coconut about Eleanor, but her calls went unanswered. She hoped she finally received her messages from the voicemail and was returning her call. "Hello?"

"Farah, it's Coconut."

Farah grinned. She had plans that night but would drop everything for a chance to kill Eleanor and put the situation behind her.

"I'm sorry I'm just getting back to you. Are you busy?"

"Coconut, what happened? I thought we were meeting Eleanor today, but I haven't heard from you."

"I don't know what happened. She called back to confirm. I told her I was bringing you with me and she hung up."

Farah sat on the edge of the bed. Coconut ruined all of her plans, and she didn't even know it.

"What's going on with y'all? Why would she hang up? She seemed like she was scared of you or something."

Irritated, she said, "I have to go, Coconut."

"Hold up. Are you mad with me now?" Silence. "Farah, what's going on?"

Farah ended the call. She was frustrated with Coconut's dumb ass. She'd come so close to getting rid of this woman, only for Coconut to fuck it all up. She lay face up on the bed and looked at the ceiling. "Where are you, Eleanor? Why don't you just die or disappear forever?"

When her phone rang again, she answered in full attitude mode. "What?"

"Wow, somebody doesn't seem too happy to hear from me," Mayoni said in a seductive voice. "Considering all of the great things we have planned for you this evening, I'd think you'd be nicer to me, Farah."

Farah sat up. "I'm sorry, girl." She giggled. "It's been a long day. To be honest, I'm kinda looking forward to hanging out."

"Well, let us make your evening better." She paused. "You ready to go out and have some fun?"

"Y . . . yes . . . I think so," she stuttered. "I don't know what we're going to do though. I've been nervous all day just thinking about how things will go down."

"There's nothing to worry about, Farah. I promise you won't be disappointed. It's time to start enjoying the rest of your life. We're just happy you're doing it with us." She paused. "Now hurry up and get ready;. We're downstairs waiting on you. Be careful though. You have some admirers still trying to follow you."

"How can we get rid of them?"

"Carlton has been shaking people off for years."

What does that mean?

"Don't worry. They won't be able to catch up."

Farah hung up, grabbed her coat and large red Celine bag, and strolled downstairs. On her way down the hall, she saw Slade walking into his apartment. His cologne was light and it didn't make her nauseated or sick like it usually did. Was she getting better? She exited her apartment and moved toward the elevator.

"I gotta talk to you," he said, eye-fucking the revealing dress she had under her coat. His dick hardened, and he wanted to push her to the floor and slide into her tightness. Instead he said, "You got a minute?"

She walked past him like he wasn't even on earth. Since he wanted to treat her like she was nonessential, she would return the favor.

"Farah, can I talk to you? It'll only take a few moments. My cousins said they saw you crawling out of some window. You know anything about that?"

Farah felt faint. She knew at that moment she could no longer avoid them. She needed to see how much they knew. She pressed the button on the elevator and lightly tapped her foot. It seemed like it took forever for the door to finally open. When it did, she stepped inside and waited for the doors to close. It wasn't until then that she sobbed long and hard. She cried because she missed him and she cried because she loved him.

Slade was the missing component in her life, and there was nothing she could do to change it. She loved

Slade more than her heart could stand, but she would no longer be his sucker. She could still feel the rawness of her knees from the last time she begged for his love, only to be rejected. In her mind it would never happen again. She was done. Fuck Slade, fuck his family, and anybody else who tried to get in her way.

The moment the elevator dinged indicating that she had reached her floor, she wiped her eyes, took a deep breath, and got ready for the world. A smile spread across her face when she stepped out in front of the building and saw Mayoni and Carlton waiting for her. They were dressed in all black with a tinge of red. In her mind it meant one thing. There was a blood party at tonight's event too.

"You look ravishing," Mayoni said, looking Farah over. "Good enough to taste."

Farah's pussy tingled. "Yes, she does," Carlton said, licking his lips. "I don't know, babes. With the exception of you, I think Farah is going to be the most beautiful girl in the room."

Farah blushed at Carlton's comment.

"I'm going to have to agree, honey," Mayoni responded.

The way they admired her reminded her of Coconut and her boyfriend. The difference was, she welcomed their advances. The attention was refreshing considering everything she'd lost in the months past. With all of the excitement, she couldn't help but consider that at some point she'd discover what they really wanted from her.

Farah followed Mayoni and Carlton to the same room she'd previously run from. The same people were present, and they all seemed friendly, putting her at complete ease. She was introduced to everyone and tried to appear relaxed. As nice as everyone was, she was looking for one person—Bones, the man she'd seen with the woman behind the glass window. Although her heart was with Slade, he was a welcome distraction.

"Where is Bones?" Farah asked them. "He's coming tonight, right?"

Carlton grinned at her. "He'll be here later. For now, just enjoy the show."

When the curtains opened, it revealed a bed in the middle of the floor, covered in black pillows and sheets. "What's this?" Farah asked.

"This is what's required for you to join us. This step is pleasurable, but it's also for your protection and ours. Consider it an initiation."

She frowned. "I agreed to be here. What more do you want from me now?"

"We are very cautious about the people we bring into our fold. Very cautious. We've watched you ever since you got blood from Grand Mike, and we've followed the stories about what's been happening in the news. We know you are the perfect match, but we must be sure."

"What do you mean, what's happening in the news?"

"The missing people," Mayoni responded quietly. "The slayings and slices to the jugular vein. The cops following you. The strange people in front of the building who can't let you out of their sights. We are down for you, but we need to know you feel the same."

"Did you say Grand Mike?" Farah thought about her first encounter with him a while back. Everything about him spelled trouble, including his missing teeth, yet she elected to do business with him anyway. For $1,600, his asking price, he gave her the fresh taste of blood. It wasn't until she spoke with her cousin Cosmo, who was in prison for multiple murders, that she discovered she was overcharged. Cosmo set the meeting up with him after realizing that Farah would never believe she alone had the power to slow down the rate of her illness. He hated himself to that day for getting her involved with him. After Cosmo learned that she killed him, he felt he got exactly what he deserved.

"How do you know him?" Farah inquired. "Grand Mike?"

"It's nothing for you to worry about," Carlton said. "He's an anything-ass nigga who would sell you New York if you let him. Even though most of the time his antics were a lie, every now and again he would come through for us when we needed small jobs."

"Of course that was when he was alive," Mayoni responded, looking into her eyes.

Nervous, Farah said, "Well, what did he tell you about me?"

"He didn't tell us a whole lot. When you first came to him about your illness, he mentioned how he was going to get money out of some sucker. Asked us if we ever heard of porphyria," he said, looking at Mayoni. "We told him yes and that we were aware of a few people with the same illness. We even verified the urban legend with him."

"What do you mean?"

"That the entire vampire legend was started as a result of people with porphyria, believing if they drank blood, they would be better." Mayoni touched her softly. "Not to worry though. He's dead anyhow."

Farah felt off balance. She wanted to deny the accusations, but figured they had their opinions about it anyway. Then she had a thought. They knew so much about her, could they be responsible for the picture she received recently? "I have a question." She swallowed. "Someone sent me a picture about something I did. Was it you?" She looked at them.

"Pictures?" Carlton frowned. "We don't know nothing about no pictures."

She wanted to ask a few more questions, but decided to put the matter out of her mind. She came to the mansion to satisfy her cravings, not defend herself. "Earlier you said whatever was going on behind the glass window was an initiation. What do you mean?"

"Trust me when I say it'll be effortless. Look now." They pointed to the room, and in walked a beautiful girl with red braids hanging down her back, in a red bathing suit. Her brown skin sparkled under the dim light as she eased on top of the bed. When her eyes met Farah's she smiled, although there was a hint of apprehension in her eyes. She seemed willing to do what was required.

"That's Sparkle," Mayoni said, nudging Farah. "Go inside. She knows what she has to do."

Farah slowly strolled toward the room. On her way there, the people present touched her softly on the shoulder. She was comforted as she opened the door and closed it softly behind her.

"Hi," Farah said, feeling out of place. She remained close to the door. "I'm Farah."

"Hello, Farah," Sparkle replied.

Farah strutted up to the bed and looked her over. She looked like a model, and the entire scene felt like she was in a movie. "What's your name?" she asked, although she knew the answer already. She didn't know what to say and was trying to strike up some conversation.

"In the real world I'm called Sparkle," she said with a half smile. "But in here, I'm called Slave or Giver."

Farah's eyebrows rose. "Okay, Slave." She cleared her throat. "I'm new at this, so what do we do now?"

"Anything you'd like." She looked at where she stood. "For starters, you can move closer. I'm not the one who bites."

Farah swallowed and stepped closer to the bed. "But I've never done this before."

"If that's the game you want to play, I'm with it." She smiled. "I'm great at role playing."

Farah lowered her head. "What do you mean, if that's the game I want to play? I'm serious. This is the first time I've ever done anything like this. I don't even know where to start."

Sparkle grinned. "They never invite anyone into the Fold unless they're sure you're ready. So if you're here, that means they're positive that you know exactly what is to be done. But the longer you delay, the more time we're wasting."

"Look, I'm not a part of anything or any fold. I'm just here to check things out."

"If that's the game you want to play, I'm with that too." She repeated what she had said earlier.

Now that Farah was closer to her, she observed her brown skin, which was covered with tiny slashes. Her body had been used many times in this fashion, and yet she was still alive. "Why do you do this?" She nodded at her body. "Let people cut you up while you just take it?"

"There are many reasons. For starters, I do it because I like to serve. Some of us are Takers and others are Givers, also known as Slaves. But the main reason I do it is because I love the pain and I love to please. We all do." She paused. "In the end, in exchange for giving, we are redeemed."

Farah looked confused.

"You're thinking too much into it." She touched her hand softly. The Slave lay flat on her back and spread her arms and legs. "All I want to do right now is make your first night here memorable." She flicked a gold razor and handed it to Farah, who softly released it from her hand. "Enjoy me."

As if they were lovers, Farah crawled on top of her. While straddling her, she looked down at her passive body. For some reason she felt powerful at the moment, and in charge. A small volt of electricity sparked between her legs, causing her to get wetter. She began searching for the perfect place on her body to draw blood. A place free from scars. After some time, she discovered a small spot on her inner thigh.

"I'm about to cut you." Farah pointed at her leg. "Right there."

She grinned. "When are you going to understand? You don't have to tell me what you want to do. Just do it. I am yours for the taking."

Emboldened, Farah raised the blade and ripped into the flesh of her thigh. The Slave whimpered softly but didn't fight an ounce. When a puddle of red blood popped up on her skin, Farah lowered her head and slid her tongue onto it. Then she sucked until the roof of her mouth ached. She did this again and again, until the Slave was sliced over ten times all over her body.

Farah was so far in her mind that she didn't see the Slave with her nipples in her mouth. She heard her soft moans, and that only turned her on even more. This was different from the past experiences. Normally Farah would have to get her rocks off before she drank their blood. With this experience, the act of drinking blood itself made her aroused.

With her mouth bloody red, Farah peeked through the glass walls to see who was watching. There wasn't an empty space because each member of the Fold observed the scene. It was then that she saw Bones, the only other man who moved her soul. He nodded at her and grinned lightly. Now she was really turned on.

Trying to give Bones a really good show, she got on her hands and knees so that her plump ass faced the window. Then she sliced again into the Slave's thigh. She positioned her body so that he could see her wet tongue as she sipped her blood.

The Slave raised her head and waved her hand toward the window. A light-skinned man entered and closed the door behind him.

"Wait. Who is that?" Farah inquired, wiping her mouth. "I'm not with the three-way shit right now."

"Don't worry." She giggled. "He's here for me, not you. He's my husband."

It wasn't until that moment that she peeped the rings on their fingers. "He doesn't mind that we hurt you like this?"

"No." She shook her head rapidly. "If you can't share your lifestyle with the one you love, then you aren't truly living."

Farah thought about Slade again. Up until that moment, she was relishing in the time she was spending with her newfound friends, but seeing the Slave with her husband made her miss him even more. She looked around at everyone else looking into the room. Then she focused on Mayoni and Carlton. They all seemed to be paired, and now she felt like the odd girl out. Could Slade accept this lifestyle? Even if he could, would they ever accept him? Her thoughts went wild, until she focused on Bones again. Maybe it was time for her to put Slade out of her mind, and move on with her life.

As the Slave's husband crawled into the bed, Farah observed the way he removed the bathing suit she wore. Despite the spectators, in that moment, they were all alone. He lovingly caressed the fresh cuts on her skin before easing his tongue into her mouth. It wasn't long before he entered her with his stiff dick, while Farah observed from the sidelines.

Farah was enamored by the scene and was about to help out, until her cell phone rang in her pocket. She excused herself from the couple, who carried on like she wasn't there anyway. When she saw it was her sister's number, she sighed.

"What is it, Mia?" She observed the couple. "I'm busy right now."

"Well, whatever you doing gotta wait," she demanded.

Farah observed Bones, who, despite the full-blown sex the couple was having on the bed, seemed to be focused on what she was doing.

"Mia, I'll come home when I want to. Have you forgotten already? I'm an adult now."

"Farah, fuck that shit you spitting. Bring your ass home now! Dr. Martin is here, and I think he spoke to the cops."

Chapter 18

Farah

"Don't I look beautiful? Isn't my skin clear and refreshed?"

Farah approached her apartment and stopped. The last thing she needed was this kind of drama, but she knew Dr. Martin all too well. If she even looked like she was up to something, or nervous, it would only make matters worse for her. So when she was ready, she took a few quick breaths and went inside. The moment she entered, she was met by arguing. In the middle of the floor were her grandmother, Dr. Martin, Mia, and Shadow.

"Farah, can you please tell this man you haven't killed anybody?" Elise said, waving her over to her direction. "He's hell bent on listening to whatever this cop Nadia Gibson had to say to him."

Farah trudged up to them and stood next to her grandmother. She could smell her beefy odor, but she was so used to it that it no longer mattered. Her mind was wrecked as she counted the people who could be responsible for her undoing. Eleanor, Rhonda, Lesa, Randy, Dr. Martin, and then Officer Nadia. Just when things were going good, one of them mothafuckas was bound to make things bad again.

"Hello, Dr. Martin," Farah said softly.

"Farah." He nodded. "You look well."

Thinking about the blood she consumed, she smiled. "I'm very well. That was, until I came home to all of this drama." She paused. "Look, I don't know what that bitch told you, but whatever it was, I promise you it's a lie. The only reason she is out to get me is because she wanted to room with me and I wouldn't allow her. Had I said yes, none of this would be going on."

Dr. Martin laughed. "Farah, when are you going to stop lying to yourself and your family? Why would the officer want to live with the suspect of a crime? It doesn't make any sense."

"You really do believe I'm some sort of sick monster don't you?" she asked him, still able to taste the Slave's blood on her tongue. "Where do you get all of this shit from anyway?"

Everyone looked at Elise, who held her head down and cleared her throat. "I'm sorry, baby," Elise said to Farah. "I didn't know you were drunk after you told me all them crazy stories about you drinking blood to get well a while back." She observed the doctor. "I was wrong, but that still don't give you no reason to be on this witch hunt you've been on regarding my granddaughter. Now, she answered your question, so can you please just leave my family alone?"

"I wish I could do that, Elise. I want nothing more than for all of this to be behind us. Unfortunately that isn't possible."

"If I can prove to you that the officer wanted to live here and is only trying to sabotage me after I denied her, would you believe me then?" Farah asked.

"If you can provide proof, I'll believe there's more to the story than what the officer told me," Dr. Martin said. "That's about all I can say to you for right now."

In the hopes of getting rid of him, Farah dodged into her room and returned with a stack of papers. She extended her arms and said, "It's all there."

Reluctantly he accepted the pile of paper. "What are these?"

"Why don't you read it, mothafucka, instead of asking a bunch of dumb-ass questions?" Shadow popped off. "Now, she told you what she went to get. What else do you think they are?"

"Shadow Cotton!" Elise yelled. "I dealt with your mother's foul mouth all of her life before she died, but I will not tolerate this type of disrespectful behavior from you. Do I make myself clear, or do I have to make you feel me?"

"Sorry, Grams."

The doctor walked over to the sofa and sat down. He removed his eyeglasses from the case in his shirt and placed them on. Then he scanned over the documents Farah handed him. Although he appeared to be reading them, it was obvious that he didn't understand what was before him. "What exactly am I looking at?"

"The officer's address, name, and personal info." Farah pointed at one sheet in particular. "Look at that one. Everything you need is right there."

He scanned the papers again with disbelieving eyes. What Farah was saying made no sense to him. "How do I know this is true?"

"Drive to her house. Call her home number. I don't care what you do. I gave you everything you're looking for." When he still seemed doubtful, Farah said, "How else would I get her home number and address unless she gave them to me? Trust me, she doesn't want you to know, but she applied for a room here and I told her she couldn't stay."

With narrow eyes, he pulled his cell phone out and dialed the number on the sheet. He waited impatiently for the phone to answer, and everyone in the room was on pins and needles. After a few more seconds he cleared his throat and said, “Nadia Gibson, please.” He paused and looked up at Farah. “Okay, thank you.” He hung up and stuffed his phone back into his pocket.

“Well?” Mia asked. “Did you find out what you wanted?”

He removed his glasses and stuffed them in the case. “A woman answered and said she doesn’t live there anymore.”

Farah exhaled and stepped back. “Now can you leave me alone? Please.”

Dr. Martin stood up and looked at the Cotton family. Without a response, he walked out of the apartment, leaving Farah’s question unanswered.

When Elise left, Farah sat in the living room with her brother and sister on the couch. They were sipping vodka and whiskey mixed and the half-empty bottles sat on the table. “Farah, what’s going on with Eleanor?” Shadow asked, shaking the liquor in his cup. “You been gone a lot lately, but this bitch is still out on the streets. Aren’t you worried about what Slade and them will do to you? Every time I turn around, I see another member of his family living in this building.”

“I don’t give a fuck about what Slade or anybody else in his family do,” Farah lied. “And I don’t know where Eleanor is. Anyway, I thought you said you would help me find her.” She looked at him and then Mia. “You too.”

“We been trying to find this bitch, but the last I heard, it wasn’t a solo job. You were supposed to be helping also,” Shadow said. “But the only thing on your mind lately seems to be the streets. She's not our responsibility, Farah, and unless you want to get arrested, you better start helping us out around here."

"I am helping." She sat back in the cushions of the sofa.

"I hear you, but your actions are telling us otherwise. So where have you been?"

"I have to do what I have to, to save myself." She looked at her siblings. "You know that."

"So basically you still doing the blood thing?" Shadow frowned. "You really are sicker than I thought. I don't understand this person you are anymore."

"Look at me," Farah said as she sat up. "Don't I look beautiful? Isn't my skin clear and refreshed? It may be a joke to you two, but I need to do this to survive."

Shadow and Mia observed her, and neither wanted to validate her statement. If they were being honest, they would definitely say she looked more radiant and almost glowed. They knew at that moment that unless something happened during one of her blood adventures, she would never stop or change.

"That's not answering the question," Shadow persisted. "Where have you been?"

"I'm around," Farah responded dryly. "But I have a question, Do you think Lesa is responsible for the picture?"

"No. I really don't. To be honest, I don't think it's Eleanor either," Mia continued. "And hopefully by Lesa being afraid, you won't have any more problems."

"Then it has to be Rhonda. I have to find her," Farah continued.

"I saw that bitch the other day on Benning Road," Shadow said. "She may be a lot of things, but sane enough to send you pictures ain't it."

"I still want her gone. Even if I have to do it myself."

"Well, there's one good thing that came from all of this," Mia said, pouring some more liquor into her cup.

"And what's that?" Farah inquired.

"Dr. Martin said before you got here that Lesa moved out of state and nobody knows where she went," Shadow replied. "He said she rolled out after you came over her house."

Farah grinned at the news.

"I can't be sure, but something tells me she's one less person you have to worry about."

"The way shit been going on for me lately, I'll take that."

"Don't get too comfortable. Shit always gets worse before it gets better," Shadow responded.

"Tell me about it."

Chapter 19

Farah

"Thanks to them, I've been treated like a queen."

Farah walked into a dining room within the mansion with Mayoni, Carlton, and Bones. A large spread of food—which included fried chicken, mashed potatoes, and greens—sat in the middle of the table on expensive cream-colored chinaware. As they all took their seats, Bones sat next to her, and she noticed a place setting at the head of the table.

Who will be joining us?

"You seem nervous," Bones said softly. He was so close to her that their arms touched and she could feel his body heat. "If you are, there's no reason to be. You're among friends now."

She looked up at him and smiled. His strength and confidence turned her on, and for some reason, she felt safe around him. She couldn't recall having a feeling close to this since Slade. "I'm not nervous." She scrutinized her surroundings. "I don't like not knowing what's going on. Maybe it's the control freak in me." She paused. "So when is everybody gonna tell me why I'm here?"

Carlton laughed as he wrapped his arm around the back of Mayoni's chair and looked at Farah. "You mean, after all this time, you still have questions about why you're here? I'd think we'd be over that bridge by now."

"You know what I mean." She laughed, playing with the fork next to her empty plate. It was just as well. She wasn't hungry anyway.

"It's nothing too deep," Carlton said, checking the red G-Shock watch on his arm. "It's just that since you officially joined us, we've wanted you to meet somebody. He should be arriving any minute."

The moment he said that, a tall black man entered the room. The red Versace shirt he wore wasn't tight, but it did reveal his muscular arms. Two beautiful women flanked him, wearing black tight dresses and extra red lipstick. His eyes focused on Farah's the entire time he moved toward the table. He took a seat at the head, and the women pushed his seat closer to the table before taking their own seats.

There was something about him that put Farah immediately at ease, and she liked him before he even opened his mouth.

"I've been waiting to meet you, Farah Cotton. I trust that you've been treated well so far." Then he observed the way Bones seemed to possess her with his closeness. "I see you have a fan already."

She looked at Bones, who stared at her like she was a superstar. "Thanks to them, I've been treated like a queen. Thank you."

"That's great, and hopefully I'll continue to give you the royal treatment. Welcome to my home, Farah Cotton." One of the women stood up and poured a wine as red as blood into their glasses. When she was done he said, "Let's toast." They all grabbed their glasses and pushed them toward the air. "To pleasurable times and a long, prosperous relationship. For everyone."

She sipped the wine. It was thick and tasted like cherries. "This is good," she said, licking her lips. "Very . . ."

"Sweet?" He raised his eyebrows.

"Yes," she said softly, placing the glass down. "When you did the toast, you said to a *prosperous* relationship. Can you tell me why you said that?"

"First, let me tell you who we are. My name is Dr. Weil, and some years back, about ten to be exact, I was in charge of an organization that was put in place to assist the mentally challenged. I saw a lot of things, Farah, some things that would make your heart ache if you even heard about them." He shook his head. "Things like men being castrated simply because they complained about hearing voices in their heads."

"Castrated?" she repeated. "As in dicks cut off?"

"I wouldn't have put it quite like that, but yes." Everyone laughed. "Back then, they believed castration would prevent them from procreating and passing the same mental illness they possessed to their offspring. All of this was done illegally."

"Wow," she said, shaking her head.

"The women weren't spared either. Females were circumcised to prevent the male workers from being tempted. And if they were raped, they were eventually killed and disposed of. It was total chaos, Farah. And I couldn't stand to go to work most days."

Farah was so stiff listening to his story that she could barely move. "So what did you do?" She swallowed. "When you worked there?"

He sighed. "A lot of things. I would hold meetings, try to get the families involved to help the patients, but nothing seemed to work. After a while, I made a decision to do something different about it myself." He sipped his wine. "It was Christmas Eve, and I knew most employees would be gone to spend time with their families, so the first thing I did was release fifteen patients."

Farah thought about the first time she entered the mansion. Including Mayoni and Carlton, there were about fifteen people present. Her body trembled, and she felt herself about to break out in hives, until Bones placed his hand softly on her thigh. "Relax," he said softly. "It's okay."

"What were the patients in for?" she asked in a faint whisper, trying not to look at Mayoni, Carlton, and Bones, although they were all focused on her.

"The fifteen I freed were inside for what I considered treatable illnesses. Or sexual preferences." He chuckled. "Things like sadism and masochism: those who enjoyed inflicting pain on others for sexual gratification, and those who enjoyed receiving. The patients left in the facility, who were originally entered for minor illnesses, were so destroyed due to the medications and neglect by hospital employees that there was no saving them. I had to put them out of their misery, so I injected them all with a general anesthesia and placed the facility on fire. I knew with that move, there was no looking back."

Farah moved around in her seat. "What . . . I mean . . ."

Answering her unasked question, he said, "Everyone there died, and we escaped, free to start all over again."

She looked at everyone who was now smiling at her as if she'd just been let in on a precious secret. "Why do you tell me this now?"

"Because there's no turning around for you. You are a part of us, and we can't let you go. I'm sure you know that if we were to find out that you betrayed our trust, there would be no use for you. And if there is no use for you, we have to dispose of you. Do you understand what I'm saying?"

She trembled and said, "What do you want from me?"

"We want you to be a part of us, but it is important that you understand how we make our living. Since leaving the facility, we had to get creative in what we did to earn money. After some time, we found a career in homicide and space to be lucrative."

"I know what homicide is, but what is space?"

He chuckled. "Quite often people want things to disappear, but not necessarily gone forever. For instance, bank robbers hire us to hide their money until they are released from prison. Or we come upon someone who wants to disappear themselves to avoid prosecution of various crimes. The possibilities in the space business are endless. I own property in every state, as well as overseas."

"So what do you want from me? Since it's obvious it's not just about what I've seen over the last few days." She couldn't help but feel slightly lied to.

"We want your services." He smiled. "You've succeeded at getting away with quite a few crimes on your own, and to do that, you must be very smart and resourceful."

"I don't know what you're talking about."

"Sure you do," he said, removing his smile. "If there is one thing I hate, it's people playing dumb with me." For the first time since she met him, she felt fearful. "And if we're going to have a relationship, it's important that you realize that honesty is the key."

Farah looked at Mayoni, Carlton, and even Bones. She hadn't connected with anyone on this level before, besides her sister and brother, and even with them, she had to hide who she was. Destroying the new relationship would leave her alone with her boring life, and she didn't want to turn back now, especially since Slade made his position clear that they were officially over. She decided it was better to be real than to continuously lie. "Okay, now what?"

"For now we enjoy the food and drinks," he said, raising his glass again. "And when the time is right and we need your services, we'll let you know." One of the women stood up and started dishing out plates.

"I'll do it on one condition," she blurted out.

Bones moved a little in his seat. Farah was pushing her luck and she didn't even know it. Dr. Weil was fair, but even he had his limits. "Babes, hold off on how you coming at him," Bones said. "We can discuss business later."

"It's okay," Dr. Weil said, raising his hand. "Either she's too stupid to realize the person I am or she's very brave. Either way, I'm intrigued." He focused on Farah. "Go ahead. What do you want from me?"

She thought about all of the people causing her problems. She considered Eleanor, but decided against getting them involved with her, because she wanted to make sure she was murdered herself. Lesa was out of town, and for now appeared to be too scared to cause her problems. There were two people left. "There's a girl. Her name is Rhonda. I can't find her and she's causing me problems. The other person is Randy, and I don't know what he's capable of either, so I want them both taken care of."

"Give Bones the information and we'll see to it that your problem is solved. Anything else?"

Farah smiled. "One last question."

"Shoot," Dr. Weil responded.

"What was the name of the facility that you all escaped from?"

"Crescent Falls. Heard of it before?"

Chapter 20

Slade

"We ain't got shit but time."

Slade sat in Markee's living room with his brothers and Judge and Grant. After all this time, they still couldn't find Eleanor, and Knox hadn't made another appearance either. There was nothing more they wanted than to solve the mystery and go back home.

Della walked into the living room and sat in the recliner next to the sofa. "Your cousin Barry just called back from Mississippi. He checked all of the old places Knox frequented, and just like I thought, he hasn't made contact." She removed the gun from her waist and set it in her lap. Ever since she was shot at, she stayed strapped. "Any news on your end?" She looked at everyone.

Grant sighed. "We been looking but have had no luck finding Eleanor," he responded. "But it won't stop us from trying. We just have to remain here until something comes up." He looked at Slade. "Farah, on the other hand, has proven to be interesting. I've observed her keeping time with several different men who all end up dead."

Slade was uneasy. "Fuck do you mean?"

Grant laughed. "It's clear. We follow her. She meets someone, and that person later dies."

"People die all the time. Whether Farah meets them should not be a question. I thought you were looking for leads on Knox."

"This is a lead. If she's killing people who later show up in the news, she could have possibly killed Knox too. You may not want to admit this, but your girl is very capable of this kind of crime."

"First off, she's not my girl, and if you think she knows something more, question her yourself."

"We've been trying to, but she's never home," Grant continued. "And whoever she's rolling with now seems to be good at shaking us when we're trying to follow her. It's easier trying to get a hold of the president."

"Well, that's on you, not me," Slade responded, relieved she couldn't be caught.

"What about this Randy?" Della asked with narrow eyes. "He took a shot at me, and I still want him taken care of."

"He hiding low. Real low," Grant said. "From what I understand, he never came out since the hit the boys took on his shop. But the nigga who handed the one they call Lollipop over to us—"

"They call him The Vet," Killa interrupted.

"Whatever his name is, we've been following him, hoping he'd lead us to him. I have somebody on him right now. The moment he finds out where Randy is, he'll let us know and we'll go take care of him too."

"Good, because although it won't make me breathe easier or bring my boy back, it will make me feel better having some blood shed around here," Della responded, looking at her family. "I know you don't want to hear this, Slade, but I'm going to take a chance at talking to Farah myself. Are you cool with that?"

He wasn't, but he wouldn't let her know. "Do what you have to, Ma."

"I always do."

He paused. "So what's up with Audio? How is he holding out? Back home?"

"He's fine," Della responded. "Don't worry about it, son. He's just mad now, but you made the right call by sending him back down South. He would've gotten himself in trouble or killed, and I support your decision one hundred percent."

They were just about to discuss more details when Markee, whom they hadn't seen in months, walked through the door. Fifty pounds lighter, he looked like life was weighing him down.

"Where the fuck have you been?" Slade asked, stepping up to him. "You had niggas thinking you were dead."

He walked into the kitchen and grabbed a water bottle. "It's a long story."

"Does it have anything to do with Randy?" Slade continued.

"Like I said, it's a long story."

"We ain't got shit but time."

Chapter 21

Randy

"Stop telling people that before they take you away. Is that what you want?"

Randy cruised down the street on the way to the Serenity Meadows senior citizens home, checking his rearview mirror repeatedly. Although he didn't want to admit it, the Baker Boys had him on the run. He knew it was a bad move to shoot at them with their mother in the car, but hindsight was twenty-twenty. When he saw he wasn't being followed, he parked his Yukon in the back of the Serenity Meadows senior citizens home. It was one of his two secret hideouts.

He'd donated more drug money to the facility than any other sponsor, past or present, so much so that the management agreed he should have his own office. He used it to discuss business with people he didn't trust in his home.

Holding a brown paper bag filled with fresh bagels, he was greeted by Harriet Tillman, the program director for the center, the moment he walked inside. "Hello, Mr. George." She took the bag from his hands and saluted him with a wide smile. "Can I get you something to drink? We just made some fresh lemonade. It's in the refrigerator. It's a little too sweet for my taste, but you might like it."

Randy walked past her and toward his office. "I'm not hungry or thirsty." She could be a pest at times because she was always interested in what he was doing.

She followed Randy toward his office. "We have been having a lot of strange people around here lately."

Chill bumps covered his skin.

"I was going to tell you earlier, but you called and said you were on your way."

"Strange people?" Randy felt like his world tilted. Slowly he approached. "What did they say?"

She stepped back into the wall. "Nothing. Just asked a bunch of questions about you. I'm s . . . sorry I didn't tell you sooner."

"Fuck sorry!" he yelled in her face "What exactly did they say?"

"They asked if we knew you and stuff like that."

He shook his head in anger.

"Don't worry. We told them nothing! I promise." When he backed away she exhaled. "We would never do anything to compromise you here. You've done so much for us already."

They walked into his large office. "I bet." He smirked. "It wouldn't have anything to do with the cash I pour into this place, now would it?"

She frowned. "I didn't mean it that way." She paused. "Of course we appreciate all of the work you've done for us, but we would keep your privacy all the same."

He laughed. "I'm just fucking with you." He took his coat off and placed it on the rack. "What did these strange people look like?"

"African American. Young." She shrugged. "They didn't sound like they were from the area, but I can't be sure."

"Country accents?"

"I'm not sure."

He placed his hand over his face. Someone found him, and he wondered if it was the Baker Boys. "Obviously I won't be able to come around for a while. That is, until I find out what's going on." He sighed. "Is Mrs. Hammond still hallucinating and causing problems in the wings with the other guests?"

"Yeah . . . but I called the doctor like you said. She seems to be getting worse by the day. And since she's senile, it's kind of hard to know what's sparking it. It's like it's happening from nowhere."

"Are you monitoring who comes in and out of her room like I suggested?" He paused. "Because I was told she had some guests who looked suspect."

"We try to watch her guests, but we also like for our patients to have family members visit. And if I'm not mistaken, the only one who comes to visit Mrs. Hammond is her daughter, Mooney. Whenever she comes, she seems happy."

Randy frowned. "The woman is crazy, Mrs. Tillman. She doesn't know what it means to be happy anymore." He grabbed a small tube of antibacterial gel off of the desk, squirted in his hands, and wiped them together. "Where is she now?"

"In her room." She looked worried. "But if I were you, I wouldn't go in there. Earlier today she was cursing everyone out and didn't seem too nice."

"I don't care how feisty she is. I can handle myself. Before she started losing her mind, she told me I was the son she never had. Remember that?"

"Yes, I do. It's just that she was very mean and her daughter left a note with the staff that she didn't want anyone bothering her today. I want to respect her wishes."

"Respect mine first," he said. "And if her daughter wants to talk to me, be sure to tell her that she wanted me to be a part of her life. Make sure you make that clear. Okay?"

She shook her head. "Yes, it's clear."

He stood up and moved toward the door. "Let me see how she's doing."

Randy walked to the cafeteria to get Mrs. Hammond's favorite treat, tapioca pudding. Before walking into her room, he stood in the doorway and watched how she sat next to the window in her chair. The sunlight beamed against her chocolate skin, and to him she was stunning. Randy always had a fetish for older women, but he kept that and a few other sick secrets to himself. Although he found her attractive, Randy had other motives. He was dirt broke, and Mrs. Hammond had a home, which up until recently had gone unused. With the heat he had on his back, without her house he would probably be dead.

When he finally entered her room, he closed and locked the door behind him. Then he placed the pudding on the table next to where she was. Her long gray hair hung down her back, just the way he liked it. Her skin was wrinkly, brown, and covered in age spots. She looked vulnerable and very seductive to him.

"Mrs. Hammond . . . are you okay?" he asked, approaching her chair. He used a softer voice whenever he first entered her room to throw her off, because she was partially blind and could not see. "I came to see how you're doing and to make sure everyone has been treating you right."

"That man came in here and took all my money," she yelled, speaking in the direction of his voice. "And I think my maids are in on it too. I want them out of my house right now! Do you hear me? I want them gone!"

"I'll fire all of them. Don't worry about it," Randy said, rubbing her hair softly. "You can trust me."

She smiled. "You promise? Because they'll take everything I have if you let them." She grew silent. "Wait . . . where is my daughter? Where is Mooney? She . . . she told me not to talk to anyone. She told me to tell her if someone came in here. Who are you anyway?"

Her memory recall frightened him. "I'm a friend, Mrs. Hammond." He unzipped his pants and removed his penis from his boxers. He was rock hard as he stepped in front of her. "You don't have to worry about anything."

"But I don't want a friend. I want my daughter."

"Mrs. Hammond, enough with all that talk." He paused, looking down at her. "You gotta take your medicine now, so open up."

Before she could protest, he shoved his penis into her mouth and moved her head back and forth. Mrs. Hammond told the staff members that some strange man was putting stuff inside of her mouth and vagina, but no one believed her. Had they taken the time to seriously evaluate her concerns, they would've discovered that she had been raped on multiple occasions. Unfortunately for her, the only thing they cared about was his money.

Tears ran down Mrs. Hammond's face as he ejaculated inside her mouth. Randy was a sick man who was abused most of his life by those coming in and out of his life and as a result, he was unable to enjoy consenting sex. If he was going to get off, he had to take advantage of the vulnerable. Bondage, rape, brutality, and humiliation were all parts of how he went about having sex.

When he was done, he eased his clothes back on, grabbed the pudding off the table, and fed Mrs. Hammond spoonful after spoonful, to mask his disgusting deed. She sobbed softly until she tasted the sweetness of her favorite treat. After it was almost gone, a smile spread on her face. Luckily for her, bad thoughts came and went, never holding her hostage for too long.

Talking in his regular voice instead of the fake one he used when he first entered her room, he asked, "Is everything okay, Mrs. Hammond? You look sad." He wanted to see what she remembered.

She trusted this voice, unable to differentiate between the two. Whispering low, she said, "The man came in my room. The one I don't like. He came back and he hurt me again. You can't let him come back, okay?"

Randy continued to feed her as she opened her mouth wider. "What are you talking about?" He eased the spoon into her mouth. "You're always talking about a man. Stop telling people that before they take you away. Is that what you want?"

"But there was a man in here," she whispered. "It's the one who hurts me over and over again." Then she stopped eating the food and her mouth hung open. She'd forgotten her thought. "I want my daughter! Where is my daughter?"

"She's not here. Relax and eat this food."

"I don't want it! I want Mooney," she yelled. "You too stupid to know anything about my daughter! Tell my maid to bring me my jewelry! And get my daughter on the phone now!"

When he saw she was riding the wave of another mental rant, he smirked and dropped the spoon. This was why he loved taking advantage of her. She couldn't keep a thought long enough to tell anybody what was actually happening to her. But he put a little something different in her treat today. Something to put her out of her misery for good. Originally he planned to kill her slowly, to prevent from getting noticed, but someone knew about his location, and time was of the essence. He could no longer come back.

Within an hour, after he was long gone, she'd be dead and he would be the beneficiary of her estate. He realized Mooney would contest the will. When that happened, Randy would call upon Mrs. Tillman to prove his case and to say that she looked upon him as one of her children. And if that didn't do the trick, and if Mooney persisted, he would put her out of her misery too.

When his cell phone rang, he removed it from his pocket and saw Markee's name. He'd been looking for him for months. He just hoped, for his sake, that he was telling him something that he wanted to hear.

Chapter 22

Farah

"I felt complete, I felt right, and I never looked back."

"You're driving too fast, boy!" Farah screamed at the top of her lungs. "Slow down 'fore you get us killed!"

He didn't decrease his speed.

"Let me out!" She laughed. "Please!"

After Farah snatched the steering wheel to the right, Bones brought the two-seated go-kart to a slow roll and parked. Laughing at her nervousness, he removed his helmet and held out his hand to help her out.

She removed her helmet and accepted his hand. "I should kick your ass. I see already you like to play too much." She stood up and dusted the back of her blue jeans off.

"Promises, promises." He chuckled as they walked to the counter and returned their equipment before walking toward his white Lexus. He opened the door for her and she slid inside. "Hungry? After all that yelling you did, your throat should at least be dry."

She playfully hit him on the arm. "I'm a little hungry, but thanks to you, I am thirstier." She smiled. "I think you were just doing that shit to hear me scream."

"I can't lie. I do love a good scream."

As he slid into traffic, she couldn't wrap her mind around the fact that she was going on a date with someone other than Slade. Although she loved everything about Bones, including his long dreads, dark chocolate complexion, and the way he carried himself, there was still a lot of mystery surrounding him.

"Where are we going?" she asked.

"First we gonna hook up with Mayoni and Carlton, and then we gonna grab something to eat. After that, the night is on you. Why? You got somewhere else you'd rather be?"

She shrugged. "Not really." She looked at her hands. "I'm kind of feeling this time we have alone. We been hanging out, but I don't really know anything about you. Can you tell me about yourself? Whatever you want me to know."

"What you want to know, Farah Cotton?"

She swallowed. "Can you tell me about your life in Crescent Falls?"

He moved a little around in the driver's seat. "What you want to know about it? It was so long ago, and I don't want to give you the wrong impression about me."

"Why were you there? And were you . . ."

He chuckled. "I wasn't castrated. I'm definitely still intact." Farah appeared relieved. "I knew eventually you would ask me about that place, but I hoped I'd have more time to explain to you." He sighed. "I was one of the first fifteen that Dr. Weil was talking about."

"Why were you in there?"

"I grew up thinking there was something wrong with me because I loved inflicting pain on my girlfriends when I was in high school. It was always consensual, but one day, my girlfriend's mother walked in and caught us fucking in her room. I had one of her father's ties wrapped around her neck and was fucking her from behind. She was loving it." He grinned, recalling the event. "But her mother didn't. And instead of fessing up that we'd played that game at least fifteen times before, she claimed I raped her. I was arrested, and everything I owned, in my room, was searched. They were trying to figure out what caused me to act that way." He shook his head. "My parents were popular in the political community, and they didn't want the flack, so to their minds, it was easier to send me away and not deal with it at all. That was ten years ago"—he sighed—"when I was seventeen. I'm twenty-seven now, and I haven't seen my family since." He looked over at her. "So what's your story?"

"I suffer from something called porphyria. All my life. My family members suffer from it too, but they seemed to do okay on the medicine the doctor gave them. It never quite worked for me." She paused. "Well, one day I met with Grand Mike, and he gave me my first taste of blood, and everything about my life changed at that moment. I felt complete, I felt right, and I never looked back."

"You grow up in a violent home?"

"Yes." She thought about Brownie. "Very violent."

"So it's not about the pain with you. It's about the blood?"

"Yes." She looked over at him. "So what is it for you?"

"Administering pain. Always." His eyes stayed on the road. "Do you think you could ever be a Slave?"

She shrugged. "I never thought about it before. I guess I would be willing to try. For you."

They continued down the road until they met up with Mayoni and Carlton in the restaurant parking lot. Both of them wore huge grins on their faces as they approached Bones and Farah. "You haven't looked at the news today, have you, Farah?"

Farah shook her head no. Carlton whipped out his phone and showed her a news article about a twenty-something female who was found on the side of the road with her throat slit. That part of the story was ordinary. There was always some dead girl on the side of the road. What stood out was the victim's name: Rhonda Marshall.

Farah looked up at them and met their grins. "Are you serious?" They leaned against the car and chuckled. "Wow, you guys work fast, don't you?"

"You haven't seen—"

Before Carlton could finish his sentence, a bullet whizzed between Carlton and Farah, removing the tip of his nose. He dropped to the ground and released the .45 on his hip. The driver in a black car bombarded the area where they stood with bullets. Firing in the direction of the shooter, Carlton had one mission: to kill. Not alone in his quest, Bones and Mayoni matched his shots blow for blow to put down whoever wanted them dead.

Farah hid behind a car and did her best to avoid getting killed, but the loud noises of the gun popping off didn't put her at ease. When Bones stood up and moved toward the car, aiming in the driver's direction, it was only then that she lifted from her spot. Suddenly it was quiet and no one was shooting. The driver was dead, and the windows were splattered with blood.

"Fuck!" Carlton said, holding his nose as blood poured from his face. "Who the fuck was that?"

Farah was just as shocked as they were, until she saw someone opening the car door and taking off running. When the person turned around and she saw her face, she felt faint. It was the person she'd been looking for the past few months—Eleanor McClendon.

A rage like she hadn't felt in a while crept over her, partly because instead of going into hiding, Eleanor had come after her. And secondly because she knew she could never tell her new friends that someone she knew was involved, for fear that they would blame her and cut her off. It was settled. No matter what she had to do, she was going to kill Eleanor McClendon, even if it was with her bare hands.

Chapter 23

Elise

". . . if you dumb enough to think that we saying the same thing, you need the help, not Farah."

Although it was cool outside, Elise had all of the windows to her apartment wide open. She did it whenever company came over, knowing that not too many could deal with the natural scent of her body. In all honesty, she didn't want to be speaking to her present guest anyway, but wanted one last attempt to talk some sense into him.

They were sitting at an old wooden table in the kitchen. "Would you like some coffee?" Elise asked Dr. Martin. "I just made a fresh pot."

"It smells delicious." He rubbed his arms for warmth. "Yes, I'll take a cup. Although I like mine with cream and no sugar."

Elise stood up and opened the refrigerator. "Will milk do?"

He smiled. "Of course." He rubbed his arms again. "Is there any reason why you have all of the windows open?"

"Is there any reason you keep interrogating my family, after getting all of the information that you needed already from Farah?" She made the cups of coffee.

"I really wish you didn't look at it that way, although I understand why you would."

When both of them held cups of coffee in beautiful pink mugs, Elise got to the question at hand. "And the windows are open for your comfort, not mine."

"If it's because of your odor, it doesn't bother me. I've been knowing you for years and understand your concern."

Elise closed all of the windows and sat back at the table. "What can I do for you, Dr. Martin? You seemed very upset on the phone earlier today."

"I am upset." He took a sip. "I spoke to the officer again when she called me to follow up, and she admits to applying for a room in Farah's apartment. What she didn't admit to is harassing her. In fact, she claims Farah's friends pulled her over at a gas station and threatened her life." He wiped his finger along the rim of the cup. "I guess I can't understand why you and your family can't seem to see what's going on with Farah. It's so obvious that she's out of control and exhibiting signs of psychosis. I mean, are you okay with your granddaughter hurting other people?"

Elise sighed heavily. "Me and my family are my business, Dr. Martin. I can't understand what you want me to say differently about it. If Farah says she isn't hurting anyone, than she isn't. I mean, does the authorities have proof?"

"It's not what I want you to say, it's what I want you to do."

"Dr. Martin, like I told you at my granddaughter's house, there was a misunderstanding on what I shared with you, and now you're taking things out of context."

He shook his head in disgust.

"Even if I wanted to control her I couldn't. She's an adult."

He placed his cup down. "I believe you have more control over her than you realize."

"What exactly do you want, Dr. Martin? If there's one thing I hate, it's a man beating around the bush."

There was an eerie silence, a silence so long it felt like a third person was in the room. "I want you to have her committed. I have the information to a great facility that can assist her. There used to be another facility for people with her mental illness, called Crescent Falls, but it was dismantled many years ago." He paused. "Anyway, Farah's the first of her kind with this type of multiple diagnosis, and I think she could benefit if she was observed around the clock."

"And what diagnosis is that? Far as I knew, you only treated her for porphyria."

"You're right, and I can't be sure without seeing her that she has anything else, although I'm fairly positive. Elise, I believe she has porphyria and a touch of something called Renfield's Syndrome."

"What is that?"

"Renfield's Syndrome is when someone believes that in order to survive, they must drink blood. It's modern vampirism. I don't know what happened in your granddaughter's life, but she's pretty delusional at this point. Was she raised up in a violent home?"

Elise thought about Brownie and Ashur. If they weren't terrorizing people in the neighborhood, they were hurting people who they believed did them wrong. Of course they were violent. In fact, Ashur was in prison for killing a family of three, just because their son scratched his car. But in her opinion most black children grew up in less-than-savory environments and learned how to survive.

"My granddaughter wasn't raised up in a home any more violent than other people. She had her problems, but then again, don't we all? It doesn't mean she needs to be committed."

"Elise, to my understanding, her mother is dead."

Elise wanted to jump across the table and snatch his throat out but she refrained.

"And, if that's the case, you're pretty much all she has left. She needs you. You are a strong woman, and I'm asking you to help me heal your granddaughter."

"I'll talk to her father," Elise responded. "He's in prison right now, but I don't want to make a decision like this without him."

He seemed irritated and twisted in his seat. "He can't even make decisions for himself. How can he for her?" he asked in a serious tone. "She needs *your* help, Elise. The kind of help that an in-house facility could provide. And right now, I'm coming to you out of respect."

"You want me to agree to have my granddaughter put in a facility over something she said to me over the phone? Are you that delusional?"

"She told you she was drinking blood. I know you said she was drunk when she shared the information, but I don't believe it. A lot of people have gone missing in her building alone. This deserves some serious attention." He looked at her with pleading eyes.

"Even if she is"—she swallowed—"drinking blood, how do you know she's hurting people?

"Because nobody in their right mind would rightfully give up their blood. That's why."

"I'm not sure." She shrugged. "If she is drinking blood, she may have ran into someone who can provide. There are a lot of people out here who may have the same fetishes she does. Whatever the situation, it's her life and she has the right to live it." Elise pushed her coffee to the side. "Now, I know you're concerned, but it's time for you to let it go." She sat back in her seat. "At this point, there is nothing else I can do."

"You need to know that I will never forget what you told me that night on the phone. I haven't told the officer yet, because I wanted to come to you and your family first." He took another sip of coffee. "But what you said keeps me up late at night and ruined any chance of me having a normal life. I want peace, Elise, and I can't have it knowing what your granddaughter is out there doing."

"What does that mean?" She frowned, feeling violence wash over her.

"It means that I have a responsibility to let someone know. Now, I want to have her checked out by a licensed professional and, hopefully, committed willfully into a facility. If we don't do it that way, the only other way I can think of is by contacting the authorities. I hope you understand, but you really leave me no other choice."

Silence stood between them for an eternity. "Dr. Martin, I had Brownie when I was twelve years old. A teacher I cared about decided that he would teach me how to be a woman by taking my virginity. It was the worst experience of my life, prior to losing my daughter and grandchild."

"I'm sorry—"

She put her hand up to silence him. "I don't need sympathy." Her hand dropped. "Before Brownie died, I shielded her from everything because I wanted her to be safe and never violated like I was. I was strict with her in some ways, lenient in others. I allowed her to say and see more things than she should have as a teenager and because of it, she developed a fucked-up sense of entitlement. Make no mistake, I feel responsible every day that my leniency may have been the cause of her murder. But yesterday I made a decision that nothing matters. My daughter is gone and my other grandchildren are still here, and I'm going to protect them to the best of my ability, and I won't let you or anybody else get in the way of that. I hope I'm making myself clear."

"And I want you to protect them, starting by getting Farah the help she needs. Don't you see, Elise, we are saying the same things?"

"Dr. Martin, if you dumb enough to think that we saying the same thing, you need the help, not Farah." She grinned. "I need you to stay far away from my family, so far that I won't see or hear from you ever again."

"What about Mia and Shadow? They have porphyria, which I have successfully treated for years."

"Not a problem of yours anymore. This is my final warning, and another will not follow it. Do you understand what I'm saying?"

He backed up in his chair. "I have a feeling you are threatening me, and I don't take well to threats."

"And you should know that I'm making a promise. Stay away from Farah. Stay away from Mia. Stay away from Shadow, and stay away from me. I will do everything I can to see to it that Farah gets the help she needs, but it will be on my time."

Dr. Martin stood up, drank the rest of his coffee, and set the mug back on the table. "Thank you for the coffee, Elise. I really appreciate it. It was the best I had in a long time." He put his coat on. "You have a good day."

"You do the same."

She was certain that it wouldn't be the last time she'd hear from him. But she put her warning into full effect, and whether he lived or died was all on him.

Chapter 24

Farah

". . . I might be willing to help you out, provided it's worth it."

The night sky enveloped Farah's car as she sat inside of it, staring at the dope house she was about to enter. Something told her Eleanor wasn't in there, but it was worth a shot. After the attempt Eleanor took on her life, she realized she had to kick her search efforts up a notch to find Eleanor before Eleanor found her again.

On the news that morning, she learned that the driver Bones murdered was a dope boy out of Chicago. She wondered how he was connected to Eleanor. Before the gun battle, Farah wrote her off as an old lady on heroin who sold small bags of weed to feed her habit. She never once considered that she had the ability to rally the troops. She couldn't make the same mistake again.

As she sat in her car, her cell phone rang. She unconsciously answered while looking out of the window. "Hello."

"Farah, why haven't you been answering your phone?" Coconut screamed. "Me and Jake have been worried sick about you. That is so rude and so wrong!"

Farah removed the phone from her ear, looked at it, and frowned. The Jake situation was getting a little creepier than she thought, and the moment she started making money with the Fold, she couldn't wait to cut them off. As it stood now, the threesome they participated in allowed her to pay her bills and put food on the table. God only knew what Shadow and Mia did with the little money they made.

She put the phone back to her ear. "I'm fine, Coconut." She sighed. "Just had a lot on my mind, that's all."

"You fucked up about Rhonda too, huh?" she asked softly. "Why you going through this alone? Times like this, you're supposed to be with friends."

Farah shook her head. "I have no idea what you talking about," she lied.

"Wait, you didn't hear about Rhonda?" She paused to catch her breath. "She was murdered last week. I wanted to talk to you instead of leaving a message on your phone, but you never answered."

"I heard about the murder." Farah was as dry as cornflakes with no milk.

Silence. "You heard about the murder *and?*"

"And what?"

"Farah, you sound like you don't give a fuck."

Silence.

"Farah, you didn't have anything to do with what happened to her, did you? I mean, you did say she stepped to you at IHOP a while back. Was this out of revenge?"

"I can't believe you even coming at me like that. Just because I'm not crying my eyes out don't mean I don't give a fuck. Now, I'm sorry to hear about Rhonda, but I have a life over here too." She paused. "Anyway, how's Knight?"

"He didn't take Rhonda's death too well. He blamed himself for throwing her out on the streets after losing the baby. The last I heard he was walking around drunk and got locked up for firing into store windows for no reason."

Farah shook her head. "He loves blaming other people for the shit that goes on in his life." Farah observed two pregnant women walking into the dope house, she guessed to get a fix. "When is the funeral?"

"It was yesterday, Farah. And it was sad too. You should've been there."

"Me coming to the funeral won't bring Rhonda back."

Silence.

"That's the second funeral you didn't go to when a friend died. You didn't go to Natasha's and now Rhonda's. I lost both of my friends in two years and you all I have left, yet you act like you don't care about me or nobody else. What's wrong with you?"

Farah sighed. "You trying to say I don't care about you? I allowed you to use me more than anybody else in my life, even to the point where you got me fucking you and your boyfriend at the same time! Don't tell me I don't care about you, Coconut. I'm sorry you miss Rhonda more than me, but I have to go. I'll call you back later."

Coconut was the least of her troubles, and if she stayed on the phone with her long enough, she would've told her so. Besides, with Rhonda gone, she hoped the pictures would stop flowing. With Lesa out of town, the only person she had to worry about was Eleanor. She eased out of the car and dipped into the dope house.

The stench in the dope house was sickening, but Farah didn't care. From the entrance of the hellhole, she stood in the middle of the floor and observed the disgusting surroundings.

"Excuse me," she said to a man sitting on the floor with his head against the wall. "You know Eleanor? An older white lady with a fat ass?" She pointed at her own. "I think she used to be a stripper or some shit like that."

He looked up at her from the floor. His head rolled around loosely on his neck and slobber rolled out of the corner of his mouth. "You got some money? Some change? If you do, I'll tell you anything you wanna know about anybody."

"I got a little change, but you gotta tell me what I want to know first."

He frowned. "Who are you anyway?" He adjusted himself on the floor. "The police or something?"

"Naw, I'm just a friend. And ain't no need in you worrying about all that. You need to be worried about what the fuck I'm asking you right now. Now, do you know her or not? I don't have all night to be fucking around with you."

"I know of her." He nodded off again. "But she ain't here right now. She just left." He wiped the corner of his mouth. "Like five minutes ago, I think. If you a friend, shouldn't you know that already?"

"I'm here, ain't I?" Farah said angrily. "Now, where is she? It's important that I get to her right away."

"Like I said, that's going to cost you. But don't worry though. I'll take you to her for the right price." He scanned over Farah's body. "So what you working with?" He grabbed the edge of her jeans and she kicked him off. She could see his dick harden in his dingy slacks and wanted to throw up.

"What exactly are you asking for?" She placed her hands on her hips. "Because if it's pussy, you can forget about it. If it's money, I might be willing to help you out, provided it's worth it."

He laughed. "I figured you weren't about to give me none of that sweet thing. My luck ain't ever been that good." He licked his lips. "Naw, sweetness, just give me a few bucks and I'll take you to her. Deal?" He stood up and extended his hand.

She looked at it but had no intention of shaking it. Her instincts told her to leave, but she ignored them. "Deal."

Eager to put Eleanor out of her misery, Farah reached into her Louis Vuitton purse to grab her wallet. The moment she did, she was struck in the back of the head with a bottle. She plummeted to the dirty floor, and her lips pressed against a used condom. She tried to get her bearings together when, suddenly, her purse was ripped from her grasp. She turned over and kicked and hit him, but it didn't seem to be helping. Seconds later, other people got in on the party. There seemed to be at least twenty people striking her from all areas of her body. In the end, she knew she was being robbed, and there was nothing she could do about it.

"Get the fuck off of me!" she yelled, trying to land blows hard enough to stop them. "Leave me alone." No one listened as they worked overtime to take everything she owned.

"We gonna leave you alone, bitch! After we take everything you got," said someone from behind her.

When they were finished, she was stripped of everything of value. Her purse was gone. Her shoes were gone. Her coat was gone, and even the jewelry around her neck and fingers. She lay on the dirty floor, crying her eyes out. It became apparent that her life was so far out of hand that it wasn't funny anymore.

After everyone was gone and she was surrounded by silence, she got up and limped out of the house.

She could barely see out of one of her eyes, and blood streamed out of her nose. The cool air attacked her arms as she hobbled down the street, looking for some help. Most people saw the condition she was in, but they stayed as far away from her as possible.

She felt lost, until suddenly someone beeped at her. "Damn, baby. You out here looking hard as shit." The voice came from a blue Mustang. "You want a ride?"

Farah looked him over. He was a light-skinned nigga with a low haircut and hazel-brown eyes. Since he didn't have a country accent and looked harmless enough, she decided to take him up on his offer. Besides, she wasn't even close to her house, and since they stole her purse, she couldn't even afford to catch a cab. "Yes, if you can take me home, I would appreciate it."

"Well, come on in." He opened the passenger door and she slid inside. "I'll take you wherever you want to go. The last thing I want is for a pretty thing like you to get sick on me."

Farah hopped into the warm car and was immediately at ease due to the heat. Although it was no longer winter, the air was still chilly.

"What happened to you, baby?" He observed her battered and bruised frame. "And why you got all those scars on your face? I know you not letting no nigga bang you out. You too pretty for all that shit."

She sat back into the seat and closed her eyes. She was trying to prevent more tears from streaming out. "It's a long story, but I'd appreciate if you would just let me ride in silence. I know it's your car and everything, but I'm not much on company right now."

He looked at her and frowned. "And who the fuck are you, some sort of queen?"

Her eyes popped open.

His total disposition changed. "Bitch, this is my ride, not yours. I call the shots in this mothafucka."

"I'm sorry. I didn't mean to come off like that." The last thing she needed was to get tossed out on her ass. She had to come correct . . . quick. "I just had a bad night."

He pulled over and parked. "I was just looking out for you, but since you got an attitude, get the fuck out."

She wasn't anywhere near home, so it was time to beg. "I'm sorry. I didn't mean it like that. I just had a long day."

"Farah, that's what you don't understand. I don't give a fuck about you or your day. As a matter of fact, when I saw the great job my peoples did to that pretty little face of yours, I couldn't have been more pleased." He grabbed her by the chin and moved her head to left and right. "Them mothafuckas were brilliant. It's amazing what people will do for a little rock."

The hairs on the back of her neck rose, and she slapped his hand off of her face. "How did you know my name?" She backed up to the window. "I didn't tell you shit about me."

He laughed. "You ain't got to tell me shit about you, bitch."

"Who are you with? Eleanor? Rhonda?" She paused. "Randy?"

He pulled a 9 mm from under the seat and aimed it in her direction. "I won't tell you again to get the fuck out of my ride."

She was so frustrated by people following her and not knowing what was going on that she'd given up. "If you gonna kill me, just do it already," she cried. "I don't give a fuck anymore!"

Calling her bluff, he fired out of his open window. "Do you really mean that?"

Realizing she was almost hit, she quickly undid her seatbelt and pushed the door open. Before the dude sped off, he threw a white envelope at her. "Enjoy the gift, bitch."

He sped off, and she grabbed the package on the ground. When she opened it, her legs gave out and she fell to the cold ground. Inside was a picture of her holding the property manager's son's hand as she led him to her car minutes before she killed him. There was also a picture of Gary, the man she met one day when she was walking with Lesa, her ex-roommate, to the store. It was the same day she killed him and sucked his blood.

The mystery of who was taking pictures was heightened. It wasn't just about Knox now. Whoever it was wanted revenge.

"Who are you?" she screamed out loud. "And what do you want from me?"

Chapter 25

Killa

"I'm telling you, it don't look too good for your boy."

Killa had just finished bagging up the dope with Major for their next sale. Slade wasn't home because he was still searching for Eleanor with Judge, Grant, and his mother. This worked out for Killa because it left him some time to speak to Markee in private.

"We done here," Killa said to Major. "You mind if I rap to Markee in private?"

"No doubt," Major said, leaving the apartment to go to his own.

"You wanna grab a beer with me right quick? I wanted to rap to you about a few things. Plus we haven't seen you in months, and you look bad, man."

"What is it? All the weight I lost done gave you some competition?" he joked.

"Not even close," Killa said, nudging him on the arm. "Come on, man. Have a beer with me."

Killa made him nervous, but he knew his offer was a demand and not a request. "I guess I can have a drink with you. I don't want beer though. I'll take a soda."

Killa walked into the kitchen and returned with two beers. He tossed one at Markee. "Fuck a soda, you gonna drink a beer. This shit is serious."

Despite his request, Markee accepted it, popped the top, and gulped half down. "Thanks, man. I guess I needed that anyway." He wiped his mouth with the back of his hand. "So what's up?"

Killa wasn't about to tell him that, prior to his mini vacation, he'd followed him. He wasn't going to tell him that he saw him go into their sworn enemy's house. Instead he decided to give him the benefit of the doubt. "What made you disappear for so long without telling family? Don't you know how mad mothafuckas were?"

"I had some shit I had to sort out." He sighed, placing the beer down. "And I finally figured out what I have to do."

Killa nodded. "Well, how you been holding up since you stopped working for Randy?"

He shrugged. "I'm not understanding the question."

"You used to get a lot of money with him. So much you were able to move out of Mississippi without looking back. I'm just checking to make sure you handling it okay without him."

"I guess I'm fine." He rubbed his knees. "Especially since you and Slade put me on. It ain't like I'm broke. It's just different money."

Killa sipped his beer. He wasn't getting the response he wanted, and he was growing agitated. "Do you have anything you want to get off of your chest, man? Anything at all?"

Markee's phone went off in his pocket, indicating he had a message. He read it and immediately seemed edgy. "No . . . I'm fine. If I wanted to rap to you about something, I know I could." He set the beer on the table. "Do you know where Slade is?"

"He's out. Why?"

"No reason." He sighed. "Look, I gotta go. Something came up that I have to see to." He stood up and moved toward the door. "I'm going to get up with you later, okay?"

Before he left, Killa said, "Markee, I know we haven't been the closest, and I want to be the first to apologize for all of the shit I did to you on my end. Almost losing Audio and trying to find Knox reminded me about how important family is, and I wanted to tell you that if you got problems I can help. If you in too deep, there ain't nothing I can't or won't do to pull you out. You understand what I'm saying? But you gotta tell me now."

Markee wanted to tell him so bad about the position Randy was putting him in, but he wanted to handle things on his own. "I know you got me, man. Just look out for your brothers, because you never know when you might not see them again." He dapped him up. "I love you, man." He left the apartment.

Slade was sitting on the couch, thinking about Farah, with a beer in his hand. Although he was still working for Willie, money didn't seem important. The only thing on his mind these days was Knox and Farah, in that order. He heard from his family that Farah had been in and out of the building with some niggas. For her sake and theirs, he prayed he never saw it with his own eyes.

Killa handed Slade a fresh beer and said, "How come we got places of our own, but we can't leave this nigga's apartment?" Killa laughed, looking around.

"I don't know." He chuckled. "I guess his spot feels more like home." They clinked the cans together. "It was the first place we landed after leaving Mississippi."

"We been holding the nigga Markee's apartment hostage forever. I think it's about time to let him have it back. Don't you?"

"I hope you talking about yourself, too," Slade said, focusing back on the TV. "Anyway, no matter where I go, there always seems to be one too many niggas around. I just want peace and quiet."

"You know anyplace you go, Ma gonna be too. She not keen on letting us out of her sight these days."

Slade sighed. "Tell me about it. Where she at now?"

"With Willie. They taking a liking to each other. What you think about that?"

Slade had a lot of theories about the matter. If he had to grab one off the top of his head, it would be that Willie was trying to do anything in his power to get the Baker Boys to stay, and that included shacking up with his mother. "Not sure what I think about it right now." He shrugged. "For his sake, I just hope he treats her right."

"I'm with you on that," Killa replied.

Slade sipped his beer and looked up at the ceiling. "Anyway, I think I will start spending most of my time at my crib." He looked over Markee's apartment. "And I know this nigga wants us out of here as soon as possible. He needs his space."

Killa sipped his beer and looked at the TV screen. "I think Markee can't be trusted, man. I don't know why, but my heart tells me he's bad news. What we gonna do about it if we have to step to him?"

Slade cut the TV off and observed his brother to be sure he was hearing him correctly. "What you mean, what we gonna do if we gotta step to him? He's still family, Killa. The nigga done so much dumb shit in the past that if we were gonna hurt him, it would've been done already. Sometimes I think we read too much into dude, and it's time to back off a little."

"He can't be trusted," Killa reiterated. "Before he disappeared for months, I followed him over Randy's. This was *after* we had beef. Why go over there and not tell us? It was the day Audio went missing. I'm telling you, it don't look too good for your boy. You know how he is."

"I don't know what's up with Markee, but I do know he would never do anything to go against the family. I put that on my life."

"I hope you don't have to."

"He's blood, Killa. Remember it."

Killa shook his head. He hated how his instincts were never respected. He was always written off when actually, he was very keen. Just like Knox. "I feel you on that, but why go over Randy's house and not tell us? And what was up with the disappearance?"

Slade drank the rest of his beer. "Answer me this: Did you ask him? You questioning me like I got a direct tap into his thinking process. Going to him directly could have given you every answer you needed. Right?"

"I guess." He shrugged. "To tell you the truth, I didn't ask him because he always got a lie for everything. I figured it would be a waste of my time."

"Well, maybe you should step to him like a man before you start pointing fingers at him like he's a child."

Chapter 26

Farah

"First you have to prove it."

After being robbed and given pictures by some unknown person, Farah lay in her room, crying her eyes out. She hadn't even seen the members of the Fold, because she couldn't concentrate on anything but the fact that someone knew more about her than she did them. Missing the unconditional love of her grandmother, she decided to call her for support, because as much as she hated to admit it, she needed her love.

The phone rang once before Elise answered in a sleepy voice.

"Grandma, it's me. Farah." She paused. "You have time to talk?"

Elise yawned. "Of course I do, baby. And there ain't no need in you saying who you are. I know my children's voices when I hear them." She giggled. "I'm glad you called, because I was going to call you myself."

"Really? What about?" She rolled over on her back.

"Tell me what's going on with you first. How do you feel? You sound sad."

"I'm awful, Grandma. I don't feel like myself." She looked at the dark skies through her window. It was her favorite time of day. "I can't really explain it."

"You're probably exhausted. You have to get the right amount of rest, Farah. Lately you've been running around nonstop."

"How do you know that, Grandma?" she asked, irritated. "This is the first time I've talked to you in a while."

"Just because you don't call me doesn't mean I don't know what's going on with you, Farah. And I know you're out a lot because every time I call, Mia or Shadow answers and tell me you're not home. A mind can't rest if a body doesn't."

"I'm trying, Grandma. I have so many things going on. You just don't understand."

Silence.

"Grandma, are you there?"

"Yes, baby, I'm still here," Elise responded. "I'm sorry if I was quiet. It's just that I want to say something to you, but I don't know how. I'm old, and sometimes my words come across the wrong way. You know what I mean?"

"Maybe you should just say it."

Elise sighed. "I know, but I wish I could take some of the pressure off of you. I always told your mother before she died to watch you. If only she would've listened."

"I don't want to talk about Brownie. She was your daughter, but she wasn't my mother."

Elise fought hard to bite her tongue. "Farah, I want to talk to you about that night. The one when you called me and told me what you did to make yourself feel better. Do you remember that night?"

Farah immediately had an attitude. "Of course I remember. You told Dr. Martin about it too."

"Farah, were you really drinking—"

"Grandma, please don't say that over the phone. Why can't you just leave that day alone? It's old news now."

"I'm not trying to upset you. You know that. It's just that Dr. Martin came over here again the other day. He said something I didn't like, and I want to see where your head is at. Are you drinking blood?"

"You just had to say it over the phone, didn't you? Why can't you ever respect my wishes? What is it about me that you don't like? It's like you never loved me!"

"You know that's not true!"

"Then what is it?" She sobbed. "I told you what I said because I thought I could trust you. I believed you when you said you were in my corner."

"Farah, I'm concerned now more than ever, because when I asked you later, you told me you were drunk and didn't mean any of it. And I don't know if you realize it or not, but he's not letting up on his quest to catch you in the act. If you are doing anything to hurt other people, I advise you stop now, while you still can."

"What are you saying?" Farah frowned. "Is he trying to get me locked up or something? Because if that's the case, I already know."

"Farah, I'm begging you to stop doing whatever you're doing. That's all I'm going to say. You can choose to listen to me or not, but keep in mind that I warned your mother, too, and she didn't take heed. Now I can only pray that God protects her soul."

"You know what? You always talk about family this and family that! Why did you tell Dr. Martin in the first place? Whatever happens because of it is all your fault!"

Silence.

Now Elise believed maybe Dr. Martin wasn't so far off. "Farah, you need long-term help. I think you should come over here so we can discuss more options."

"Long-term help?" She sat up straight in the bed. "Just what the fuck is that supposed to mean?"

"Farah—"

"I knew I should've never trusted you! I hate you, you old, stinky bitch!" She threw the phone against the wall and stomped around her room. Her face started itching, followed by her arms. Needing some fresh air, she threw on her sweatpants and a white T-shirt. Before going out, she grabbed her spare keys.

The moment she opened the door, Nadia Gibson and another officer greeted her. "Farah Cotton, just the person I wanted to see. I hope you're not about to go anywhere special, because if you are, it's gonna have to wait."

Farah swallowed. "What do you want with me, Nadia? I got shit to do." She moved to walk around them, but they blocked her path.

"I won't be ignored, Farah," Nadia said. "And I know you know I'm not here for my health."

"Well, what the fuck do you want with me then?"

"We need to talk to you at the station." The grin on Nadia's face was beyond irritating. Every tooth in her mouth was present as she anticipated taking her archenemy down. She observed Farah's outfit. "Judging by your current choice of clothing, you weren't going anywhere special anyway."

"Am I under arrest?" Farah questioned.

She grinned. "That remains to be seen. But what do you have to worry about? You're innocent, right?"

***

Farah sat in the police station, shivering. She wasn't sure, but she had a feeling Nadia kept turning the air conditioner down so that it would be cooler in the room. Although she was uncomfortable, she was trying her best to save face. She knew this moment would either make or break her, so she had to play it smart.

"So, Farah, as you may know, sixteen people went missing after visiting or while living in Platinum Lofts."

"Why would I know that?"

Nadia grinned. "You're good." She pointed at her. "Really good."

Farah knew immediately she was an amateur. After all, she hadn't done anything yet. "And you're telling me this because?"

"I'm telling you this because several witnesses say that either you or somebody in your apartment was last seen with the missing victims. Considering the amount of people who have come to us, some of whom are very close to you, we find it hard to believe that you don't know anything."

"Some of them like who?" she asked as if she had no idea. "There is no use in beating around the bush, Nadia. I'm here now, so you might as well shoot it to me straight."

"Well, for starters, Amico Glasser, whose family hasn't seen him since he left the movie theater, is missing." She scanned through the documents in her folder as if she didn't know the information already. "The last his mother was told, he was with Lesa. Of course, we verified it with her and know she never met him before."

"Is that all?" She sighed.

"Not even close." She laughed. "Then we have Kirk Griffin, who police officers arrested after an attempted rape on you in your apartment. It was during some party or something."

"He did try to rape me," she shouted. "In the closet in my bedroom. If my sister Mia hadn't come in, he would've gotten away with it."

"So you say." She paused. "Anyway, then there's Vivian Baker's son. His name is Antonio. He also went missing. Last but not least, a really close friend of yours, Rhonda Marshall, was found with her throat slit." She placed the folder down. "I don't know, Farah, but if you ask me, it seems like you are either bad luck or responsible. Which one is it?"

Farah tried to remain calm. She considered the fact that if they had anything concrete, she'd be in jail already. So, she took two deep breaths, folded her hands on the table in front of her, and said, "I don't know anything about any of the people you just listed, and it's not my responsibility. I am my own person, Nadia. I'm not a killer, and I'm not a suspect. Now, you have bothered my grandmother, my ex-roommates, and even my doctor with all of this shit, and I want it to stop. If it doesn't, you will pay for it. Trust me."

Nadia grinned, although she was horrified. "What you gonna do, get rid of me too? Or have your friends threaten me again at a gas station?"

"You know, the funny thing about my friends, if you were in the right that night, why did you pull off?" Farah asked. "You seem very guilty."

"I'm going to bring you down," Nadia promised.

"I'm warning you, Nadia. Leave me alone."

"Unfortunately, I'm not going to be able to do that." She paused. "Furthermore, if you don't have any information about these or the other cases, why was this handed off to us as evidence that you do?" She slapped a piece of paper on the table.

Farah's skin crawled. Farah observed the pink stationery with green flowers embedded on the sheet. It belonged to Lesa. "This stationery belongs to my ex-roommate, who would have plenty of reasons to lie on me."

"I know how you feel about your roommate. Remember? I was there. In fact, after you showed up at her house, she moved out of the state."

Farah tried not to smile. "What can I say? For some reason, people get angry with me when I kick them out of my life. You know about that feeling all too well, Officer. Don't you?" She slid the sheet back over to Nadia.

She placed the paper back in her folder. "You think this a game, don't you?"

"No, but I think you're ridiculous, and I'm not going to allow you to take up much more of my time." She stood up. "Now, is there anything else? Because if not, I'm going home."

"You think you're so smart, don't you? You think you've got everybody fooled. Well, you don't. I know what kind of person you are, Farah Cotton, and when it comes out that all of this is your fault, there won't be anything anybody can do to save your ass from going to jail. I don't care what I have to do. You will go down as being responsible for this crime."

Farah had a moment of clarity. There was no way Nadia would ever leave her alone. "I don't know about saving my ass from jail, but I would like to save my ass from this tired-ass interrogation for the time being."

"Always the jokester. You're going to go down for these crimes, Farah Cotton. Believe that."

"You have one problem, Officer."

"And what's that?"

Farah leaned in so that only she could hear her voice. "First you have to prove it."

Chapter 27

Slade

"What you just say to me, nigga?"

Slade was on the way out of his apartment to go to the bar with his brothers and cousins. At first he didn't want to be bothered, because the guilt of not finding Knox always stayed in his mind. But he figured he needed a break, and it might as well be with family.

They were all headed for the door when Slade tapped his pockets. "I forgot my wallet." He looked at them by the door. "I'll meet y'all outside."

"Hurry up too," Killa joked. "You take longer than a bitch to get ready."

"Fuck you, nigga." He laughed.

When they left, he dipped back into his room to grab his wallet. When he opened the door, he saw Farah talking to some dude in long dreads. She was crying and looked frazzled. The last time he saw her like that, she had gotten into a fight at a baby shower. His temperature was so high that if it was taken, it would be over one hundred degrees.

"You sure you okay, Farah?" Bones asked, pulling her toward his body as they walked down the hall. "Is there anything I can do for you?"

"No . . . I just wanna go home." She sobbed lightly, holding on to him.

"Farah!" Slade roared, stopping their movements.

She turned around slowly, knowing immediately whom the voice belonged to. "What do you want?"

He took two steps closer. "Are you okay?" He observed the nigga in all black with the red watch.

"Even if she wasn't, I got her," Bones said, standing in front of her. "You go 'head about your business."

Slade ran up to him quicker than a star athlete on his way to a touchdown. He was so close to his face that if Bones would've moved forward, he could've kissed him. "What you just say to me, nigga?"

Bones stepped back, but Slade saw something different in his eyes. The move he made wasn't out of fear. It was something darker. Slade knew a killer when he saw one, and he would bet money that Bones felt the same way.

"Bones, just go in my house," Farah said softly, handing him her house keys. When he seemed to be more interested in Slade than her, she raised her voice a little louder. "Bones, please."

"You sure you okay?"

"Nigga, you heard her?" Slade added. "Kick rocks."

Bones smirked at Slade as he walked backward all the way to Farah's apartment. Slade didn't take his eyes off of him until he disappeared inside. He would have problems with him in the future. He was sure of it.

"What do you want, Slade?" Farah asked, crossing her arms over her chest. She'd just left the precinct and was worried about her freedom. The last thing she needed was to be fussing with a nigga who dumped her. "I'm busy right now."

He gritted his teeth and focused on her eyes. He loved her more than he was willing to let on, but he had no right to come at her sideways when she didn't belong to him anymore. If only he could get his heart to listen.

"Slade, what do you want with me? I got company."

Still thinking about the chemistry he saw between her and Bones, he said, "I don't have shit else to say to you. Go fuck that nigga you was just with. I'm glad I dumped your ass."

Chapter 28

Randy

"I'm ready for whatever."

Markee sat on a chair across from Randy and his men, with a hand towel draped over his shoulder. He was sweating so much it looked like he showered with his clothes on. He hated having to meet with him for anything, especially matters pertaining to his cousins.

"I see you lost a lot of weight," Randy said, looking him over. "Where were you? At some fat camp?" Randy asked in an accusatory voice.

"I just needed to get away. A lot of shit been on my mind."

"Is there any particular reason you haven't arranged a meeting with Slade like I asked? Despite the fact that this nigga robbed my stash houses and killed another one of my men? Where . . . is . . . Slade?"

"He's been trying to find my cousin Knox and—"

"That nigga is dead!" Randy yelled. Markee shifted in his seat, and The Vet moved closer to him, in case Randy gave the word to put him out of his misery. "Even if he was alive, it don't stop the fact that my business has been stopped behind this shit. Are you refusing to set the meeting up?"

He swallowed and rubbed his face with his hand towel. "I can't do it, man." Markee sobbed. "I can't do what you're asking. Slade is my cousin, and he was the only nigga who looked after me when I was a kid. I can't betray him or my family like that. I hope you can respect that."

"I can't respect shit about you. You're a weak-ass nigga, Markee. Always have been and always will be. Have you forgotten how you landed here from Mississippi with nothing but a pair of overalls and thick-ass accent? It was me who put you on, not your cousins. And this is how you repay me? By being disloyal? Why would I respect a nigga like that?"

"I appreciate everything you did for me, man. I really do. Maybe I can set up a meeting with both of you in an open place or something like that. I haven't spoken to Slade about it yet, so I don't know if he'll be with it, but I can't blindside him." He wiped his face again. "If something happened to him it would devastate my Aunt Della and the rest of the family. We lost too many already."

There was a place in the pit of Randy's stomach that brewed with jealousy. He didn't have an honest member in his family or his life. His father had chosen sides with the Baker family, and he was officially alone. What was it about the Baker men that people couldn't betray? He was such an evil-minded person that he didn't understand their undying loyalty.

"Let me work off whatever you think they stole from you, man," Markee suggested. "I'll do whatever you want. Just don't kill me."

Randy strutted up to him and rubbed his head. "Look at you all nervous and shit. You need to relax, man. I'm not going to hurt you." He grinned. "Breathe, my nigga."

Markee took his advice and breathed a sigh of relief. "Oh my God! You don't know how bad you had my heart kicking." He laughed. "I'm gonna make this up to you. I promise! I'll see to it whatever you lost will be paid back in full."

"It's not a problem. Rest easy, man. You're safe with me."

Randy sat on the sofa in Mrs. Hammond's house, drinking a glass of Rémy, while looking at a black TV screen. When she died, he wasted no time setting up inside her home officially. He drank so much lately that his thoughts were all over the place. Something told him that he would not live too much longer if he didn't get a hold of his affairs, but he didn't even know where to start. Getting a hold of one of the Baker Boys seemed next to impossible.

"I took care of it," The Vet said. "We dumped his body in front of Platinum Lofts like you asked. You need anything else?"

"Wasn't nobody out there?" he asked, sipping his tipsy juice again. "I mean, you weren't followed, were you?"

"Nobody followed me after I dumped him. Me and Musty wore pizza uniforms." He walked closer to him and looked at the condition his leader was in. "But you know we just turned up the dial on this war, right? Them niggas are gonna flip when they see the condition we left him in."

"You plucked out his eyes and heart?"

"Yes." The Vet nodded.

"Well, you did what I wanted, and I don't give a fuck what they think," Randy replied. "They took out two of my men!" he yelled, raising two fingers. "Lollipop and Tornado." He shook his head. "Not only that, I'm sick of these mothafuckas thinking we had something to do with this Knox nigga going missing. Now they got something to be mad about."

When there was a knock at the door, Randy sat up straight. "Is Musty still with you?"

"No. I dropped him off at his crib before I came." He put his hand on the weapon under his jacket.

"Well, go see who that is." Randy nodded toward the door.

The Vet moved toward the door slowly. When he was close enough, he looked through the peephole. "It's your father." He removed the gun from the holster. "I don't trust this shit, Randy. I don't think we should let him in."

"How the fuck did he find out where I lived?" Randy stood up. "You sure you weren't followed?"

"On my daughter's heart I made sure nobody was following me. What you want me to do? I ain't got no problem laying him down, if that's what you want. It's your call." The Vet was eager to get revenge for Willie fucking his wife and impregnating her.

Randy saw it a different way. He and his father had beef, but he wasn't sure about killing him. Not yet anyway. What he really wanted was to repair the bond. He wished he could talk to him to find out where his mind was. After all this time, Randy still feared his father's presence, but he wasn't some little boy looking for love anymore. He was a man who lost everything at his father's hands.

Randy brushed his shoulders off. "Naw, don't send him away. Open the door. I want to see what the fuck this nigga got to say for himself."

The Vet opened the door, and Willie strolled in with a brown suit with fine blue pinstripes. He glided up to Randy and extended his hand. Randy hesitantly accepted, and when their hands embraced, Willie wouldn't let it go. "Did you have something to do with the Baker boy being thrown in front of the apartment building tonight for his entire family to see?"

Randy snatched his hand away from his father and wiped it on his jeans. "You come over my house to insult me?"

"Your house?" He laughed, looking around. "You mean the one you stole from that old bitch in that home? I don't know if you realize it or not, but the FBI is seconds away from bringing you down. You done dropped drugs and got into fraud?"

"I don't know what you're talking about," Randy lied.

"Sure you do, son."

"Why do you hate me so much?"

"It's not like you haven't given me plenty reason," Willie said calmly. When he felt the extra heat in the room, he looked over to The Vet. "Leave me alone with my boy. We have to talk in private." The Vet didn't move, and he focused back on Randy. "After all this time, you still working with a nigga who used to be my friend and betrayed me?" Willie asked Randy. "This is one of the reasons we will never have the relationship you want. You're not loyal."

"You're the one who slept with my wife," The Vet reminded him. "And you're talking to us about loyalty?"

"Always a smug mothafucka!" Willie shook his head.

"You can leave," Randy told The Vet, who walked out slowly.

"Did you have something to do with that Baker boy being murdered tonight?" Willie asked again.

"Maybe I did, maybe I didn't." He stuffed his hands into his pockets so he wouldn't see them shaking. "If I did, what makes you think I would tell you?"

Willie shook his head. "What about Knox Baker? I guess you had something to do with him going missing too, huh?"

"Pops, I haven't seen you in months, and when I do, you ask me about two niggas I couldn't give a fuck about. This is not how Ma would've wanted us to carry shit. But you don't care, do you?"

"Is this beef you have with the Baker Boys over Farah? Or Knox? If it is, you need to get over it. Nothing is worth what's getting ready to happen if you keep this up. Especially not some bloodsucking bitch."

"Even if our beef had anything to do with Farah, which it doesn't, I don't know shit about no Knox." Randy sat down. "She's Slade's problem now."

"From what I understand, they aren't together anymore, and it's because of Knox." Willie paused. "Anyway, it doesn't matter. What does is that you stay as far away from them as possible." He looked around the house. "I'm not sure how you looking on money, but I'll give you whatever I can to keep you away."

Randy raised his eyebrows. "Why would you do that? You haven't done anything for me in years."

"Is it too late to start?" Willie grinned. "Just stay away, Randy."

Randy looked into his hands. "I don't know nothing about no Knox, but I do know I had a lot of product stolen from me, and to this day I haven't received a decent explanation about what happened."

The grin Willie wore on his face up to that moment was gone. "You really are fucked up in the head, aren't you?"

"What are you talking about?"

"Ain't nobody took shit from you! I just took back what was mine."

Now he wished he didn't send The Vet away, because he may have given the order to have him taken out. "At least you finally admitted the truth. So I guess Slade helped you, too."

"I told you what I want from you: for you to stay away," Willie said, ignoring his question. "I'll give you enough money to see that you're okay." Willie would never tell him that he wanted Randy to remain in hiding so that the Baker Boys would not have a reason to return home. He just hoped he was greedy and smart enough to accept his offer. "If you don't accept my offering and decide to jump into the bed with the Baker Boys, then that's on you. Just know that I've seen your crew lately, and if you ask me, it's looking a little light. Be careful about starting a war you aren't prepared for, son."

"I'm ready for whatever."

"You know what? For the first time ever you sounded like my son. Too bad it's too late."

"It's never too late," Randy said arrogantly.

"You give yourself too much credit. If it wasn't for the fact that you're holding my last name, you'd be dead already. Stay away from me and my business, or I won't continue to extend you my good graces."

Chapter 29

Farah

". . . this may be deeper than where I'm trying to go right now."

Lately Farah had been spending an extended amount of time with the Fold. If they weren't drinking and mixing pain with sex, they were getting high and indulging excessively in alcohol. She was dressed and ready to meet Mayoni and Carlton for brunch when she opened her door and was met by Della, Judge, and Grant instead. They were dressed in all black like they were going to a funeral.

"Who died?" she joked.

"Markee," Della said flatly. "My nephew and Slade's cousin."

Farah stumbled backward. She wasn't close to him, but she could only imagine what Slade was going through. "I'm so sorry, Ms. Della." She paused. "How is Slade doing?"

"He's holding up as best as he can. We just got back from Mississippi from burying him." Della sighed. "Anyway, I'm sorry to bother you, darling"—she held firmly on to her cane—"but can we come in? We have matters to discuss with you and shouldn't be long."

She stomped back into her apartment, and they followed. Once inside, Farah flopped on the sofa and folded her arms over her chest. “Where is Slade now? Still in Mississippi?”

“He’s not here, and that’s all you should be concerned about. I told him we would handle you fairly though.” Della smiled, although her disposition was far from kind. “Have you seen Eleanor?”

The Baker family was making her ass itch. “I’ve been looking for her, Miss Della. I really have. Just the other day I went to a dope house, but things didn’t go as planned.”

“What does that mean?” Della questioned.

“Let’s just say I was robbed, beat, and almost raped trying to find this woman.” Farah cried for sympathy points, but Della wasn’t giving them. “I’m trying my best, but at this point, I don’t think there’s anything else I can do. All I want to be right now is left alone.”

“Left alone?” She laughed. “Bitch, you better be glad my hands aren’t wrapped around your throat right now. My son may still think you’re innocent, but I know evil when I see it. It’s all in your eyes. If only Slade could see you for who you really are, I’d put you out of your misery right now. Fortunately for you, he’s still in love.”

“Please just leave!”

“Fuck please!” Della laughed. “You got a week to find this Eleanor person, and if you don’t, I promise you this, I will see to it that you’re never found again. I’m talking about the place where bodies are not found. Do you understand me?”

Farah straightened her shoulders and stood up. She stepped toward Della until she was pushed back a little by Judge's massive hand. "Della, I don't like threats." She wiped the fake tears off of her face. "Whatever you gonna do, just do it already."

"Be careful what you ask for, little girl," Della told her. "Where I'm from, wishes like yours are granted every day."

"So I'm supposed to be scared of you now?"

"You may not feel the need to be scared of her, but you should be frightened of us," Grant interrupted, stepping between them. "I know all about the people you were with who were killed later."

"So what are you gonna do?" Farah asked. "Snitch on me?"

He gripped her throat until she reddened. When he realized he was about to kill her without knowing anything, he let her go. "Don't ever disrespect me like that again," Grant told her.

She laughed. "If you not gonna snitch, what do you want with me now?"

Grant took a deep breath. Farah's cool demeanor put him out of character. "We didn't come all this way to play games with you. We came for one purpose and one purpose only, and that's to find our cousin."

"And we not leaving without him," Judge added.

"Then knock yourselves out."

After the Baker family left, she couldn't make brunch with the Fold. Since she was broke anyway, she decided to visit her cash cows, Coconut and Jake. She finished taking care of business and was waiting to be cashed out for her services.

"Well, I'm about to go." Farah eased into her jeans. When she was dressed, she stood at the edge of the bed and looked up at them. "Can I have my money? I got a lot of stuff to do today."

"Sit down for a second, Farah," Jake said with his hand outstretched to her. "You always rolling out, and we never have time to rap."

"Yeah, Farah," Coconut said, playing with the hairs on Jake's chest. "What's the rush? I haven't had a chance to talk to you since before Rhonda died. Chill with us for a minute. We were thinking about grabbing something to eat."

"There's no rush," she lied, "I just figured you guys wanted some privacy. It's not like I'm hitting and running." She giggled.

"Why would we want privacy when you're good company?" He patted the bed. "Now, sit your sexy ass down. I want to rap to you about a few things." He opened the covers for her to reenter.

Instead she took a seat on the edge of the bed and looked at both of them. *Damn, these mothafuckas freaked out. Just leave me the fuck alone.* "What's up?"

"Like Coconut said, I wanted to take both of my girls out to dinner and maybe catch that new hood movie that just dropped. I think it's called *Pitbulls in a Skirt*."

Coconut crawled up under him. "I'm with that shit, baby!" She looked down at her friend. "What about you, Farah?"

It wasn't like they were the worst people to be around. In fact, she really enjoyed the way they handled business in the bedroom. It was just that she had a lot of things to handle, and the last thing she wanted was to be snuggled up under the sex-crazed couple.

"I kinda want to go home." Farah shrugged. "I didn't want to tell you guys, but I think I'm coming down with a cold or something." She stood up again. "Can I please have my money now?"

Jake sighed. "I'm not going to lie, Farah. Your response kind of hurts my feelings." He grabbed the belt loop of Farah's jeans, forcing her into the space on the bed next to him. "Because I was thinking about taking my babies out shopping too." He kissed her on the neck and small chills traveled down her body. "Now, are you sure you can't make a little more time for me?"

He won her over, because although she wanted to be alone, Jake spending paper on her was not a bad idea. She hadn't been shopping since Randy cut her off. "Can I ask both of you something?" They nodded simultaneously. "How do I fit into this equation with you two? Am I a fuck buddy, a fuck homie, or what?"

Jake looked at her inquisitively before focusing on Coconut. "Wait, you didn't tell her?"

"I didn't get a chance to," she responded, looking nervously into her eyes. "Farah has been hard to find these days." He seemed irritated. "Let me explain it to her now, baby." Coconut exhaled. "Farah, I think I gave you the wrong impression on what Jake was looking for when we first spoke."

"Can you just spit the shit out?" Farah said combatively. "You're scaring me."

"Okay." She sighed. "Jake . . . I mean . . . *we're* looking for an exclusive thing. Not just a sexual thing."

"An exclusive thing?" She laughed, looking between them. In her book this was utterly ridiculous. "How can it be exclusive if there's three people involved?"

"When I was coming up, my father always had these types of relationships," Jake said. "And it worked because nobody ever had a reason to cheat. All three people were stimulated on a consistent basis. In my mind, it keeps the excitement alive."

"You mean you grew up like a Mormon?"

He laughed. "Not exactly. I don't remember them being real religious or nothing like that. There were a lot of swinger parties, but that was it. Anyway, I knew as a kid that I wanted the same." He rubbed Coconut's hair. "When I met Coco, I told her from the jump what I was about. She told me she had the perfect person for us, and when I saw your face, I knew it would work. But Park was with me, and since I didn't tell him my plan, he put his bid in and y'all started kicking it. That was then and this is now. I really hope you can get wit' this."

"So that means I got to be in a relationship with you and my best friend?"

He nodded. "Trust me, if we try hard enough we can make this shit work. Niggas do it all the time, but they never involve the women. I'm not like that. I'm trying to keep shit on the up and up."

Farah immediately thought about Slade. Although he saw her with Bones and told her to fuck off, she didn't want to be in a relationship with anyone else until she was sure. Then there was Bones. She still had yet to see what was up with him. What Jake wanted could complicate everything.

"I'm gonna be honest. This may be deeper than where I'm trying to go right now. Can I have time to think about it first?"

Coconut shook her head. "Farah, don't mess this up for me, please. Jake has been good to you. Plus you kind of owe me."

Farah grimaced. "Why do I owe you?"

Coconut sat up in the bed and crossed her arms over her chest. "After that video that was placed on YouTube? Of you smacking me? You mean to tell me that you don't remember that shit? Technically we aren't supposed to be even talking right now, but I forgave you."

"Coconut, I wasn't the one who uploaded that video, so you can't hardly blame me for that."

"Let me come at you a different way," Jake interrupted, not feeling the petty girl shit. "You obviously can't take care of yourself, because you always asking for money. I'm in a position to look out, but if I do, I need to know I'm getting what I want in return. A full-time scenario, on a permanent basis." He rubbed her long hair. "And that means you not giving up the pussy to nobody but me." With a serious face, he asked, "Do we have a deal or not?"

Farah had no intention of staying true to this deal no matter what she told him, but to get money, for now, she would tell him anything he wanted to hear.

Chapter 30

Slade

"You just have to be clear on what you want in the beginning and stand on it."

The music in the car was pumping, and although Shannon was riding shotgun, Slade still felt alone. Losing Markee had shortened his patience, and he couldn't wait to get his hands on Randy. It was a good thing he was hiding, because he had plans to dismember him while he was still alive and feed his body parts to the sharks.

His mind was still on the funeral when she ran her hand up his thigh. He looked over at her. "I'm not feeling that shit right now." He stopped at a light. "I'm driving."

She snatched her hand away. "Since when are you not feeling getting your dick sucked? You would do it five times a day if I could stand it."

"You just love saying stupid shit, don't you?" He pulled into traffic. "I can't never get you to act like a lady."

She threw her weight back into her seat, pouted, and crossed her arms over her breasts. She didn't care if she was the in-between girl. She wanted to be with him, so she would do whatever she could to keep him. But it bugged her out that unless he was about to nut, she always seemed to be irritating him. "Whatever you want, Slade. You're the boss." She sighed. "Anyway, where we going out to eat?"

"I was thinking we could grab some steaks." He looked over at her. If there was one thing that could be said about Shannon, it was that she was sexy. The jeans she wore hugged her thick thighs, and her waist was virtually nonexistent. She wasn't no Farah Cotton, but she was a great substitute. "Why, you wanted something else?"

"I'll take whatever you give me." She laughed, happy he was willing to compromise. "So," she said as she rubbed his thigh again, "when you gonna make me your girl?"

He turned the music down. "You playing, right?" He looked into her eyes as he steered his truck. When she didn't crack a smile, he said, "Wait, you're fucking serious?"

"Why wouldn't I be? I don't suck your dick and let you treat me like a fuck toy just for fun. I do it because I like you, and someday I want you to take me seriously."

"I thought it was about the bread I put into your pockets. Now, if that ain't enough, I don't know what else to tell you."

"And I appreciate it—"

"Well, you better start acting like it, Shannon," he said in a voice that rocked her core. "Because I told you I'm not trying to be in no relationship."

"You mean you not trying to be in no relationship with me. If I were Farah, it would be all good."

Just the fact that she uttered her name plagued him with guilt. "How come whenever I turn around, you talking about Farah? Are you that fucking insecure that you can't even exist without knowing how I feel about her?" He paused briefly. "I'm not going to keep justifying where you stand in my life, versus what I feel about her."

"What does that mean?"

"It means that I will always love Farah. It means that you will never measure up. And it means that if you mention her name again, just once, I'm pulling this truck over and throwing you the fuck out."

Slade didn't relax until he made it to the restaurant and had two glasses of Hennessy in his system. Suddenly, when he looked over at Shannon, she didn't seem so irritating. In fact, she looked beautiful as she silently sipped her soup.

"What you over there thinking about?" he asked, hoping she wouldn't ruin the night. "You been quiet ever since we got here."

She released the spoon and it clinked against the inside of the bowl. "I don't know." She shrugged. "I guess I can't believe that I'm sitting at the table with somebody like you." Shannon sipped her Moscato. "I ask myself over and over, why me? And I want to know so badly what I can do to make you happy. I just don't know how."

"What you mean, somebody like me? I'm just an average nigga."

"Slade, you may be a lot of things, but average you're not." She looked him over. "I mean, look at you. You have the height, that sexy chocolate skin, and even that scar on your neck. Girls like me don't normally find themselves in the company of niggas like you."

"You a bad chick, Shannon. I can see a rack of niggas wanting to get with you. You just have to be clear on what you want in the beginning and stand on it."

She shook her head because it hurt her feelings that he was talking to her about other niggas. In her mind, it meant that he would never be serious about her. "Naw, they never like bitches like me, except if they're trying to fuck. I guess you can relate, since that's all you want, right?"

He sipped his liquor. She was a beast at finding ways to bring up the topic of commitment. "Yeah, a'ight, Shannon."

"I'm serious," she continued, tossing her wine up, leaving only a droplet in the glass. "Can I ask you something? Before you say yes, I want an honest response, even if you think it will hurt my feelings."

"Don't say you can take it if you can't."

"I promise I can take whatever answer you give me. I'm tired of being lied to, and I know, no matter what, you do care about me. Even if it is only a little bit."

He sat back in his chair. "Okay, give it to me."

She exhaled. "Can you tell me why you would never take me seriously? As a girlfriend? I don't want you to beat around the bush, Slade."

He gulped his Hennessy and flagged the waiter over for another glass. "I'm gonna tell you this because contrary to what you believe, I do like you. A lot." When his drink came, he took a slow sip. "I could never see you as wifey because of how you got down when we first met."

Her eyebrows rose and she was confused. In her mind, they had a great night, which ended with his dick in her mouth and her friends fucking his brothers. "Are you talking about when you picked me and my friends up and took me to your cousin's house?" She paused. "Because I thought everything was cool. As a matter of fact, you said that was the only reason we still kick it."

"You right, you did hook me up, but what I'm talking about is *how* you and your friends got down when you came over my cousin's place." He paused. "If you wanted to be wifey, you had to carry yourself that way."

"So you saying you'll never be with me like that because I sucked your dick on the first date? Even though that's what you wanted me to do and you liked it?"

He shrugged.

"That's so fucking wrong, Slade. If that's how you felt, why didn't you tell me while I was doing it?"

"It's not my responsibility to express what you want for yourself." He pointed at her. "*You* gotta put it to niggas how you want to be treated, or else you'll be taken advantage of."

"So you're admitting that you took advantage of me?"

"I'm being real with you, Shannon. That's what you asked, remember?"

"Wow, you never really know a person." She took his glass and drank the rest of his Hennessy. "At least you being real."

"I've always kept shit real with you. You just figuring it out now."

Slade knew she was talking, but suddenly he could no longer hear her, because across the room was the woman he thought about every day, hugged up with *another* nigga. Since it wasn't even the same dude, he was confused. *What is she, some kind of freak?* The six foot five inch dude had her wrapped in his arms like a scarf, and she was smiling so wide her teeth sparkled.

"Excuse me for a minute, Shannon." He stood up.

Shannon grabbed his hand and said, "Slade, please don't leave me. We came together."

He shook her off and approached them. When he was close enough to breathe on both of them, he asked, "You look like you're really enjoying yourself, Farah."

Farah almost tripped over her feet when she saw him. "Nobody's asking you, Slade." She focused back on Jake and Coconut, who were both grilling Slade.

"Farah, what are you doing with this nigga? Wasn't you just pinned up with another dude the other night? Don't you got shit to take care of back home?"

Farah looked in the direction he came from. When she saw Shannon, she frowned. "What I'm doing over here is none of your business, but it looks like you having yourself a good time too." She laughed to herself. "You love fucking the consolation prize, don't you?" She looked at Shannon, who was grinning from ear to ear. Part of her wanted to snatch her face off, but the other part wanted to remain cool. Besides, he was the one pressing her out, not the other way around.

"My man, not for nothing, but I'm having an evening with my ladies right now," Jake said to Slade.

Prior to him opening his mouth, Slade forgot he was even there. "Your lady?" Slade laughed. "Nigga, I think you feeling yourself right about now. Back up before I embarrass you."

"I think you feeling yourself," Jake persisted. "And if you don't step the fuck away from the table, there's going to be a situation."

Farah, wanting to save Jake from a beat down, interfered. "Jake, please let me handle this alone."

"Naw, baby girl, this nigga way off beat. It's time for me to set him straight."

When he put his finger on Slade's arm, Slade gripped it and bent it backward. He didn't stop until he heard the pop of his bones.

"Ahhhh! What the fuck," he screamed, jumping in place. "You just broke my finger!" His limp finger moved around loosely. "I can't believe you just broke my finger!"

Slade was about to drop him on his back until Farah said, "Slade, please stop this shit. What is wrong with you? We're not together, remember?"

"Get your shit and come with me, Farah," Slade demanded. "Unless you want me to hurt somebody else!" He walked toward the exit without looking back.

Farah hopped up so quickly she knocked over a glass of water. If there was one thing she was certain of, it was that he was capable of everything he said.

On his heels, Slade grabbed Farah by the hand and snatched her out of the restaurant. He forgot all about Shannon until he was ten blocks down the street. Slight guilt covered him, and he texted his brother and told him to pick her up and take her wherever she wanted to go.

He responded with, I'm on it, but you gonna pay for that shit. I don't trust that chick.

Annoyed even more, Slade threw the phone in his console and drove silently down the street.

"I heard about your cousin," Farah said softly. "I'm sorry that happened to your family, Slade."

He looked at her and faced the road again. "I don't want to talk about it."

He drove in silence for five more minutes before she said, "Can you please talk to me and tell me what's going on?" She looked over at him. "What was that shit back there?"

"What you mean, what's going on?" His driving grew erratic. "I should be asking why you out on nightcaps when you still haven't found that bitch." Slade couldn't give a fuck about Eleanor at that moment, but he couldn't let her know that. The only thing on his mind was Farah Cotton and losing her for good.

"You mean to tell me that all of that back there was because of Eleanor?" Farah was heartbroken.

"Yeah . . . What you think it was about?"

"Pull over, Slade, or I'm jumping out of this bitch." She tugged on the door handle.

"I'm taking you home. You can do whatever you want once you there."

"Slade, either pull over or I'm jumping out. I'm not fucking around."

Calling her bluff, he said, "Then you do what the fuck you gotta do, because I'm not stopping for shit."

True to her word, she opened the door and rolled out onto the street.

"What the fuck is wrong with this bitch?" he yelled, pulling the car over to the side of the road. His heart pumped wildly and he prayed she was okay. Once outside, he ran to the patch of grass she landed in and looked down at her limp body. "What the fuck is up with you?" He helped her up, checking her over for injuries. "Why would you just do that shit? Huh? You could've killed yourself!"

He embraced her in his arms and she lost control. She cried long and hard as she pulled him closer to her body. "Slade, I'm so sorry for my part in everything. I don't know who you want me to be or what you want me to do, but you gotta stop fucking with my mind! You have to!"

He hugged her tightly and sniffed her hair. It felt so right to be with her, but wrong at the same time. "I can't play these fucking games with you no more either, baby. I just don't know what to do. So much shit is going on right now."

"If you want me and I want you, what's the problem?" She sobbed. "We're adults, Slade." She wiped her tears. "Let's do this shit and not worry about other people."

He pulled away from her and looked into her eyes. "I'm tired of living for everybody else too, but I gotta know, are you fucking that nigga back there?"

"What? N–no," she stuttered, leaning against his chest. "It's not even like that. He's Coconut's boyfriend and I was just with them while they were celebrating their anniversary." Lies rolled off of her tongue so effortlessly she believed them.

"What about the other nigga? Back at the Lofts?" He paused. "I saw the look in his eyes when I called your name. He looked at you like I do. Are you with him?"

"No, baby, he's just a friend."

"Does he know that?"

"He should, but if you want, I don't have a problem telling him."

"Are you lying to me, Farah? Because you know how much I hate liars." He gripped her tighter. "I can't do the secrets no more, Farah. I'm done!" He paused. "If I find out you lying, it's over for good. I'm putting everything on the line to be with you this time, and I don't want to find out it ain't worth it."

"I promise on everything, there's nobody I want to be with more than you. I was just waiting for you to realize that you want me too." She stepped away from him and grabbed his hands. "But there's something I want to share with you. Something you must know about me."

"What is it?" He looked nervous.

"Let's make up the right way first."

As Slade and Farah hugged on the side of the road, Bones remained in his car and observed the scene from a distance. He had been following her since she left Coconut's house. He always followed her, because it was important to him to know everything about her. He knew there was much more to the relationship with Slade than what she let on, and when the time was right, he would see it brought to an end in the most violent way imaginable.

Slade parted Farah's pussy lips and ran his tongue into the center of her wetness. She gripped at the sheets to pull away from him, but with both hands, he yanked her back. Making his tongue as stiff as possible, he went in and out of her hole before circling her clit.

"Slade, damn, that shit feels so good." She pulled his head closer toward her warmth and wiggled her hips. He flicked his tongue back and forth, causing her button to stiffen in his mouth.

Her syrup oozed from between her legs and fell over his lips and then on the bed. He lapped up as much as possible, and Farah was driven wild. "Turn over," he demanded.

When she flipped over, he spread her ass cheeks and licked from the top of her ass to the opening of her hole. "Oh, my goodness, Slade. What are you doing to me?"

He didn't respond. He was so in love with this woman that he was gone. His tongue circled in and around her hole until her entire body shivered.

"I love you, Slade, so much." She moaned.

"Turn over," he demanded.

Now putty in his hands, she quickly turned over and he looked down at her. His dick was as stiff as a hammer, and he stroked it back and forth before power-driving into her walls. "You my fucking bitch. Let me hear you say it."

"I'm yours," she said, feeling every inch of his iron. She clawed at his back and pulled him closer. Now a semi-pro, she worked her hips like a master as she met him thrust for thrust.

He gripped her hair roughly and said, "Tell me you're my bitch, Farah. Now!"

"I'm your bitch, baby. I'm all yours."

He pulled out of her wetness and entered her asshole from the front. At first he was slow, but after the third pump, he couldn't care less how she felt. He hated her for making him choose between her and his family. He hated her for being so secretive, and he hated her for having so much power over him.

"Damn, you feel so good," he said, pumping her harder. "I fucking love you."

"I love you more than anything, Slade," she professed, although she was in major pain. "My body is yours to do whatever you please. I don't even care."

Even if she hadn't said it, he knew it was true. He could tell by how wet she'd gotten. "I'm cumming, baby," he said. "Fuck, I'm cumming."

She quickly jumped up and got on her knees. With her mouth wide open, she welcomed him. The glistening of her wet tongue turned him wild. When he was ready, he poured his cream into her mouth and she swallowed every drop.

She was in ecstasy, until there was a heavy knock at the door.

"What are you doing here, Bones?" Farah whispered, looking behind her for Slade. "I'm kind of busy right now."

"I was worried about you," he said in a soft tone. "You sounded out of it when I called earlier to tell you we couldn't meet up." He scanned over her. "I'm just checking to make sure you're okay."

She was shaking so hard it looked like she would explode. Although she didn't know what was going on with her and Slade, she knew she didn't want to mess things up with him already. "I'm fine. I just—"

Shit got worse when Vivian walked up behind Bones. "Farah, I have to talk to you about this month's rent."

Bones stepped to the side and observed her with scrutinizing eyes.

Farah sighed and looked up to the ceiling. "Are you serious? Don't you see I got company right now? Plus it's only the first of the month. I have fourteen days left."

"First off, the fifteen-day time frame is a grace period," she said, stepping closer. "It's not actually when your rent is due. And if I waited on your company to leave, I'd never get to talk to you." She looked over Bones and rolled her eyes. "I'll be back later."

Farah sighed. "I hate that bitch!"

"Is everything cool?" he asked, watching the property manager walk down the hall and enter her room. "You need anything?"

"I'm good, but I really have to go, Bones. I'll call you later, okay?"

She moved to close the door, and he stopped it by pushing it open. “You deserve better, Farah. And whether you know it or not, I’m gonna be the one to give it to you, not the same nigga you told me dumped you for his family. Think about that while he’s using you for your body.”

Chapter 31

Farah

"Sorry, bitch. That nigga belongs to me."

After their fuck fest, Farah and Slade decided to grab breakfast. As he drove down the street in his shiny Escalade, she remembered how things used to be, when he drove a broken green Ford Expedition. Although he had more money, to her it didn't seem like he changed.

When they arrived at Mama's Kitchen, Slade went inside to order the food. Farah remained in the car and stared at him from the window. He was perfection; the kind of man who turned heads every time he moved. Although he was physically attracted to her, she also loved the little things he did, like how he would break from what he was doing to open doors for elderly women, or how he kept his hands in his pockets, for fear he'd break something. Then there was the way he'd look every so often at the truck and smile. She wondered if he was making sure that she was still there, like she did him.

She was still focusing on the restaurant when her cell vibrated. She removed it from her purse and saw it was a text message from Bones: Thirsty?

Immediately her pussy jumped and her mind wandered. If there was one thing she enjoyed doing with them, it was drinking blood. When she looked at the mirror on the visor, her skin did look a little dry. Maybe it was time. Sure. What time?

I'll hit you later with the details. Get rid of him first.

Farah threw her phone down and looked around for his truck. The more time she spent with them, the more she was starting to believe that the Fold could've been responsible for sending the pictures. If that was the case, she decided to keep them on her good side, no matter what.

Slade was still at the counter when a girl with tight black jeans strutted inside with her hood rat friends. Farah's skin heated up when the girl walked up to Slade, but a smile spread across her face when he pointed at his truck, indicating he was taken. Farah threw the "fuck you" finger up in the air. "Sorry, bitch. That nigga belongs to me."

The girl shook her head and walked to another counter.

Farah thought about their plans for later. First they would enjoy their food; then they would go back to his new apartment and fuck all day. When they were done, they would eat some more and fuck again. Her daydreams were sweet, until she saw the one person who could change everything: Eleanor McClendon. She blinked twice, not believing her eyes. If Slade saw her, it would be a wrap, and there was no way she could let that happen.

She looked at the restaurant and saw that Slade seemed to be occupied with the cashier. Slowly she pushed the door open and eased out of the truck. She was so worried that Eleanor would get away that she didn't close the door. She moved as quietly as a cat on the pursuit to kill her.

She was five steps away from Eleanor when Slade walked out with the food in his hand. When he saw who Farah was chasing, he dropped the bag and screamed, "Eleanor! Wait!"

Eleanor looked behind her and saw them coming at her full speed ahead. She ran with the speed of an Olympic track star.

Why the fuck did this bitch come back in town? Why didn't she stay away? Although Farah questioned her reason for returning, she knew none of it mattered. At the end of the day, Eleanor possessed some information that Farah didn't want Slade to have.

Slade and Farah zipped in and around cars trying to catch her. Since Farah was closer, Slade yelled, "Don't let her go, babe! Stay on that bitch!"

Chapter 32

Present Day

Mooney

Cutie's mouth hung open as Mooney placed the clothes in the dryer. "Well?" She stepped so close to Mooney that their arms were touching. "I'm waiting."

"Give me a second," Mooney said, throwing rags into the dryer. "And back off. You see me over here working."

She hopped back on the dryer. "Don't do me like this again, Mooney. You always start the story, make it good, and then leave me hanging. That's why a part of me don't even want to hear it."

"What you talking about, girl?" She thought it was hilarious that Cutie was so much into a story that didn't involve her. "Calm down before you pass out somewhere."

"Mooney, please stop playing!" She hopped down again and helped her put the rest of her rags in the dryer. When she was done, she closed the door. "Did Farah catch Eleanor? Or did Slade get her? Because it's too close now for her to get away. I been waiting for this moment for the longest!"

"You would want to know, wouldn't you?" She shook her head. "Just be patient, Cutie. You'll find out everything you want to know."

"Mooney!" She stomped her foot. "You are the worst storyteller ever! I can't wait to find out something you want to know because I'm never gonna tell you. Watch!"

Mooney laughed. "Okay, okay. Walk with me upstairs and I'll tell you the rest."

Cutie was irritated, but knew she had to be patient. Once they made it to the apartment, Cutie sat on the sofa and waited quietly for five minutes.

Mooney felt she made her wait long enough. "Well, as you know, Farah knew she had to get a hold of that woman before Slade did. Remember, the last time Farah was over Eleanor's place, Slade was with her. But Eleanor already told Slade everything she knew about his brother. And if she had his phone, she would've definitely given it to him. So, of course, it was crucial that Farah kill her."

"I remember the day, but what happens now? If Slade catches Eleanor, she's going to tell him that Farah tried to kill her, even though she tried to kill her too."

"Farah is sick and lives in the moment. Most liars do. She doesn't understand that her lies will come back to haunt her. She'll do whatever she can to get out of the situation. The only thing on her mind is keeping Slade and cleaning up her mess. But when you do so much dirt, it's hard to clean it all up."

"I'm scared for Farah," Cutie said, sipping her soda. "Part of me thinks she deserves to be alone, but the other part of me is sad."

"How are you scared for her when you don't even know her?" She laughed, sitting in the recliner.

"I know it's crazy." She sighed. "But I feel like I know her. She had a hard life, and I do too." She placed her soda on the table. "It's like we are . . ."

"The same?" Mooney questioned. "I told you when I first began the story that you both were alike."

"That's kind of scary though." She pouted. "What about the Fold? The Bones character sounds scary."

Mooney laughed. "He is." She paused. "And what did you mean by saying you have a hard life?"

Cutie looked into her soda can. "I don't want to talk about that kind of stuff right now." She seemed saddened. "Maybe later."

"Okay, but I want you to know you can talk to me about anything, Cutie," Mooney said honestly.

"About anything?"

"You name it."

"Well, can you start by telling me the rest of the story?" She laughed.

"That was good." She chuckled. "Anyway, wanting Eleanor and catching her had proven to be two different things."

Chapter 33

Farah

"The last thing we need is for the cops to be circling around here."

It seemed as if Farah had been chasing Eleanor forever. When Farah originally spotted Eleanor, she chased her down the street, but before Farah could catch her, Eleanor dipped into an apartment building. There was no way Farah could lose her now, so she stayed on Eleanor's trail.

Farah ran up and down the hallways of the property trying to find Eleanor. To her dismay, she realized she'd lost Eleanor. She felt like kicking herself in the head. In the end, all she could ask herself was, *How does she keep getting away?* She was about to search another floor when Slade found her on the fourth.

"Where the fuck did she go, baby?" he asked, walking up behind her. "You didn't let her get away, did you?"

Farah had an idea of which floor she hid on, but she had no intention of telling him. "I'm sorry, baby. I tried to stay on her trail, but she was too fast. You saw how quick she was running." She punched at the air. "I feel like I let you down again."

"Don't worry about it, babes. I'm going to knock on every door in this mothafuckin' building until I get her.

That's on my mother." He looked around where he stood, trying to determine which door to knock on first.

She saw the determination in his eyes and had to put a stop to it. "No, Slade! You can't do it this way."

"Why?" He frowned, looking down at her. "If we let her get away, we'll never be able to find her again."

"Because . . . because . . . uh . . . when we started chasing her," she stuttered, "somebody said they were gonna call the police. For all we know, they may be on their way here right now."

"I don't give a fuck about no police, babes! I dream about this bitch every night!" Slade yelled. "And she gonna tell me why she had my brother's phone or I'ma light this building on fire. I know this bitch know more than she told us. Why else would she be hiding?"

"You're right. She's hiding because she does know something," Farah encouraged him. "I been telling you that from the jump, and I'm glad you're able to see it for yourself now, but we have to be smart, baby. The last thing we need is for the cops to be circling around here. You don't want to get locked up for threatening no white woman." She pulled him closer. "Then you really won't be able to find Knox's body."

He pushed her back. "What you mean find Knox's body?"

The hair on the back of her neck rose. "I didn't mean it like that. I meant find Knox. I'm sorry, baby."

He was still skeptical about her response, but said, "My brother is alive somewhere, and I'm going to find him. Don't ever say *body* and my brother's name in the same sentence again. Understand?"

"Yes, baby. I do. I know you want her, but you not going to be able to get her if the cops catch you."

There were two things that she said that scared him to death since he was from the South, and they were getting locked up for threatening a white woman and not being able to help his family. Slade paced the floor angrily because he knew she was telling the truth.

"You right. Let's get the fuck out of here. I got a plan." They rushed to the truck, but once they were inside, he didn't pull off. Instead, he got on the phone and called his brothers. "Major, the family with you?" Slade sounded anxious.

"Yeah. We all here! Everything cool? You sound out of it."

"No. I need y'all to come down here to Mama's Kitchen. This bitch Eleanor just went into this building, and I don't want to take my eyes off of it until she walks out. Bring Judge and Grant too. We need as many people as possible on this shit. I don't care if we have to stay out here all night. I want niggas in the front and in the back. You got me?"

"Say no more. We on our way!"

When he ended the call, Farah was sweating so hard she was about to pass out. This was the one thing she was trying to avoid. She had to think quickly on her feet or else a bag of shit was about to blow up in her face. *Think. Think. What can you do to save yourself?* She was hard pressed for an excuse to get the fuck out of dodge, until she broke out in hives all over her arms and face. Back in the day, it was the worst thing that could happen. Now it was a blessing in disguise.

"Slade," she exhaled, "baby, I gotta go home."

"Not now, Farah," he said, eyes still glued on the building. "I'm waiting on my brothers to get here first. We finally about to get some answers around here."

"I know, but I'm not feeling too good. I got to go now," she said in a low voice as she watched him continuously looking at the building.

"I told you I can't." He stopped short of yelling at her when he looked at her face. She was covered in red splotches and looked like an entirely different person. He'd never seen anything like it in all of his life. "Oh shit, are you okay?" He grabbed her arms. "Damn, baby, what the fuck is going on?"

"I'm having an allergic reaction. I'm not feeling too well."

"But we didn't eat anything yet." His eyes continued to roll over her body.

"I know. It's probably something in that building." She shrugged. "I don't know. I just gotta get out of here."

"You want me to take you to a hospital or something?" he asked, concern heavy in his voice.

"No, I got some stuff at my house though, but we gotta leave so I can get it, or else it's gonna get worse. I know you want to wait on Eleanor, but I'm in so much pain, baby. If I don't get what I need, my throat may close up."

He looked over at the building and his right leg moved rapidly. This was the last thing he needed to happen, but he also didn't want the love of his life to be in pain. What if her heart kicked into overdrive or something and she died?

He pulled out of the parking space and drove into traffic. Agitated, he took his phone out of his pocket and called his brothers again. "Major, something came up, man. I gotta go."

Major sounded frustrated. "What you mean, you gotta go? We almost there. Give us a few minutes."

"I can't. Just know that an emergency came up or else I wouldn't leave. The building is right next to the restaurant. She's a white older woman and she's wearing blue jeans and a white T-shirt. Question every white person who fits the description. Matter of fact, question everybody. Whatever you do, don't let her get past you. I don't give a fuck what you have to do."

"Are you sure she went into the building?"

"I'm positive!" Slade told him. "You hear the pump in my voice. This shit is the real deal. Something tells me we're finally about to find out what happened to Knox."

"Okay, we on it. I'll get up with you later with an update."

When Slade was done, he hung up and continued on the way to the house. Two minutes later, his phone rang again and he answered. "Hello."

"Slade, you gonna pay for leaving me at the restaurant. I promise," Shannon screamed into the phone.

"Suck my dick, you whore-ass bitch," he yelled, ending the call.

Farah looked over at him. "Who was that? Shannon?"

He rubbed her leg. "Don't worry about all that. I need your mind at ease." He snatched his hand away and moved angrily down the road.

Farah could tell he was annoyed, so she kept quiet so he could concentrate on driving. The last thing she needed was to irritate him even more, especially since it was because of her he had to leave. When they made it to Platinum Lofts and then her apartment, she just knew he would go back to the building. Instead he followed her inside the apartment.

"Are you going back?" she asked. "I figure you'd want to as soon as possible." She wanted him gone so she could pack her shit and get the fuck out of dodge.

"You playing, right? My girl in here fucked up and you want me to leave? Naw, baby. I gotta make sure you're okay first."

She threw her keys on the table next to the door.

"What you got for your condition? And why you didn't tell me you had allergies like that? You gotta be careful out here."

"I don't always know when it's gonna kick in. My stuff is in the bathroom though." She walked down the hall, but he was right on her heels. Needing space, she said, "Baby, can you bring me something to drink? A bottle of water from the fridge?" She tried to make a joke. "Try not to break that one. It's new."

He laughed. "At least you got a sense of humor right now."

"Seriously, I need water to take my medicine," Farah said.

"No problem. I got you, babes."

When he walked into the kitchen, she dipped into the bathroom and locked the door. She slammed the medicine cabinet a few times to make noise and sat on the toilet to clear her head. *What can I say to get rid of this nigga?*

A minute later, Slade was wiggling the doorknob. "You okay in there, baby?"

She loved him to pieces, but at the moment, wanted nothing more than for him to go away. "I'm fine, Slade. I have to use the bathroom too. Can you just hold the water for me until I come out?"

"You sure you okay?" Slade inquired. "Because you got my head fucked up out here."

"I really am fine. Just give me a few moments."

"Okay, I'll be in the living room in case you need me. And if the medicine doesn't work, I don't care what you say, I'm taking you to the hospital."

Fuck. Having spent most of her childhood in hospitals, the last thing she wanted was to go to one. "Okay, baby. I'll see you when I get out."

Farah had to come up with a plan. She had no doubt in her mind that his brothers would be grabbing that old woman and hauling her there in any second. When that happened, what was she going to do? What was she going to say?

After faking long enough in the bathroom, she walked out and into the living room with a sad look on her face. She stood in front of him while he observed her beauty.

"Even now you're beautiful." He reached his hand out to her, and she sat next to him on the sofa. "Drink up." He handed her the bottle of water, and she curled up into a ball and lay on his chest. "I didn't fuck up the fridge." He nodded toward it. "But I did break a glass getting you some ice."

She laughed. "Leave it to your cock-strong ass to break some shit."

"Where is your medicine?"

"I took it already." She felt the cool bottle in her hand. "I used faucet water." She placed it on the table.

"Well, how do you feel now?"

"I'll be better in a little while." She lied so much she couldn't stand herself anymore. "I don't want you to worry, Slade. I go through this all the time."

"Baby, I'ma always worry about you. Even when we weren't together, I worried." He rubbed her face. "What you take?"

"It's something the doctor prescribed. I can't even remember the name of it." Farah swallowed.

"You should always know what you take. Go get me the bottle. I want to see what they giving you."

I know this is you, Knox, trying to ruin my relationship from the dead! "Slade, I just want to lay up under you. Can you give me that?"

"You right, baby." He rubbed her back. "What did you want to tell me the other night when your crazy ass jumped out my ride on the side of the road?"

Originally she wanted to tell him about her lifestyle, but what if he didn't understand? What if he left her and this time for good? "I do things, sometimes, to make me feel better."

When she stopped, he said, "Things like what? Drugs? Weed?" He chuckled. "We all do a little something different when times are hard. As long as you not fucking with dope or crack, I'm good with it."

"It's nothing like that." She shook her head. "It's like . . . like . . ."

"You can tell me anything, Farah, so don't hold back with me anymore. I want us to be stronger, and we do that by staying honest." He was in his head about their relationship, when for some reason, he thought about what Shannon told him a while back. He never asked her about it before because it was too farfetched to be true. "I heard something a while back that I never said to you because it didn't make any sense."

She sat up straight and looked at him. "What was it?"

"Somebody told me you drank . . . that you were drinking blood."

Farah's heart dropped. Out of all of the things in the world, she didn't imagine he would ask her that. She considered telling him the truth, since he heard the rumor a while back and never stopped loving her. She was about to confirm the story, until she considered the way he looked at her at the moment. His expression was filled with slight disgust, and she knew telling him about her lifestyle would be the death of the relationship.

"Slade, don't ask me anything so crazy like that again," she spat.

He laughed and appeared relieved. "I knew it was dumb, but I wanted to check with you anyway. So what did you want to tell me?"

"Can we do it later?" She paused, rubbing his leg. "For some reason, my head is starting to hurt even more."

"No problem, babes."

After a few more minutes passed, she said, "So . . . you talk to your brothers yet? Were they able to catch Eleanor?"

He took his phone out of his pocket. "I'm waiting on them to call right now. I don't want you to be worried about all that though."

Yeah, right. It's the only thing I can think about.

His phone rang. "Speak of the devil." He answered it. "What's up, man? You got her?"

"Is Farah with you?" Killa questioned.

He looked down at her and rubbed her hair softly. "Yeah, why?"

"Keep her there, man. We on our way now."

He looked at the phone strangely and put it back in his pocket. Suddenly there was a shift in his body mechanics. He wasn't as loving as he was earlier, and Farah felt it. "Who was that?"

"My brother Killa."

He didn't tell her what he said, but he didn't need to. She was a wizard at knowing when something was wrong.

"You sure you okay?" Farah asked him. "You seem different now that you're off the phone."

"I'm fine." Slade smiled. "I told you to stop worrying." Slade pulled her closer. "You not going anywhere right now, are you?"

She shook her head. "No. Why you ask? I don't even feel like leaving the house."

"Good. I'll be glad when all of this shit is behind us."

"You and me both, Slade."

When Killa arrived, he was flanked by Major and Judge and Grant, and they all looked ready for business. Although the four of them made it obvious they didn't fuck with her, it was the scraggly-looking man with the nappy hair who held her attention. It was the same man who robbed her in the dope house.

"What's up?" Slade looked at the stranger. "Who the fuck is this? And where's the bitch?"

Killa walked past Slade and up to Farah's spotty face. His jaw clenched, and for a second she felt like he was about to lay hands on her in a bad way. "When are you gonna start being real with us, Farah? We know you had something to do with Knox going missing. Just shoot us straight. If you love my brother like you said you do, you'll speak the truth."

She stepped back. "I don't know what you're talking about." She looked at Slade. "I don't even know this man, baby." She didn't want to tell him that they'd met each other before.

Killa looked at the unwanted visitor. "Come here, man. Tell her what you told us at the building."

The man who robbed her cautiously stepped closer to Farah. “Eleanor was at my apartment earlier.” His voice was low and fragile. It was as if he was afraid of her, and she guessed it was because he robbed her. “She’s been living with me for the past few months. Anyway, she told me when she saw you earlier that she was in fear for her life. She said you’re trying to blame her for something she didn’t do.”

“Are you sure it’s not the fact that she tried to kill me?” Farah responded.

“She did that because you were after her, so she called her nephews from Chicago.”

“They were black,” Farah responded.

“We all got a little black and white in us, don’t we?” He laughed. “If you must know, they were in-laws from a past marriage. Anyway, when you killed him, she’s been bad ever since.”

“What you talking about, babe?” Slade asked, pulling her to him. “Who the fuck shot at you, Farah?”

“Eleanor, and apparently her nephew. I didn’t tell you because we weren’t together and I didn’t think you’d care.”

“I always care about what happens to you, even if we not together.” He paced the floor. “I swear to God I wish I could kill this nigga again. Who killed her nephew?”

She was silent.

“Who was it, Farah?”

“Bones . . . the person you saw me with in the hallway the other day.”

He was a new level of demented now. He knew the moment he looked into his eyes he was a killer, and now he had proof. “Fuck that nigga,” Slade said. His jaw jumped. “I’m just glad you okay.” He gritted his teeth and tried to calm down. Although he loved her, the fact that she was keeping things from him ruined all trust.

Farah faced the stranger again. “Is that all she said? You should’ve asked her why she keeps running when all we want to do is talk to her. She’s the one who fired first that night.”

“That’s not what she’s saying,” the unwanted visitor added.

Farah wanted to snatch his dry lips off.

“She says you probably have something to do with Knox missing, and that’s why you’re trying to kill her.”

“If that’s how she feels, then why isn’t she here to defend herself?” Farah continued. “Why hide?”

“Eleanor gave him a message before he came out to meet us,” Grant responded. “She is willing to talk to us when it’s safe.”

“Yeah, she told him that she’ll call when she’s ready to meet with us,” Killa said.

“Okay, and then we can put this shit to rest,” Farah responded.

“For your sake, Farah, everything that you’re saying better be true, because if you had something to do with my brother going missing, not even Slade will be able to hold me back.”

Chapter 34

Farah

"I'm going through some serious shit over here."

Farah sat on her bed with balls of used Kleenex all around her. Once again she was crying to her sister and brother and trying to figure out how to get herself out of the situation. "I don't know what to do, y'all." She sobbed, wiping her nose. "In a few weeks this bitch is going to meet up with Slade, and they gonna find out I was involved with Knox's death."

"Involved?" Shadow said, sitting on the edge of the bed. "You killed the nigga."

"Shadow, don't be ignorant," Mia responded, hitting her brother on the arm. "You see she's fucked up."

"She knows I'm playing with her," he said, nudging Farah's leg.

"Well, I don't feel like playing right now, Shadow," Farah yelled. "I'm going through some serious shit over here. I need this bitch Eleanor like yesterday!"

"I know it's serious, but my thing is this, even if they catch her, it will be your word against a dopehead. If you ask me, Slade and them should give you credit for that alone. Try not to work yourself all up when it might be for nothing."

"Well, what if it's not for nothing?" She looked at both of them. "What can I do to get out of it then?"

Shadow stood up and walked toward the window. "I can murder Slade if that's what you want." He looked at Farah and then Mia. "If you ask me, that will probably solve all of our problems too."

Farah wiped her nose with a Kleenex, stood up, and slapped him in the face. "I don't want to ever hear you say that shit again." She pointed at him. "Ever."

He stomped toward the window. "Then what's your plan?" he asked with an attitude. "Because, if you ask me, you shouldn't have had his phone anyway. You would've been free and clear of all this shit had you not taken his shit."

"Is this really necessary?" Mia asked. "I mean, what is it helping to say what she should've done?"

"Answer the question, Farah."

Farah sat back down and sighed. "Before I killed Knox, he said something was in the phone that could save Slade." He looked over at him. "It turns out he was right. Had I not taken the phone, he would've been dealing with some shit with a sheriff back in Mississippi. With the phone, they were able to prove their innocence."

"Yeah, but did you ever stop to think how you were going to give him the phone? Did it ever occur to you that there was no earthly reason for you to have it, but for the fact that you killed him?" he asked with a combative tone in his voice.

"Shadow, we both know Farah do dumb shit from time to time, but it ain't no reason to keep beating her up about it. Let's just put our heads together and come up with a plan that will work this time." She looked at Farah. "So did the dopehead give Slade and them an exact time when they'd meet?"

"No, but I think it will be in a couple of weeks. The dopehead said she gets her social security check then, and that's when she normally comes around. It's being sent to his house."

"So we'll be watching for her to come back. Put some people on it."

"Even if we do intercept the meeting, what about the person who keeps dropping pictures off on me? At first I thought it was Rhonda, but more came after that."

"How you know it isn't Eleanor?" Shadow asked, walking over to the bed.

"I don't know, but what if it isn't? If she had all of the things on me the pictures show, why not go to the cops?"

"I don't know, Farah," Mia responded, rubbing her hand over her face. "She is a dopehead. The more you tell me, the more I'm thinking it is her. I mean, could it be anybody else?"

Her mind roamed to the Fold, but she shook the thought out of her mind. "I can't think of anybody else." She sighed. "And that ain't all. Nadia Gibson's broke ass is making it her mission to pin every murder in this building on me, including the person Slade killed with his bare hands in the hallway."

"Is there anybody else who could've sent the picture?" Mia asked.

"Yes. I'm still worried about Randy."

She sighed. "It's settled. We're going to come up with a plan that will take care of everything," Mia said in an exhausted tone.

"And everybody," Shadow added.

"Y'all telling me something I already know. My question is how?"

Mia walked away and paced the floor. When she couldn't concentrate, she walked into the living room to be alone. An hour later, she returned to Farah's room with a smile on her face.

Waving her finger, Mia said, "I got a plan so sweet, by the time it's all said and done, the only person they won't be looking at for these murders is you. And if we do this right, the mysterious picture person will disappear too." She paused. "But you'll have to stay out of trouble, Farah. No more drinking blood and no more hanging around them freaks in the all black and red."

"But . . . why?" She paused. "I . . . I have to drink blood. If I don't, I'll look like Mama did before she died. Don't you see? It's not because I want to, it's because I have to."

"Farah, that blood shit doesn't work!" Shadow roared. "To be honest, it was cool at first because I just came home from jail, but now it's weird."

"I don't know—"

"You either do shit my way, or you do it on your own," Mia snapped and looked at Farah.

It took Farah five minutes to say, "Okay. I won't drink blood." Even though she knew, like everything else, it was a lie.

"Good, because if you follow my plan to a T just like I outline, you'll be indebted to me for the rest of your life."

Farah was hopeful seeing how excited Mia was. "Well, what's your plan?"

"First you have to reconnect with your biological father." Mia started pacing the floor.

Farah was confused. She never told anybody that she knew Ashur was not her biological father. "Wait. I never told you about him," Farah responded with wide eyes. "How did you know?"

"We been knew," Shadow added. "Nobody gives a fuck though. You still our sister."

"Does Daddy know too?" Farah inquired, looking at her siblings.

"We never told him." Mia sighed. "And if it's all the same to you, we want to keep this secret to ourselves. Ashur would be devastated."

Farah agreed. "So why reconnect with my real father?"

"Because he's rich and you're going to need a lot of money for an attorney and an investigator. Don't worry. I'm confident that he'll help you."

Farah was doubtful, but continued to listen.

"Then we need to go to Jean's apartment," Mia continued. "Because I don't care what he's telling police, he has that surveillance tape from the night he went missing. And if my theory is correct, it's in his apartment. You're going to have to seduce this nigga and go get it."

"Mia, I don't know about this shit. It seems like too much."

"Farah, desperate times calls for desperate measures, and unfortunately you don't have a choice. Getting with this dude is not an option." Mia paused. "The last part of my plan is Randy," she continued. "It won't do us any good to get you out of this drama if Randy is still in the picture. You'll have to visit him."

"But he moved," Farah responded. "And if I see him, he'll probably want to kill me."

"That nigga is in love with you," Mia reminded her. "And from what I'm told, he's broke. He would love to see you. Now, are you sure you don't know where he is?"

Farah remembered the last call she had with him that was interrupted. The person in the background said, "Welcome to Serenity Meadows." She wondered if there was a lead there. "You know what? Let me put something together. I might be able to find him."

"Good, because he's important," Mia said, sitting on the edge of the bed. "Now, the last part of the plan means you'll have to go to the precinct," Mia told her, knowing she wouldn't like it. "To turn yourself in."

"What? Why?" Farah yelled. "If I do that, I'll have to go to prison." She was so worked up she was panting.

"Just trust me, Farah." Mia touched her leg. "I got you, and everything will be okay."

Farah sighed.

"Trust me, Farah. I got you. Now, are you down or not?" Mia asked.

Farah thought about her options. She realized she didn't have any. "I don't have a choice."

Chapter 35

Farah

"All my life I've been an outcast."

Farah rehearsed over and over in her mind what Mia told her as she steered her car down the highway. She was meeting a man she hadn't spoken to in years. It took a lot of work to locate him, considering he was a congressman for DC, but in the end it paid off. Farah had wanted to talk to him personally for a long time, but her loyalty to Ashur prevented her from making the move. With her current situation, everything had changed.

When she pulled up in front of his beautiful brick home in the suburbs of Maryland, she wondered what kind of life he had. Was he married? Single? Did she have brothers and sisters? Her mind moved nonstop considering the possibilities. When she calmed herself down, she took a few quick deep breaths and walked up the stairs leading to his door. She didn't have to knock, because the man she knew as Coach Jaffrey was standing in front of her, waiting.

Jaffrey was an extremely attractive white man with coal-black hair and brown eyes. He looked upon her with admiration and at the same time a bit of sadness. For a second, standing in the doorway, he observed her, and when his lips finally parted, she was afraid he would shoo her away. Instead he said, "Farah, I didn't know about you. I mean . . . when I heard Brownie was pregnant again, I knew we shared moments together, but she promised me that you were not mine. I didn't press the issue because she was married and I didn't want to destroy her relationship."

She swallowed. How could he not want to destroy her marriage and still fuck a married woman? "Didn't you think I looked like you?"

"I never once considered the fact that you could be my daughter. Not once. Now that I look at you, I wonder why I never realized it all along." His smile was weak, but she could feel the kindness behind his eyes. "I'm so sorry that you lived your whole life without me in it. You gotta believe me when I say, had I known I would've been there."

Farah felt warm inside. There was something validating about being wanted. Yes, she knew Ashur loved her, and her heart told her that her siblings adored her too, but he was her biological father, and it made his acceptance different.

She cleared her throat. "I believe you would've been there for me had you known." She looked into his home. "Can I come inside?"

"Oh, I'm so sorry." He laughed. "I was so caught up I lost my manners." He opened the door and allowed her into his beautiful home. The theme was white and mahogany, and the furnishings were breathtaking. To be honest, it reminded her of her own apartment, and she smiled, considering they possibly had the same taste. The closer she looked, she was sure that there was a woman in his life.

"I hope I didn't come at a bad time," Farah said. "When I called and you said it was okay to come over, I should've told you that it would be now."

"It's definitely not a bad time." He shook his head. "I am happy you came. Since you called, it was all I could think about." He looked her over, and she wondered what he thought about her. "So tell me about your life. How are things going? Are you safe? Happy?"

There was no way she could tell him that she was a murderous freak who loved blood. Instead she did what she always did: lied. "My life is going okay, but my sister died not too long ago. And Brownie, too. I don't know if anyone told you yet."

He stumbled a little and took a seat at the dining room table. She sat next to him. "What? I don't understand. H . . . how did she die?"

"My mother died some months back." Farah was cold when she read off the details about her late mother. She couldn't care less about Brownie's cold bones or the life she led, but when she saw the hurt in his face, she tried to appear more compassionate. "You cared about her, didn't you? My mother?"

He looked behind him, she guessed for his girlfriend or wife. "I never stopped loving your mother. I just wasn't ready to be with her at the time. I was young. We both were, and we allowed people to shape how we felt."

"What do you mean?" Farah replied.

"I wanted to be with your mother, but she didn't trust me. Every day it was a fight. She fought with this person and that person, until it was difficult even walking outside with her. Being with your mother meant being in fear for your life constantly, and me trying to defend her always turned into a black and white issue. It was too much."

"Wait . . . I thought you didn't want to be with her because she had dark skin."

His eyebrows rose. "Who told you that?"

She remained silent.

"Farah, whoever told you that lied to you. I've given up everything for what I like, including my family members. They've proven themselves to be racist over and over again, even with my current wife." He shook his head. "No, the reason I couldn't make it with your mother was because she loved violence. And she wasn't comfortable in her own skin." When he remembered he was talking to her daughter, he calmed down. "I'm sorry I have to be so cold, but it's important that I put you on to the truth." He touched her hand. "But enough of that. Tell me what's going on in your life."

"I wasn't totally honest about myself. I'm not well at all."

His eyes widened. "What do you mean, you're not well?"

"I suffer from an illness. It's a very rare illness, but it ruined most of my life."

He backed up. "Please tell me you don't have HIV."

She shook her head. "Oh, no, nothing like that. I just have some blood thing that doesn't allow me to make blood well on my own. Not only that, but I can't be around certain smells, wear certain perfumes or cosmetics. I can't even eat certain foods. This illness is draining."

"I see. I remember you always being sickly in middle school, but I never knew why." He looked her over again, and she wondered the meaning behind his stares. "So, what's the name of the illness?"

"Porphyria."

He frowned. "I never heard of it before."

"Most people haven't. That doesn't stop it from ruining my life. I try to be strong because it seems that stress makes it worse, but I haven't been too successful."

"I can't imagine. Are you on medications?"

She thought about how she refused everything Dr. Martin had ever given her and lied again. "Yes, I'm taking a few things." She paused. "It's hard living my life and not being like other people. All my life I've been an outcast. Even in school." She started crying. "Not having you in my life and as a support system really messed me up, and I guess I never knew that before now." She wiped her tears. "Do you know how I felt when I learned that my coach was actually my father? Do you know how much that hurt my feelings? Even now it's hard to deal with when I look at you."

He jumped up and held her in his arms. She smelled the cologne on his body, but it didn't bother her as much. For some reason, his embrace made her feel safe. "Farah, I swear on everything I love, including my wife, that there won't be a thing you can do to get me out of your life. Me and my wife haven't been able to have kids, and it's something I always wanted. Of course I want you."

"So where do we go from here?" she asked honestly.

"Well, for starters, we can start building on our relationship. Get to know each other and things like that. With time, maybe you will start to look at me as your father. I'm willing to try if you are, but whatever you decide, there will be no pressure on my end. Just know that I'm here for you, no matter what you need."

"Daddy," she said in a low voice, "actually there is something I need you to do for me. If you can."

Chapter 36

Farah

"I don't know about you, but I could certainly use the company."

Farah waited across from the mall at a coffee shop for her mark to complete the second part of her plan. She'd been watching him handle his employees, and it seemed like she'd been there forever, when in actuality it had only been thirty minutes.

When Jean Hershey finally walked out of the building, she checked her makeup in the mirror, smoothed the side of her red tight jeans, and strutted past him. If she still had "it," he'd be under her spell in seconds, and banking on it. If it didn't work, she planned to play the "Don't I know you from somewhere?" routine.

The moment she walked past him, just as she hoped, he was on her.

"Damn, shawty. I haven't seen anything as fine as you in all my life."

Farah hated corny niggas, but whatever, this was business not pleasure. "I hear you, but I wonder how much of what you saying is true."

He scratched his peezy head. "What that mean?"

"A nigga as fine as you can get anybody you want. But I'm sure you know that already."

He looked over the dirty movie theater uniform he donned. Although he was a manager, he failed miserably when it came to keeping his appearance up, and had been pulled in the office ten times in the last six months for the same problem. "Everything I say is true. And you right, I can pick any bitch I want, and luckily for yourself, I've chosen you." He licked his lips. "My only reservation is that I hope you don't break my heart. Pretty girls like you always smash the picture."

Oh, how she wished she could just dead his ass. He was laying it on too thick. "I'm not a heartbreaker. For real, I was hoping to grab a few drinks." She stepped closer and fixed his wrinkled tie. "I don't know about you, but I could certainly use the company."

He put his arms around her waist and pulled her toward him like they were lovers. When he saw his male coworkers peeping the scene, he gripped both of her meaty ass cheeks and squeezed. "You ain't said nothing but a word."

"Where we going?"

"To my place."

It took everything in her power to hide her smile.

An hour later she was in his filthy apartment. Jean was on his third drink and could barely sit up straight on his own sofa. His smile was overexposed, and he had zero control of his neck, because it rolled all over his shoulders. She laced his last drink, and she couldn't wait for him to pass out. She used the same drug on him that she'd used with her victims in the past, and it didn't take nearly as long. He seemed to have a stomach of steel.

"You ready to take a nap, pretty lady?" he asked, kissing her neck. "I'm trying to see how soft them sugar walls really are."

Her skin crawled, and she pushed him off in outrage. “I was kind of hoping we could drink some more before going to bed.” She looked around his dirty living room. “You got roommates? Because I wouldn’t want someone walking in on us.”

“I live alone, sweetheart.” He placed his head in her lap. “So don’t even worry about all that.”

Please go the fuck to sleep. “That’s good to know. But you look so tired.”

He lifted his head, moved it toward her face, and sucked her bottom lip. “Baby, I can stay up for the next five hours,” he boasted. “I drink my friends under the table and am always the last one standing.”

Her lip smelled like pickles when he finished. “Prove it.” She poured another cup of vodka, and when he closed his eyes for a second, she dropped two more pills into his drink. “Here you go.” She handed it to him. “Toss it back.”

“I don’t know if I can do another one right now.”

“Wait, you mean to tell me you lied that quick?” she joked. “You just said you can drink your friends under the table. I want to see you do it,” she said, rubbing his dick. “Besides, I always fuck better high.”

With that promise, he wasted no time throwing it back. It took less than two minutes for him to pass out. She waited five minutes before beginning the mission to find the tape he claimed was missing to the police. She figured there had to be a reason he was hiding the tape, and she was determined to find the reason.

She went through room after room, and it was starting to look like she would never find what she was looking for. Luckily she never gave up.

“Where would you keep the tape?” she asked, huffing and puffing in the middle of the living room. “Think creep. Think creep!”

She checked every area of the house except the refrigerator. An hour later, she found what she was looking for in the vegetable drawer in the refrigerator. It was stuffed under some spoiled collard greens.

"I got you," she said to herself.

Quickly she rushed to the DVD/VCR in the living room. Before placing it inside, she looked back at him. He was still asleep. She placed it in the player and fast-forwarded in search of that certain thing. Thirty minutes later, she saw her sister Chloe and Amico walking out of the movie theater together. Chloe looked so vibrant and so alive, and she wept quietly. With everything going on in her life, she still didn't have a chance to grieve.

Farah also saw the reason he wanted to hide the tape because there he was, in a back office, having sex with another man. Farah had seen worse, so she wasn't interested in what he was doing; although if he made any noise about the tape being missing, she had plans to blackmail him by telling people he was into men.

She was about to leave until she heard Jean say, "What you doing with that tape, bitch?"

Farah stood in Jean's living room with Mia and Shadow. They were staring down at Jean's lifeless body. The plan almost folded, but luckily they came through when she needed them. They were hiding outside of Jean's apartment door, ready to enter when Farah gave the word.

The plan Mia outlined entailed them coming into the house to check for the tape after he was passed out from the medicine, but Farah got so caught up in what she was seeing on the tape that she forgot all about them. Had it not been for quick thinking on their part, she would've been dead.

"Why would you look at the tape here?" Shadow asked, looking at the blood pouring from Jean's forehead, courtesy of the bullet he'd just fired into it. "We could've checked that shit out at home."

"I'm sorry." She breathed heavily. "I saw Chloe and got lost. If y'all didn't kick that door in, I would've . . ." Just thinking about her fate had her shaken. "I don't know how to thank you." She looked down at him again. "I gave this nigga three pills and he still woke up."

"Thank us later. For now we gotta get out of here," Mia said, "in case someone called the police."

They were on their way out the door when Shadow said, "Oh, before I forget: the nigga Slade and Major were talking in the hallway on the way to Markee's crib. I was behind them after getting off the elevator, and they didn't hear me. I'm not sure, but I think they planning to meet Eleanor in that building tomorrow."

Farah's heart rate sped up. "Are you sure?"

"I wasn't exactly invited into the conversation, so I ear hustled as best I could, but yes, I'm pretty sure," Shadow clarified.

"Shit!" Farah yelled. She felt faint. "This is it. I'm over."

"Don't worry. We still good." Mia placed her hand on her shoulder. "It's just time to activate part three of my plan a little earlier, that's all."

Chapter 37

Randy

"In the past I said it and had everything to lose. Now I have nothing."

Since Willie regained control over his business, Randy was stuck with the money he provided to care for himself. He knew his father wasn't into good deeds, so he figured there was a reason for the arrangement, although Willie never let him in on it. To make matters worse, with the exception of The Vet, most of his men abandoned him because he was unable to pay them.

Frustrated, he was preparing to take a shower, when suddenly there was a knock at the door. He turned the water off to be sure he heard it correctly. When the knock grew louder, he grabbed his gun on the sink and moved cautiously toward the door. When he looked out of the peephole and saw Farah, he thought he was seeing things.

He snatched the door open. "What the fuck you doing at my house?" He looked behind her on the street. "And how did you know where I lived?" He walked into the house and she followed, closing the door behind her.

"If you don't want me here, just kill me, Randy. I don't even care anymore. As a matter of fact, you'll be doing me a favor, because my life is real fucked up right now." She walked closer to him.

He turned around to look at her. "You not answering the fucking question, bitch. I know you fucking with Slade, so what are you doing at my house?"

"Randy, if you even thought I was still dealing with Slade, you would've shot me through the door." She looked around the living room. "Nice house . . . How did you come up on it?"

"I inherited it," he said in a flat tone as he entered the kitchen.

She sighed. "I was thinking about you the other day. The one thing I can say about us is we are unstable together. But worse apart."

He looked behind her. "How do I know you don't have a rack of niggas outside my house right now?"

"Because nobody knows where you live, Randy."

"How did you find me?"

"After my sister died, you called me on the phone and someone yelled in the background, 'Welcome to Serenity Meadows,'" she said, mocking Mrs. Tillman's voice. "So I had a few friends check on you, but you weren't there." She ran her hand over the marble countertop. "So we came back, hassled her a little more, and she gave up the address."

He shook his head. "So that was you?" He laughed to himself. "All this time and I thought it was Slade. What did you have planned for me?" He grabbed the vodka from the freezer and one glass.

"Nothing. I just wanted to say hello." She walked up to him and he stepped back.

"You think you're smart, don't you?" He walked into the living room and she was on his heels.

"No . . . just cute." She laughed. "What do you think about me?"

He sat on his couch. "You got a lot of shit with you, Farah. Luckily for you, tonight I'm in the mood for entertainment." He poured himself a glass of vodka.

Farah sat next to him and placed her purse on the floor. "I miss you, Randy. A lot."

He shook his head. "If you coming over here for some money, you can forget about it. I'm not breaking you off anymore." He looked her over. "Besides, dead bitches can't spend cash no how." He swallowed his whole drink.

"You really are considering killing me, aren't you?" She sat up straight.

"What do you want?" He leaned back.

"I came here to apologize for everything I did to you. I was thinking we could put our heads together and maybe start all over."

He laughed in her face. "You must really think I'm some gump-ass nigga, don't you? I may have hit hard times, but it doesn't mean I'm down and out."

"Before you get all out of hand, I'm not talking about being back in a relationship with you. I know what we had is done, and I'm okay with that, but I gotta be honest. Since I stopped fucking with you, I haven't been in the company of a real nigga, and I miss that." She saw his chest swell up a bit, and she loved it. Stroking his ego always did wonders.

"You must think I'm the type of nigga you can say anything to and I'll believe you."

"Why you say that, Randy?" She reached for the vodka bottle to pour herself a glass, and he slapped her hand.

"Because I know you fucking the dude Slade, that's why."

She rubbed her hand and made herself a drink anyway. "So wait. I tell you that I haven't been in the company of a real nigga, and you talking about Slade?" She shook her head. "You think he's a realer nigga than you?"

He pointed at her. "You pushing it, bitch. My limits with you are already extended."

"I'm not pushing shit, Randy." She sipped her vodka and set the glass down. "When I said I haven't been in the company of a real nigga, that included Slade. That's why I'm here. I can't stay away from you no more. And don't even fake like you don't miss me, because I know you do."

"Well, maybe you should try. The way I feel these days, I'm liable to do anything to anybody."

"Randy, I'm serious. Just let me enjoy you for tonight, and if you still want to kill me afterward, you're welcome to it."

"I'm welcome to it whether you want me to or not, Farah." He was trying to play tough, but she had him right where she wanted him, in the palm of her hand.

"You just don't get it, do you? I don't care what you do to me. You're like my favorite drug. I just have to have you all the time." She smiled and massaged his leg. "And I know I'm yours too."

"You know if I find out that you're here for anything other than dick, I'm gonna hurt you. Really bad."

"You say that all the time."

He separated from her. "In the past I said it and had everything to lose. Now I have nothing. That makes me deadly."

"Randy, what can I do to gain your trust again?"

"You really want to know?"

"Yes."

"Tell me why you're really here."

"I got one better." She smiled, pulling him toward her. "How about I tell you where you can find the Baker Boys all at once?"

His eyes widened. "You playing, right?"

"Why would I play? I'm trying to prove to you where my mind is, and maybe if I do this, you'd believe me and we can start all over."

"Why should I trust you?"

"Because I got my own beef with Slade, and I want him squashed. And he's meeting with someone I can't have found. Is that good enough for you?"

Randy crawled into the building with five niggas by his side. Because he wasn't sure if the information was a setup, he had The Vet and another goon waiting outside of the building. The men all agreed to help him with the promise of being paid once he took down the Baker Boys and reclaimed his drug operation. Randy was determined not to let the opportunity pass to rid the world of the Baker Boys. Slade intruded in his life when it came to Farah, and he intruded in his life when it came to his father.

At first he thought Farah was trying to set him up; after all, she was as sneaky a bitch as they came. She never did anything without having an angle for herself. So when she explained to him that they actually blamed her for Knox's disappearance, and because Willie confirmed it when he showed up at his house, he believed her.

"We have to split up to cover more ground," Randy told his cronies in a low whisper as they stood in the stairwell. "Search everywhere for them." They quietly followed his orders.

After they split up, Randy opened the door leading to the fourth floor. He freed his weapon from his jeans and held it in his hands. He didn't want shit for Christmas but Slade's head on a pedestal.

He passed the first door in the hallway and then the third. He knew they were somewhere in the building, because Slade's truck was out front. From what Farah told him, they were waiting for some bitch named Eleanor to show up. She didn't know the exact address, which was why he was led on a small goose chase, but Randy didn't care just as long as, at the end of it all, he took him out.

When he passed the fifth door, he heard a couple yelling loudly.

"Where the fuck were you, Dave? I know you weren't over your mother's house like you said you were. I called. So just tell the truth for once in your miserable life! I mean, it don't make no fucking sense."

"Bitch, stop playing with me. I been told you I had to visit my mother."

"Well, why didn't she answer the fucking phone? Plus I remember you telling me she had Bingo on Sundays."

"I don't feel like this shit! If you don't believe me, then that's on you."

"Well, I don't believe you then!" she yelled. "You can keep the fake shit for somebody else."

Randy was so involved in a conversation that didn't have anything to do with him that he didn't hear the two niggas creeping behind him with .45s aimed at the back of his head. By the time he turned around, he was facing Slade, Killa, Major, Judge, Grant, and his father. They entered the hallway out of an apartment on that wing. To make matters worse, Farah, Mia, and Shadow entered out of the apartment where the conversation took place. It was Mia's and Shadow's voices that held Randy's attention and caused him to drop his guard.

"So what about my men?" Randy asked his father. He knew what was about to happen before it was said. He was set up. "The Vet and Musty?"

Willie laughed at him. "I guess you did have two loyal men after all. Unlike the others, they wouldn't flip, so we had to kill them."

Randy felt queasy as he stared at Farah. "I can't believe you did this to me."

"Yes, you do, Randy," she said coldly. "If you ask me, you wanted to die."

"I told you not to trust her," Willie added. He looked at Farah. "No offense, beautiful."

She remained silent, although Shadow wanted to snatch his old face off.

Randy could do nothing but laugh and shake his head. Once again he'd fallen victim to Farah and her scheming-ass ways. He faced Slade and said, "I don't suppose there's anything I can say to convince you to let me live."

"Nigga, you killed my cousin and threw him outside the building like he was trash. Ain't shit I want to hear from you but the sound of blood gushing out your body."

Randy looked down at the floor and then at the Bakers. All of them had guns aimed at him. "Who set this up?" He looked at Farah. "Because I know she's not smart enough to come up with this."

"The who's and why's are not important anymore."

Willie Gregory stepped into the hallway and approached his only son. It was obvious, if it wasn't before, that he hated his only child.

"Dad, you doing me like this? I mean, I know we haven't had the best relationship, but I would have never thought you'd stoop so low."

Willie stepped closer. He wanted him to see that there was nothing he could say to get him to change his mind. He loathed him like a lifetime enemy. When he was close enough, he whispered so that only he could hear his voice. "I told you to stay away. That's all you had to do. Instead you let that bitch bring you out of your hole. What a fool."

Randy tried to stop the tears from pouring down. "You can't do this. I know you can't." He beat his chest. "I'm your own blood."

"Then I guess you don't know me very well, do you?" With that, Willie raised his hand and bullets flew into Randy's chest cavity and out of the flesh on his back.

"Wait!" Slade yelled, but it was too late. Willie promised to give him to Slade so that he could avenge his cousin, but he had other plans.

"Sorry, Slade," Willie said, looking back at him. "I got caught up in the moment."

With Randy's dead body at his feet, Willie walked up to him and spit in his face. "Weak-ass nigga. I can't believe you was actually my son." He laughed, looking at Slade. "I guess it don't matter no more now, does it?" He looked back at him. "What's done is done, and it suits me just fine."

"It may be done, but it couldn't have come at a worse time. We were scheduled to meet someone here today, but Farah called and told us Randy got information about it and decided to meet us here." He looked at her. "It's a good thing that she did."

"I don't know who you were meeting, but you scored big time on this one. Be grateful. One of your biggest enemies is gone. And since I killed him myself, it should prove where my loyalty lies. Right?"

Slade observed the expression on his face. He always knew Willie couldn't be trusted, but killing his own son made him pure evil. At some point he was going to have to sever ties with him, or suffer the same fate as Randy.

After killing Randy, Willie walked into his house. Soft music played in the air, and he smiled slightly. At first he didn't want her in his home, but after learning how bad the Bakers wanted her, he decided he could humor her for a little while. Besides, the longer she went missing, the longer the Baker Boys would be in town.

He threw his jacket over the edge of the sofa and approached Eleanor at the stove in the kitchen. From behind her, being in his house reminded him of old times, when he was cheating on his wife with her. It was before the dope and before he went to prison. "What you cooking? Smells good."

She turned around and smiled. "Your favorite. Sweet spaghetti and meatballs." She turned off the eyes of the stove. "Thanks for letting me stay here." She wiped her hand on the towel. "I can't tell you how much I appreciate you taking me in. It's the only place I feel safe."

"I know." He smiled slyly.

"I don't know how I'm going to do it yet, Willie, but I'll find a way to repay you."

"I know you will." He reached into his pocket and handed her a bag of dope. "In the meantime, go take care of yourself. And when you're finished, drop to your knees and give me a little dessert."

She accepted the bag and grinned. "You got it, daddy."

Chapter 38

Nadia Gibson

". . . you fucking with the wrong person."

Nadia strutted into the precinct, high off coke and ready to do everything in her power to put Farah Cotton underneath the jail. Once inside, she was surprised at all of the strange expressions from her coworkers. Each person she walked by had the look of knowing something she didn't, and to say this bothered her would be an understatement.

She walked to her desk and threw her purse and car keys on top of it. When she saw her boss's straight face, she grew nervous. He left his house before she did, and apparently knew something she didn't. "What the fuck is up with you?" She turned around and looked at everyone. "And why is everyone acting so strangely?"

He laughed and placed his hand on her shoulder. "So you really don't know, do you?"

"I wouldn't ask if I did." She pushed his hand off of her. "Now stop fucking around and tell me what's going on. You're scaring the hell out of me." She looked at her coworkers again. All of the deceitful things she did in the dark put her on edge.

"How about I show you?" He handed her a sheet of paper.

She snatched it out of his hand and sat down. Before reading it, she gave him one last suspicious glare. Then she submerged herself into the sheet, hoping to find answers. When she finally saw what was written, she was startled. She'd had visions of how this moment would play out, and she never thought it would go down like this. The document floated out of her hand and fell to the floor. "What . . . I . . . I don't understand."

He picked up the sheet. "It's easy to see why you don't understand." He laughed. "I didn't either, but essentially you're getting what you wanted. If anything, you need to be celebrating. This is a career case."

"I know." She rubbed her hands over her face. "I wanted this for the longest, but how did it happen? I mean, she swore before God and all His angels that she had nothing to do with Amico Glasser's disappearance. So what changed now?"

"I don't know, Gibson. What I do know is that she's saying something different now."

"Where is she?" She looked up at him. "I don't trust this, and I have to see her."

"She's in a holding cell in the back." He placed the sheet back in the folder. "Why?"

Nadia stood up and rushed toward the back where they kept the prisoners. She passed cell after cell, until she was staring directly in Farah's face. The first thing she noticed was that she didn't look anything like a woman in fear for her freedom. "What are you doing here, Farah? Why the change of heart?"

Farah stood up and walked toward the bars. "I'd think you'd be happy to see me, Nadia. After all, you've been on a mission to ruin my life for the longest, and it looks like you succeeded." She looked around, "Doesn't it?"

"I asked you a question," Nadia said seriously. "What the fuck is up?"

Farah chuckled. "Wow, you don't even know when you've won, do you? I realized that you are so much smarter than me and that I must surrender. You truly are a great cop, Nadia. I'm sure they'll give you an award for this and everything." Nadia stepped closer to the bars and Farah did also. "Smile, Nadia Gibson, you finally got what you wanted: me behind bars."

"Why would you sign a confession, Farah? Just be straight with me and tell me the truth."

"Because you wanted me to."

Nadia frowned. "Because I wanted you to? What the fuck are you talking about?"

Suddenly Farah's disposition moved from cocky to bashful. It was as if she were playing up for an audience. "You told me that if I didn't admit to knowing something about Amico's disappearance, you would hurt me. I'm afraid for my life, so I admitted to something I didn't do."

The little hairs on the back of Nadia's neck rose. "I didn't say I would hurt you, Farah! If anything I said you need to confess and stop hurting other people!"

"But you did blackmail me, Nadia. You said you would hurt me if I didn't turn myself in, and since you roll with killers, I was afraid for my life."

Nadia stepped so close to Farah, she could feel her warm breath on her nose. "What are you trying to do?"

"I know everything about you," Farah whispered into her face. Her breath tickled her eyelashes. "And you know nothing about me. You have no clue what I'm capable of. But guess what? You're getting ready to find out."

"I don't know what you got planned." Nadia pointed in her face. "But you fucking with the wrong person."

"If I was fucking with the wrong person you wouldn't be a worthy adversary." Farah giggled. "Now, if you'll excuse me, I'm waiting for the perfect time for everything to blow up in your face."

Nadia laughed loosely even though she was petrified. "I'm not even worried about this shit, because nobody will believe anything you say." She tried to speak louder so anyone listening could take notes. "I'm a decorated officer and you're a coldblooded murderer. We're two totally different people."

"If you truly feel that way, why are you trying to prove it to me?" Farah paused. "I will give you a little tip, you got something white on your nose." Nadia rubbed her nose so hard it reddened.

When she was done, Farah was in stitches laughing so hard. "You see, Officer, I got your number, and soon everyone else will too. When I'm done with you, you'll wish you never saw me."

Chapter 39

Nadia Gibson

"I'm in the process of losing everything!"

Nadia Gibson was on her sofa after snorting as much cocaine as she could breathe into her nostrils in one sitting. She couldn't believe her life had actually turned into diarrhea in a matter of weeks. One moment she was a decorated officer who brought down the DC Vampire, also known as Farah Cotton, and the next minute she was being investigated for blackmailing Farah.

Not only was she about to lose her job, but also, thanks to the pictures Farah obtained of her copping cocaine, courtesy of a private investigator, she was facing drug charges. In the end, Farah was released from jail after staying only two nights, and vindicated of all charges. Farah was right when she said she wasn't to be fucked with, because somehow she was also able to get her hands on the video that showed Chloe with Amico Glasser in the movie theater together, as opposed to her. In the end, Farah's confession looked like it came from a drug addicted officer who was on the take.

She was stretched out on the sofa, considering her fucked-up life, when her phone rang. When she saw it was Beverly Glasser, she immediately grew irritated.

In her opinion, had it not been for Beverly's insistence that Farah was responsible for Amico's disappearance, things may not have been so bad.

She picked up the phone. "What do you want, Beverly? I really don't feel like it right now."

"Well, I'm sorry to hear all of that, but I need to know what's going on with Farah. I heard they released her the other day. Can you tell me why? She wasn't in jail for even a month."

"Beverly, that's not something I can help you with. And like I said, I don't feel like it right now." She turned on her back and looked up at the ceiling.

"Fuck you mean, you don't feel like it?" She paused. "This bitch killed my son, and I want justice! The justice you promised me!"

Nadia placed the call on speaker and threw the handset on her stomach. "She didn't do it, Beverly. Her and this high-powered attorney she hired made me look ridiculous in court! You've had it in for her for the longest, and I guess you were wrong."

Beverly started laughing. "Wait . . . you're claiming that I'm the one who was after her? I told you from the start that Lesa was the person my son was last seen with. He said it when he sent the last text message from his phone."

"Well, her name is not Lesa. It's Chloe, who, as you know, is dead. Apparently she lied to your son and gave him the wrong name. Perhaps she had ill intentions the entire time. One will never know. I do know this: we were wrong about it being Farah, and it's all your fault."

"I can't believe you're blaming me for this." Beverly fired back. "It was you who convinced me after some time that it was Farah instead of Lesa. Now, I'll be honest. After looking into her eyes, I was a believer too, but that's after the fact."

"You say that shit now, but every other day you were coming after me to go at her. Now I'm in the process of losing everything! My life, my job, and even my respect." She was now laughing so hard that the pinks of her gums were visible. "Not only that, but she was able to get her hands on some pictures of me copping from a drug dealer."

"So wait, you're blaming me for your drug habit, too?"

"I'm not saying that. What I am saying is that my life was fine before you came into it."

"Let me clarify some things, Nadia. Yes, I do want the person who murdered my son arrested, and if I'm wrong for that, sue me. If you are receiving some type of fly back because of your wrong hunch, then blame yourself. You're the officer, remember? Not me." She paused. "Now, if that Chloe girl murdered my son before she died, then justice was served because she's dead too, but if I find out that Farah had even one thing to do with his disappearance, there will be nothing Jesus could do to keep me from her. Regarding your career, I raise my cup to Farah, because at least she did one thing right."

Nadia knew the moment she saw her boss and ex-lover's face that something terrible was rolling her way. Still, she pushed herself into his office, despite wanting to run the other way. "I tried to get into your house last night with my key, but you changed the locks."

"Have a seat, Nadia."

She could tell immediately the romance was over. "That's cool." She gave him a knowing glance. "I'll remain standing." She looked around for one indication of what was coming. "You wanted to meet with me?"

He couldn't look at her at first. "Yes, uh, I need your badge and your gun."

"So I guess the department doesn't even want to hear what I have to say about all of this, right?"

"We've heard your position already, and the decision has been made. Not to mention the fact that because you harassed Farah Cotton, she and her attorney are suing this department for millions."

"But don't you see? That's why she confessed. If I was really harassing her like she claimed, she would've submitted her claim before being arrested. She knew the big money came in only if she turned herself in."

"It doesn't matter, Nadia. The evidence is stacked against you. Now, quit wasting time and hand over your badge and gun. The least you could do is go out with some dignity and respect."

"And if I don't give you my gun and badge?"

"Then I'll be forced to have them removed from you." He looked over her shoulder at two officers in the distance.

Here it was; she'd fucked this nigga more times than not, and yet he stood on the other side of the desk ready to judge her like a stranger. Where was his part in all of this? He fed her cocaine on many nights just to enhance their sex life, and now he was perpetrating the worst fraud by acting like he wasn't aware of her habit.

"So what's going to happen to me now?"

"Gibson, that's not what we're here to discuss." He paused. "I need your badge and your gun right now, and I won't ask you again."

"You never loved me, did you? You just used me for my body."

When he didn't answer, she could feel two people approaching her from behind. Her worst fear was being realized. She was about to be arrested. There was nothing worse than an officer going to prison and having to deal daily with the people they helped put behind bars. She couldn't see her life going down like this.

In that moment, she made a decision. If she was going to go to prison, she would make it worth her while. She raised her weapon and fired into her superior's head. His blood, guts, and life splattered out of his body and slapped against the wall. She was immediately pushed forward, and the gun flew out of her hand. Although it wouldn't change her situation, it did make her feel better.

Chapter 40

Farah

"What you trying to do, play some kinky game or something?"

Farah lay on the rug in her apartment with Shadow and Mia as they smoked a blunt and stared up at the ceiling. Everything Mia had planned worked, and Farah could finally move on with her life. "Mia, your plan was the most vicious shit ever!" Farah cheered. "I still don't know how you came up with it. At first I was worried, but now, damn!"

"I told you to trust me, and luckily for yourself you did," Mia bragged. "Besides, with Chloe and Mama dead and Daddy in jail, I can't lose another family member."

"I'm so glad I'm on your good side, because you're the most manipulating bitch ever! Even Dr. Martin's ass disappeared when I was released from jail. Left his practice and everything." Farah giggled.

"It's a good thing he left, too, because Grandma acted like she had plans for him if he didn't," Mia said.

Farah accepted the blunt from Mia, and they talked about how everything went down. Thanks to her biological father, she was able to pay for an attorney and a private investigator. With a pending lawsuit against the police department, she stood to make millions.

"I will never doubt you again, Mia. Ever," Farah said honestly. "I don't know what I would do without you two." She looked at Shadow. "I don't know what I would do without both of you."

"You won't have to worry about it." Mia nudged her and sat up. "Oh, before I forget. Somebody named Bones called you. He called a lot when you were in jail."

"I know. I never told him where I went," Farah said sadly. She hoped she didn't burn her bridges with him.

"Well, he said he was coming over to check on you tonight. He found out you're home."

"Oh, shit," she said, covering her mouth.

"You don't want to see him? Because we can spin him around," Shadow said.

"I'm gonna try to reach him now and tell him I'll get up with him later."

She got out her phone and sent a message.

Bones, hit me back when you can.

"Oh . . . Vivian said she coming by later to get the rent. You got it?" Shadow asked.

"I don't have no choice, because God knows you two don't have shit. Jaffrey gave me a couple of bucks to last for a few months," she said, looking at them. "But when y'all gonna start helping me out around here? To be honest, I don't know what y'all do."

"Let's see, we got rid of unwanted people for you and cleaned up your loose edges so you could stay out of prison," Mia said. "If you ask me, we helped out enough around here."

"I guess you right about that."

"I am." Mia laughed. "But just so you know, me and Shadow got some things in the works with Willie."

Farah's eyebrows rose. "You sure that's a good thing to be getting into business with him, seeing how he murdered his own son?"

"Money is money, Farah," Shadow replied.

"Whatever. Y'all grown people, and there's nothing I can do to change your minds."

"Exactly." Mia grabbed the empty vodka bottle. "Now, since it was my plan to set you free and it worked, who going to the store to get another bottle?"

Knock. Knock. Knock.

Farah jumped up to answer the door. "Unfortunately it won't be me, because I have to get the door." When she opened it, Slade was on the other side.

"Can I talk to you for a minute?" He looked inside and saw Shadow and Mia. He hadn't seen her since she helped him bring down Randy.

Farah felt he looked so good, and he was only wearing blue jeans and a white T-shirt.

"I can come back later if you too busy." He paused. "Although I really want to be with you, and I miss you like crazy, Farah."

She hadn't had sex in a while, so she saw the look in his eyes and knew what time it was. "Slade's here," Farah said, trying to keep her calm. "Didn't y'all say something earlier about going to the store to get some liquor?"

Farah was in the bed with her legs wrapped around Slade. This was the best part about being with him: the tender moments like this, where she had him all to herself in an empty house.

"So when are you going back home?" she asked him. "To Mississippi?"

He sighed. "My mother is going tomorrow. Me and my brothers are staying behind."

"Really?" she asked hopefully. "Why the change of heart?"

"Because we're still hoping that this bitch will show up." Farah seemed sad. "And even if she did, I'm not sure if I can pull myself away from you."

She looked into his eyes and kissed him on the lips. "You don't know how good it feels to hear you say that. It's one thing to be here for business, it's a whole other thing to be here for me."

"It's the truth." He rubbed her hair. "But I'm glad it makes you feel good."

"I gotta ask you something," she said in a low voice. "Why are you with me? I mean, you have Shannon and God knows how many other groupies who would kill to be with you." She rubbed his chest.

"Why you saying stupid shit?" He was beyond annoyed. Shannon hadn't stopped giving him grief ever since he left her at the restaurant. If she wasn't calling his apartment every five minutes, she was calling Markee's crib where Major stayed alone. "Shannon is the last bitch on the face of the earth I'm thinking about. And I'm with you because I love you. Stop asking me stupid-ass questions."

She hated his generic answer. "This is why I don't like to talk to you sometimes. Every time I try to express how I feel, you shoot me down. It's like it don't even matter."

He lifted her chin so she could look into his eyes. "It's like this, we won't always agree on things, babes. And yes, some things you say may rub me the wrong way."

"And vice versa," she admitted.

"And I'm cool with you not always agreeing with me. Most couples don't. I'm offering you love, Farah. Unconditional love. Maybe you aren't used to it, but it is true." He lifted her onto the tip of his dick. "I thought I was in love with my ex-girlfriend." He moved inside of her. "And to be honest, I thought there wasn't a woman alive who could come close to what I felt for her, and you know what you taught me?"

"No," she said, biting her bottom lip as she rode him.

"You taught me I don't know shit. I'm in love with a bitch who I'm sure is bad news, and I don't even care anymore."

Farah tried to keep a straight face, despite the fact that he was talking real shit and fucking her at the same time.

"I stepped to my family for you, Farah. My brothers are telling me that I shouldn't be with you, and my mother said she'll never respect you. But guess what? I'm a real nigga, and I have chosen. I'd rather be with you for the rest of my life than to be with some bitch I'm not feeling for another minute."

She kissed him passionately without responding, and he had his answer. "I can't believe after all of this time, I'm really in love."

"Now, that's what I like to hear."

They were just about to get into it real heavy when there was a knock at the door.

"Who is that?" Slade asked.

"If they knocking, it can't be Shadow or Mia." Farah was nowhere near being presentable, so she said, "It's probably Vivian. Can you hand her the rent money on the kitchen counter?"

"You keep that. I got a few bucks on me. I'll pay you up for the next two months."

She grinned. "Why do I feel spoiled?"

"I haven't begun to spoil you yet." He tapped her on the ass. "Let me hurry up and get rid of this bitch so we can finish where we left off. I'll meet you back here."

Farah jumped up and went to the bathroom to wash their lovemaking session off her body. She took a look at herself in the mirror and smiled. "You really did it, didn't you? I guess you're smarter than people give you credit for." Her skin was clear and barely held a blemish.

When she was done with her whore's bath, she walked back into the bedroom, but Slade wasn't there. "Baby, where you at?" She looked in the closet and even under the bed. She laughed to herself when she realized there was no way he was squeezing his big ass under her mattress. "What you trying to do, play some kinky game or something?"

She walked into the hallway and saw her man standing by the kitchen counter. He was talking low, and she wondered what was up. She started to go back into the room, not feeling like seeing Vivian, until she saw the look on his face. When she continued on her journey and saw him holding one of the mysterious red boxes she'd received, her legs gave out from under her body and she fell. Somehow she was able to push herself up and walk into the living room. That's when she saw *his* face.

The moment she laid eyes on him, it all made sense. After everything she and her family did to him as a child, why wouldn't he want revenge? It was Theo Cunningham, the boy she kicked in the penis as a child, because her mother told her to. The boy who lost his mother by the hands of her family.

When Slade took the lid off of the box and pulled out a picture, it was over. From where she stood, she could see it clearly. It was a duplicate of the first picture she'd received and destroyed. It was the photo where she stood over Knox's bloodied body, covering his nose.

Slade held the picture out and looked in her direction, and the box fell from his hands. "Baby, what is this?" Tears poured out of his eyes. "What is he showing me?"

She moved cautiously toward Slade. "I don't know," Farah lied. "What's going on, Theo? Uh . . . what are you doing at my house? Bringing me fake pictures again?"

"It's not fake, Farah," Theo replied. "You and me both know that the photo is authentic. Just tell him the truth."

She looked at Theo, but her heart was with Slade. There she was, worried about Eleanor, Lesa, and Randy, when all this time it was Theo Cunningham. He wanted revenge, and he'd gotten his wish.

"Farah, why are you standing over Knox's bloodied body?"

"Baby, I don't know what this nigga is trying to do, but I bet money that picture is a fake. Don't let somebody step us back again. We came too far to be together!"

"I'm not telling a lie," Theo combatted in his two-piece blue suit. Although he was there to ruin her life, he looked like money, like life had been good to him. "These pictures are real, and I have more if you want to see them, Slade. Farah and her family are evil, man, real evil, and it's time you knew the truth."

"Farah, is this my brother Knox?" Slade yelled, interrupting him. His voice rocked her eardrums and caused them to itch. "I want you to stop playing games with me! Please . . . please . . . tell me the truth!"

"Slade, can we at least talk about this first? I think this nigga is giving you the wrong impression about me, and I want an opportunity to make it right. There's so much I want to tell you, but I need to do it in private."

"I want you to stop telling lies, Farah. Did you or did you not have something to do with my brother going missing?"

Farah remained silent.

"The least you can do is tell the truth, baby," Slade pleaded. "I'm dying over here."

"And I'm telling you the truth, but you not listening."

She never saw a grown man cry that hard before. Sure, she witnessed weaker men shed tears, but never, ever, in all of her life had she witnessed a man she respected cry from his soul. Although she hated to witness it, she understood where the pain came from. She didn't lose Chloe in the same way, but her death hurt her just as deep. She could only imagine how it must've felt to lose a family member at the hands of a woman who stole his heart.

"Be decent, Farah," he said with a voice full of bass. "Are me and my family looking for a dead man?"

Now she was crying. "Baby . . ."

"Answer the fucking question!"

The boom in his voice rocked her back a few feet. She was trembling. This was it. This was the moment she feared. "I don't know about the picture, Slade. All I know is—"

"What?" he cut her off. "What do you know?"

"All I know is that I love you." She stepped up to him. "And that I've never loved another human being more than you. Not even my family, Slade." He stepped away, and she pulled him back and put her head on his chest. She could hear his heart thumping wildly. He tried to walk away, but she pulled him and held on to him so tightly that her nails dug into his skin. "Don't walk out on me again . . . please." In a low whisper, she said, "I made a mistake. Please . . . don't take yourself away from me again." She paused to look into his eyes.

Finally he pulled himself away from her. "Did you kill my brother?"

Softly she said, "Yes."

He stepped to her, preparing to do her harm, when there was a knock at the door. Without approval, Theo opened it, and in walked two police officers with angry faces. "Slade Baker, you're under arrest for the murder of Warren Farmer." They forcefully grabbed him, threw him up against the kitchen counter, and placed handcuffs on his wrists.

"Where are you taking him?" Farah asked, walking into their space. "Please stop! You're hurting him!"

"He's going to jail, ma'am! And if you don't back the fuck up, you going too."

"I don't know nobody named Warren!" Slade had screamed, trying to wrap his mind around everything that was happening. First he discovered that his family had been right about Farah all along, and now he was being arrested for a crime he didn't commit.

"You may not know him as Warren Farmer, but you should know him as Tornado," one of the officers yelled. "If that doesn't jog your memory, maybe you'll recall the man you beat to death with your bare hands in the hallway."

Slade felt weak at the knees, because he knew immediately where he went wrong. Because he left Shannon in the restaurant, she did the unspeakable and snitched on him to the cops. She was there the day he killed Tornado, and now he would pay. If he was able to make it out of the situation, he had plans for her, and Farah, too.

"Now you coming with us!" Slade was whisked out of the apartment, and the door slammed behind them. Farah leaned on the door and sobbed her eyes out. Just when she thought her life was together, she realized it was falling apart.

Now she was alone with Theo. "Don't be sad, Farah." Theo giggled. "At least you still have me. As long as you're committing crimes, you'll always have me."

Farah shook her head. "I can't believe you've done this to me." Her chest moved rapidly up and down. "Why?"

"Now you know how it feels to have lost." Theo laughed. "Killing your mother didn't faze you, so I had to take it a step further."

"You killed Brownie?"

"Of course I did!" He laughed. "The funny thing is, I was in the closet when you came in and slit her throat. Apparently you hated your mother as much as I did." He continued sitting on the kitchen counter. "I dreamt about the day where I would get the woman who killed my mother."

"Theo, I didn't have anything to do with your mother being killed. You're right, my mother was responsible for that shit. But what do you want from me now? Why are you ruining my life?"

"I want her children." He laughed harder. "That's why I clipped the truck your sister was in with her boyfriend that night, causing them to get into an accident."

Farah stumbled backward.

"I thought they would both be dead, but when Chloe almost made it in the hospital, I cut the cord to her oxygen, and the hospital covered it up. You know how they hate lawsuits."

"Theo . . . I . . . I can't—"

"There's no need in you saying anything I want to hear. Most of the things coming out of your mouth are lies anyway. Since I ruined your relationship with Slade by showing him that you were responsible for his brother's death, now I have to finish what I started. "

Farah couldn't get over the fact that he killed Chloe. "I can't believe you killed my sister! She loved you! For a while you were in a relationship and everything."

"Chloe was a whore! Just like you." He laughed. "She told me when we were kids what all of you did, said she had to get it off her chest." He shook his head. "The only reason I didn't kill you mothafuckas sooner was because she said she loved me. I was confused. But when she left me for Audio, I got wiser." He hopped down off the counter. "I'll be in touch, Farah. For now, I'm going to leave you to it."

Theo was about to walk out when Mia, Shadow, and Bones walked in the apartment. It was obvious that Mia didn't see Theo, because she said, "We found your friend Bones in the hallway. He was on his way up." She paused. "He got some smoke, too." She was all smiles, until she saw Theo standing in her apartment. "Wait, what is he doing here?"

Farah pushed the pain down in her gut and said, "I'm glad y'all are here. We have a situation that needs to be handled immediately."

"What's going on?" Shadow asked, remembering what they all did to Theo as a child.

"This mothafucka killed Mama! And Chloe, too. I want him dead!"

Shadow rubbed his hands together. "Consider it done."

Epilogue

Present Day

Mooney's House

Mooney sipped from a cup full of brandy and tea as she eyed Cutie.

"You know I hate you, right?" Cutie laughed, throwing herself back into her seat. "I don't know why I bother with you sometimes."

"Why would you say something so mean?" Mooney grinned. "I thought we were friends."

"Because you know I want to hear the rest." She crossed her arms over her chest. "And you and these long pauses are going to be the death of me."

"And I'm going to tell you everything you want to know tonight. Haven't I done it already?"

"Tonight?" She looked at the clock on the wall. "But it's late."

"Your mother called earlier and said she is working late. Asked me to sit with you and the twins. So you'll learn the entire story tonight."

Cutie clapped wildly. "Thank you, Mooney! I have so many questions. Like, I know your mother died, but since Randy did too, weren't you able to get her estate put back in your name? It seems to me that the house and everything went to waste."

"Who said the house isn't in my name?"

Cutie looked around the apartment. "So you prefer to live in the projects?"

"If I told you yes, you still wouldn't believe me. If I said no, it would lead to other questions. So for now I'll say nothing."

"Mooney, can I ask you a question?"

"Wow, the young lady has manners tonight. That's certainly a start." She placed her drink on the table.

"I'm serious."

"And so am I. Normally you're cussing and fussing. To hear you use appropriate language for a change throws me off. I gotta say that I like it."

Cutie was hoping the way she worded her statement would make Mooney be honest, so she swallowed and asked, "How do I know anything you're saying is true? I mean, this sounds like a real tall tale, and my foster mother said whenever somebody pulling your dress real hard, they want some pussy."

Mooney chuckled. "Well, I'm sure you know that's the last thing on my mind."

"To be honest, I don't know what your thing is." She shrugged. "You do seem to like me an awful lot. I'm just saying."

"Well, you can be sure whatever I want, that ain't it." Mooney spit back. "Having sex with a child is atrocious, and the mere thought makes my skin crawl. The sad part is, I just gave you credit for nothing! You still the same rude bitch you were when I found you rolling around with the rats downstairs in the basement." She paused. "And for your information, when I first started telling you the story, I showed you a newspaper clipping." She got up and showed her the newspaper clipping again along with another. "Here's the article about my arm."

Cutie looked over it. The headline read, WOMAN LOSES ARM AFTER ATTEMPTED BURGLARY. "So you broke into her house?"

"That's what they want you to believe."

"How come you didn't tell me that part of the story? About how your arm was cut?"

"Because we didn't get to that part yet. You'll find out tonight, remember?"

Scanning over the papers she said, "Well, how do you know the rest of the stuff?"

Mooney frowned and stood up and stared at her. For a second Cutie thought she was about to punish her physically. Instead she went to her room and came back with a boxful of Farah's diaries under her arm. She set it at the teenager's feet. The journals were in assorted colors and Cutie picked one up. "Oh my God! How did you get these?" She examined the blue book from front to back.

"I took them. All of them. And since Vivian wanted some dirt on Farah anyway, she helped me out."

"She hated Farah that much?"

"Wouldn't you if—"

One minute Cutie was looking at Mooney's living body, and the next she was looking at her head being split open like a watermelon. Her body fell to the floor, and her blood spilled all over the diaries.

"Ahhhhhh!" Cutie screamed, trembling uncontrollably with bodily guts all over her face and arms. When she turned around and looked through the massive hole in the doorway, she saw Naylor staring at her. Having gotten his revenge, he winked, grinned, and ran away.

ORDER FORM
URBAN BOOKS, LLC
78 E. Industry Ct
Deer Park, NY 11729

Name: (please print):______________________________________

Address: ______________________________________

City/State: ______________________________________

Zip: ______________________________________

QTY	TITLES	PRICE
	16 On The Block	$14.95
	A Girl From Flint	$14.95
	A Pimp's Life	$14.95
	Baltimore Chronicles	$14.95
	Baltimore Chronicles 2	$14.95
	Betrayal	$14.95
	Black Diamond	$14.95
	Black Diamond 2	$14.95
	Black Friday	$14.95
	Both Sides Of The Fence	$14.95
	Both Sides Of The Fence 2	$14.95
	California Connection	$14.95

Shipping and handling-add $3.50 for 1st book, then $1.75 for each additional book.
Please send a check payable to:
Urban Books, LLC
Please allow 4-6 weeks for delivery

ORDER FORM
URBAN BOOKS, LLC
78 E. Industry Ct
Deer Park, NY 11729

Name: (please print):____________________________________

Address: ____________________________________

City/State: ____________________________________

Zip: ____________________________________

QTY	TITLES	PRICE
	California Connection 2	$14.95
	Cheesecake And Teardrops	$14.95
	Congratulations	$14.95
	Crazy In Love	$14.95
	Cyber Case	$14.95
	Denim Diaries	$14.95
	Diary Of A Mad First Lady	$14.95
	Diary Of A Stalker	$14.95
	Diary Of A Street Diva	$14.95
	Diary Of A Young Girl	$14.95
	Dirty Money	$14.95
	Dirty To The Grave	$14.95

Shipping and handling-add $3.50 for 1st book, then $1.75 for each additional book.
Please send a check payable to:
Urban Books, LLC
Please allow 4-6 weeks for delivery

ORDER FORM
URBAN BOOKS, LLC
78 E. Industry Ct
Deer Park, NY 11729

Name: (please print):_______________________________

Address: _______________________________

City/State: _______________________________

Zip: _______________________________

QTY	TITLES	PRICE
	Gunz And Roses	$14.95
	Happily Ever Now	$14.95
	Hell Has No Fury	$14.95
	Hush	$14.95
	If It Isn't love	$14.95
	Kiss Kiss Bang Bang	$14.95
	Last Breath	$14.95
	Little Black Girl Lost	$14.95
	Little Black Girl Lost 2	$14.95
	Little Black Girl Lost 3	$14.95
	Little Black Girl Lost 4	$14.95
	Little Black Girl Lost 5	$14.95

Shipping and handling-add $3.50 for 1st book, then $1.75 for each additional book.
Please send a check payable to:

Urban Books, LLC

Please allow 4-6 weeks for delivery